# Love Me Beneath
# the Irish Moon

# Love Me Beneath the Irish Moon

## A Love Always, Ireland Romance

## Karen Foley

TULE
PUBLISHING

# Dedication

For every young woman who has left behind all that is safe and familiar to follow her dreams. And for Brenna Leigh, whose talent constantly amazes and inspires me.

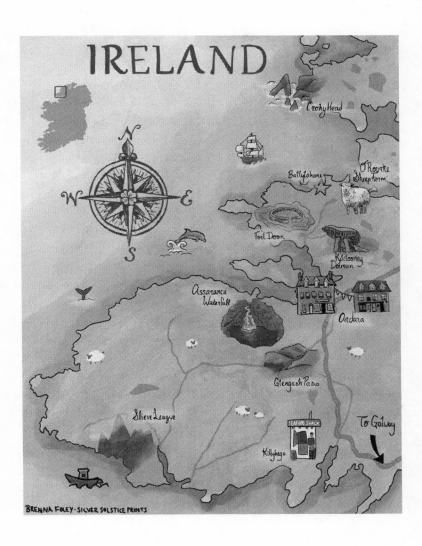

# Chapter One

*J UST BREATHE.*

In through the nose and out through the mouth.

Lori Woods clasped her hands in her lap and strove to look composed even as her heart raced and a mini volcano erupted inside her. She told herself again there was no reason to feel so anxious and unsettled. She would get the job.

She had worked hard for the job.

She *deserved* this job, and surely her father, the president and CEO of Lakeside Industries, knew that.

She glanced around the executive conference room. The assorted vice presidents, directors, and managers employed by the luxury textile firm sat expectantly at the gleaming conference table or stood shoulder to shoulder around the perimeter of the room, awaiting the appearance of Jack Woods. Lori had made sure to arrive early and she sat near the head of the table, nearest to where her father would soon make the long-awaited announcement on the selection of the new commodities manager.

On the opposite side of the room, she caught Seth Bieler's eye. He gave her a wink, likely meant to be reassuring, but which only annoyed her. He wore a new suit for the occasion and Lori grudgingly acknowledged he looked good. She only wished he didn't look so confident. He also wanted the coveted position and had done everything in his power to ingratiate himself with her father. Lori gave a soft huff of disgust because she'd unwittingly helped him in that endeavor by dating him for the past six months.

She cast him another surreptitious look. Medium height and lean, he had sandy-brown hair and brown eyes, and a ready smile. Everyone liked him, including her mother and her four older brothers. She had liked him well enough, too, until she'd discovered he was competing against her for the job she'd wanted for so long. She looked quickly away in case he saw the resentment in her eyes. Since returning from a business related trip to Ireland five weeks ago, she'd tried to put some distance between them, but he'd been like a prickly bur, hooking into her and becoming even more tightly attached.

Her thoughts were interrupted as Jack Woods breezed into the conference room and came to stand mere feet away at the head of the table. Her father wasn't a tall man, but he exuded a warm vitality and keen intelligence that inspired loyalty in those who worked for him.

"Good afternoon," he said now, his gaze sweeping the room, lingering for just a second on Lori. "Thank you for being here. As you know, we've been conducting a search for someone to fill the commodities manager position, and not just someone. Someone perfect. Someone who demonstrates the values and commitment to excellence we hold so dear here at Lakeside Industries. Someone who understands what it means to provide superior products to our customer base, and who can develop those critical relationships to source the very best raw materials that are the hallmark of our luxury textiles." He paused for a moment, steepling his fingers together. "Our selection committee has not had an easy job. We had some truly outstanding candidates."

Realizing she had her hands gripped tightly together, Lori forced herself to relax. She took some deep breaths and smoothed her palms over her thighs. It would be her. It had to be her.

"In the end, however," Jack continued, "there was one candidate who stood out among the others. This person has the winning combination of experience, education, and attitude considered essential for success in this position. This person exemplifies the values that have made us a leader in our industry and, I'm convinced, will make us even more successful in the future." He paused. "Please join me in congratulating our new commodities manager, Seth Bieler. Seth, come up and join me, please."

Later, Lori couldn't have said if she'd clapped or if she'd just sat there, stunned, as Seth made his way through the crowded conference room, accepting the handshakes and backslaps with a boyish grin and appropriate words of thanks. When he reached her father's side, he tried to make eye contact with her, but Lori averted her gaze. There was a loud buzzing in her head. Her face felt scalded with humiliation and a hard knot had formed in her throat. Only excessive pride kept her in her seat when every fiber of her being wanted to bolt from the room. Her father had not looked at her again, but was instead smiling broadly as he pumped Seth's hand and congratulated him. Lori stared blindly at her own hands, unwilling to acknowledge the curious or sympathetic looks that must surely be directed at her from the others in the room. Everyone had known how much she'd wanted this job.

Seth turned toward the assembled group. "Wow," he said, looking sheepish and overwhelmed and pleased. "I'm honored and thankful, and so excited for this opportunity. I look forward to working with each of you in this new capacity and I promise you, I won't let you down. But there's one person I especially want to recognize right now, because none of this would mean anything without her."

Lori shifted uncomfortably in her seat as Seth stepped forward to stand directly in front of her chair. What was he doing? Why would he single her out like this, knowing how much his selection had hurt her? Behind Seth, her father stood with his hands clasped loosely in front of him, beaming. A niggling suspicion pricked the back of her thoughts.

"Lori," Seth began, his expression intent and serious, "I know you wanted this job, and I know how lucky I am to have been selected, considering your own qualifications. But

I'm hoping that you'll support me going forward."

*No, no, a hundred times no.*

"Seth—"

"I want us to be partners," he said urgently. "In everything. I knew a long time ago that your family—that you—were special. There's nothing I want more than to take on this new role with you by my side."

Lori watched in astonishment as he reached into the pocket of his jacket and withdrew a small velvet box. Dropping to one knee in front of her, he opened the box to reveal a round diamond set in a halo of smaller diamonds. Light caught the facets of the center stone and threw shards of brilliant color across the room. She barely heard the soft gasps from those around her.

"Lori Woods," he said solemnly, "would you do me the honor of becoming my wife?"

Speechless, Lori lifted her mortified gaze from the ring to Seth's face. She glanced at her father, who stood looking on with an expression of pride. He gave her a barely perceptible nod. The conference room had gone completely silent as the entire leadership team of Lakeside Industries awaited her response.

She desperately wished a meteor would hit the building or a sinkhole would open beneath it and drag her to the center of the earth. She wished she was anywhere but here. She hadn't thought there could be anything worse than being passed over for the job, but she'd been wrong. This was much worse. A part of her wanted to snatch the ring from Seth's hand and hurl it across the room. None of this was fair. He'd taken advantage of the situation—had taken advantage of *her*—knowing she wouldn't refuse him in front of so many people.

And he was right.

Seeing the hopeful expression on Seth's face, she knew she couldn't humiliate him in front of the entire leadership team any more than she could embarrass her father, who so obviously believed she would welcome the proposal. In that moment, she hated herself almost as much as she despised Seth for deliberately putting her in this position.

"Okay," she heard herself say, so quietly it was a wonder Seth caught it, but in the next instant he had slid the ring onto her finger and then snatched her out of her chair to pull her into a bone-crushing embrace before planting a hard kiss on her mouth.

"She said yes!" he exclaimed to the room. Lori didn't have the heart to correct him. There would be time to end it later, when they didn't have witnesses.

"Thank you," he said into her ear. "You won't regret this."

She already regretted it, but she smiled tightly and endured the hugs and congratulations of her coworkers, until finally, the whole nonsensical farce was over and only the two of them and her father remained in the conference room.

"I know this came as a surprise," Seth said quickly, "but I've been planning to propose for at least a month, since you returned from Ireland."

In other words, since she'd decided to put the brakes on their relationship and had started making excuses as to why she could no longer spend as much time with him. She told herself again it had nothing to do with who she'd met or what had happened during those brief weeks in Ireland. She and Seth just weren't as compatible as she'd originally thought.

"Well, I think it's wonderful," Jack said. "In fact, why don't we celebrate with dinner tonight?"

He named a Michelin 2-star restaurant that boasted a typical reservation period of six weeks, promising a table for four at eight o'clock before he hugged Lori and left her alone with her surprise fiancé.

They stood in awkward silence for a moment before they both began to speak at once.

"I know this isn't what you expected—"

"You know I can't accept—"

They both broke off, embarrassed.

"Ladies first," Seth said.

Lori fiddled with the ring on her finger. It was at least a size too large and the heavy stone kept sliding to one side. "I can't accept this, Seth. You must know that."

"Oh, I see." He took her hand in his larger one. "I messed up on the sizing. Your mother said you wore a size seven, but I think you're closer to a six. No worries, I'll take it back to the jeweler and have it resized."

Lori stared at him, bemused. "You talked to my mother about this?"

He raised innocent eyes to hers. "Of course I did. I asked your father for his permission about three weeks ago. You must have guessed my intentions."

"No," she spluttered. "Why would I? We've had some fun dates, but it's never been serious between us. If I somehow gave you the impression that I expected this, I'm sorry."

But instead of being angry, Seth gave her a reassuring smile and drew the ring from her finger. She watched as he tucked it back into its velvet lining and returned the tiny box to his jacket pocket. "You have nothing to apologize for. I did this all wrong. I see that now." He gave a self-deprecating laugh. "What was I thinking of, proposing to you in front of the whole office? I just thought it would make you feel special, the way some guys use the Jumbotron at Soldier Field to pop the question."

"No, no," Lori protested, growing exasperated. "It's not that. I can't marry you, Seth. You're a sweet guy and I really like you, but marriage was never on my radar."

"Well, it's been on my radar since we first danced at the company Christmas party last year," he declared. "I admire everything about you, Lori. Your parents are great, and your dad has treated me like his own son. Your mother is beautiful and classy, and I can see you becoming more like her as

you get older. And you know how I feel about your brothers—we like the same sports teams and have similar tastes
and standards. I actually enjoy hanging out with them."

Lori looked at him quizzically. Did he even realize the
things he professed to admire pertained to her family and not
to her? Or that his so-called proposal had lacked any mention of love? She'd always suspected he was more attracted to
her family than he was to her, and now she knew it was the
truth.

"Seth," she said gently, "I'm glad you like my family.
They like you, too, but that's not a reason to marry someone.
Honestly, you don't even know me. Not really."

Seth laughed, but it sounded slightly less confident.
"Sure I do. I know we haven't taken our relationship to the
next level, but that's something I actually admire and respect
about you—that it means something to you. I never thought
I'd say this, but I don't mind waiting until we're married."
Catching her hand, he carried it to his mouth. "I know it's
going to be great."

Pulling her hand free, Lori couldn't hide her growing
annoyance. "We're not getting married, okay? The whole
idea is insane. I'm sorry, but you need to return the ring. I'll
tell my parents it was a misunderstanding, that we're better
off as friends. They'll understand."

"Is it because I got the job?" he asked.

"No!" That hadn't helped his cause, but she would have
refused him regardless.

"Okay, good. I was worried that might influence your decision, but I want to assure you that whenever I need to travel for work, you'll come with me. We'll see the world together."

"And what about my job? Do you think I'd be able to just pick up and take off anytime you need to travel?" She knew she was being unfair, since she had no intention of taking off anywhere with Seth Bieler. Ever. But he seemed not to notice her indignation.

"Well, that's another thing. You wouldn't actually need to work," he replied, looking a little smug. "I would always take care of you."

Lori's eyes widened, and for a moment, she just stared at him, speechless, realizing he had no idea how old-fashioned and misogynistic he sounded. "Oh, golly," she said, clasping her hands together and giving him a wide-eyed look of adoration. "How can I resist an offer like that?"

"Is that a yes?" he asked hopefully.

"No, that was sarcasm. And we're done with this conversation," she said, losing her patience. "I am not going to marry you. I only said I would because I didn't want to embarrass you in front of all those people. You can tell them whatever you want about why we broke things off, but I need you to be clear about this—we are not engaged."

To her surprise, he took her by the shoulders and tipped his head so that he could look into her eyes. "Don't make any decisions yet. It's been a stressful day, and you're probably still upset about the job, but I have an idea. I'll get the ring resized and when I propose again, I'll do it right—flowers and candlelight and all the romance a girl could want. Okay?"

Shrugging free, Lori stepped out of reach. "No, it's not okay. None of that matters, Seth, because I'm not in love with you."

"But we'd make such a great team, Lori. Maybe you don't understand—this company is like a family to me. I have so much respect and admiration for your father, and nothing would make me happier than to become part of the Woods family."

It was too much. His persistence, coupled with the fact her father apparently did prefer him over her, snapped what remained of her fragile temper. "Fine, then marry one of them! But not me, Seth."

Turning on her heel, she all but ran from the conference room.

THE RESTAURANT WHERE Lori waited for her mother to arrive a scant hour later was only moderately busy since it was past the lunch hour but not quite late enough for the dinner crowd. She hadn't been able to remain at work but hadn't wanted to go home to an empty apartment, and Rachel hadn't answered when she made the long-distance call to Ireland. But she needed to talk to someone. So she'd called her mother, who had promised to meet her at the chic downtown bistro right away.

Lori had nabbed a table beneath a bank of massive industrial windows where she had a clear view of the Chicago River and the surrounding skyscrapers. The cherry blossoms were in bloom along the riverfront despite the fact there was still ice on the lake and a biting wind that whistled through the city streets.

"Hello, darling. I came as soon as I could, but traffic was a nightmare."

Lori looked up to see her mother pulling off her gloves and coat, her face a study in sympathy. Still attractive at sixty-four, Kathleen Woods looked effortlessly elegant in a black turtleneck paired with a herringbone skirt and boots. Now she unwound her scarf and fluffed her dark hair before sitting down and signaling to the waitstaff.

"What are you drinking?" she asked, eyeing Lori's cocktail.

"A vodka tonic with a splash of cranberry." Lifting her glass, she took another long swallow as a waiter approached their table. "I'll have another, please."

"And a chardonnay for me," her mother said.

After the waiter left, she leaned forward and laid a hand over Lori's fingers, squeezing gently. "I heard what happened. Your father said you initially accepted Seth's proposal, but then changed your mind?"

"Mom, he ambushed me in front of everyone! What was I supposed to do?" Realizing she'd raised her voice to the point where people were glancing in her direction, she leaned forward and hissed, "It was so humiliating!"

"What, the proposal or the fact you didn't get the job?"

Lori blew out a frustrated breath. "All of it. I was so sure that job was mine. And to have Dad stand up there and hand it to Seth, and then for Seth to do that—in front of everyone—" She gave a light shudder. "It was awful."

"I thought you liked him." Her mother's voice was gently probing. "You've been seeing him since before the holidays."

"Why can't I date someone without everyone thinking I want to marry the guy?" She waited as their drinks arrived before continuing. "I know you like him, but he's not for me."

"Your father thinks he has a real future with the company. You'd be well taken care of."

Lori knew her mother meant well, so she resisted the urge to say something snarky. Her mother wouldn't understand, having always been happy in her role as wife and mother. She enjoyed playing hostess to her father's many clients and seemed to derive a sense of purpose from her various charities and fundraisers. But Lori knew that lifestyle wasn't for her. She needed a man who would challenge her. A man who would see her as a true equal and not be afraid to let her make mistakes. A man who understood her need for independence. A man like—she shut the thought down before it could fully form.

"I'm not like you, Mom," she finally said, choosing her words carefully. "I don't want to be taken care of. I want to make my own way. I want to travel, to have a career I can be proud of. The commodities manager position would have given me all that. Now what am I supposed to do?"

"You still have a job working for your father," Kathleen reminded her gently. "But the commodities manager position would have had you traveling alone to countries that aren't always safe, especially for a young woman."

And just like that, Lori understood why she hadn't been selected for the job. She would always be, first and foremost, her father's little girl. He would never see her as an adult, capable of making her own decisions. He wanted to keep her safe and he wanted to keep her close.

She thought of her cousin, Rachel, who was the same age as herself and had been raised almost as a sister to Lori. Rachel's father had been Jack Woods's younger brother, but had died unexpectedly when Rachel was just fourteen. Jack had stepped in as more than an uncle—he'd been like a surrogate father to Rachel. But he hadn't objected when Rachel's graduate research had taken her to India and Pakistan, or when she'd accepted her current internship in Ireland. In fact, the only solo travel Lori had ever done was when she'd visited her cousin in Ireland the previous month. She realized now that she'd only been permitted to go because Rachel—the responsible one—had been there to keep an eye on her.

"I understand Dad's concerns," she said now, "but he needs to understand I'm a grown woman. I'm more than capable of managing on my own. He can't control my life forever."

Kathleen gave her a sympathetic smile. "Try telling him that. He only wants what's best for you, darling."

"What's best for me right now is to get away for a while," Lori said slowly. "What would you say if I told you I want to go back to Ireland?"

To her surprise, her mother reached across the table and took her hand. "I'd say that decision is long overdue."

# Chapter Two

L ORI HAD NEVER done anything so impulsive—so deliberately out of character—in her entire life. She'd needed to escape, to get as far away from Chicago as possible. So with her mother's blessing, and before she could talk herself out of it, she'd booked a seat on the next flight to Ireland.

Just the memory of that humiliating moment in the conference room made her want to scream. Instead, she tightened her hands on the steering wheel of her rental car and tried not to freak out that she was actually driving a stick shift.

With her left hand.

On the wrong side of the road.

In Ireland.

"Look right, turn left," she reminded herself as she approached yet another traffic circle—or roundabout, as the vehicle's voice navigation called it. She slowed to a stop as she approached the circle, on the lookout for other vehicles, but when she tried to shift the car into first gear, she inadvertently hit fifth instead. The engine roared, but gained no momentum.

"Oh, no, no," she moaned softly, looking in her rearview mirror at the cars stacking up behind her. Her stress level skyrocketed.

Unaccustomed to driving a stick shift, and having never shifted with her left hand before today, Lori tried to correct her error but ground the gears instead as the cars behind her began to blow their horns. Finally, she succeeded in finding first gear and the car exploded into motion so that she almost broadsided another vehicle already in the roundabout.

"Sorry! Sorry!" she called out as she negotiated the circle in fits and starts and emerged miraculously unscathed on the other side. "Clueless tourist here!"

She'd arrived at Dublin Airport just after dawn following an overnight flight from Chicago and, despite feeling depressed and jet-lagged, had opted to drive herself the one hundred sixty miles across Ireland to the small village of Ballylahane, on the northwestern coast. She'd been at it now for almost four hours, and was despairing of ever reaching her destination, when up ahead was a sign. Ballylahane was just five miles away.

"Finally," she breathed. "Please, just let me get there in one piece."

As she entered the quaint little town with its church spires, colorful shops, and sparkling river that wound through the town center, everything looked exactly the same and yet completely different. In the five weeks since she'd last visited Ballylahane, the landscape had exploded with lush greenery, and there were flowers *everywhere*. The town was preparing for a festival, with colorful buntings fluttering over the main road and flags flying over the storefronts. An enormous banner strung across the center of town read FESTIVAL OF FIRE—APR 28 THRU MAY 1.

"Festival of Fire?" Lori wondered aloud. "What the heck is that?"

She only hoped whatever it was wouldn't impact her ability to book a room in town. She didn't yet know how long she'd stay in Ireland, but three weeks sounded about right. She needed time to process what had happened, and three weeks would give her father a chance to miss her and— she hoped—understand how much he'd hurt her.

He knew how badly she had wanted that job. She'd worked her butt off for that job. More importantly, she'd have been perfect for the job. Instead, he'd selected Seth, which had been bad enough, but for Seth to have popped the marriage question had been salt in the wound. Had he somehow guessed she was getting ready to break up with him? Is that why he'd chosen to propose to her in front of her father and the company executives? Because he knew she wouldn't publicly refuse him? Just thinking about it made her eyes sting and her throat close up, but not because she was sad.

She was *furious*.

She pulled the car to a stop in front of O'Leary's B&B,

where her cousin, Rachel, was staying while she completed an internship at McDermott Mills, the oldest weaving mill in County Donegal. For a moment, she sat in the car and watched Mrs. O'Leary's three sheep as they grazed in the front yard. She hadn't told Rachel she was coming over. Her cousin would be shocked to see her, but right now she was the only person who would understand her grief and disappointment over losing the job. They were cousins, but they were also best friends. They'd shared an apartment in Chicago for years before Rachel had accepted the internship here in Ballylahane. Lori hadn't known who else to turn to. Rachel had always been the sensible one. She would know what to do.

Pulling in a deep breath, Lori climbed out of the car and opened the gate to the front yard, careful not to let the sheep escape. But before she could ring the bell, the door opened and Rachel stood there, staring at Lori as if she couldn't believe her eyes. She took one look at Lori's face and wordlessly opened her arms. Lori moved into the embrace and promptly burst into tears.

"DID AUNT KATHLEEN really say you should come back over?" Rachel asked when Lori had calmed down enough to tell her what had happened. "That seems so out of character. I can't believe Uncle Jack would have approved."

Lori made a scoffing sound. "He's lost his right to have a say about anything in my life, since he's the one who went ahead and ruined it."

Mrs. O'Leary had prepared a pot of tea and had put together a plate of breakfast pastries and fruit for the two of them, and now they sat in the breakfast room of the B&B, eating and talking, although Lori had little appetite.

Rachel looked at Lori with admiration. "I still can't believe you drove here from Dublin."

Lori gave her a reluctant smile. "I wanted to get here fast, and I didn't want to be without a car while I'm here." She grew silent for a moment, recalling her previous visit to Ballylahane the previous month, when she'd taken a taxi all the way from Dublin. Without a vehicle, she'd been limited in seeing the surrounding countryside until a local friend of the McDermott family, Flynn O'Rourke, had offered to take her sightseeing. Pushing the memory aside, she gave Rachel what she hoped was a bright smile. "At least now I have my independence."

"Tell me what happened with Seth. Did he really propose in front of all those people? I thought you said the two of you weren't serious?"

Lori shrugged, not wanting to admit to Rachel that since she had returned from visiting Ireland several weeks earlier, Seth had become more possessive and more demanding of her time. It was almost as if he *knew* she had met someone else. Not that Flynn O'Rourke could possibly count as romantic competition, even if he did look like a movie star and kissed like a dream. His family owned a sprawling sheep farm on the outskirts of Ballylahane, and just because they'd spent time together during her last visit didn't mean she wanted to marry the guy. He'd been a sexy—if oftentimes aggravating—diversion. End of story. She was certain Flynn had not thought of *her* again after she'd left Ireland.

Despite dating Seth for almost six months, Lori stopped short of actually calling him her boyfriend, even though her friends and family—especially her father—thought it was an excellent match. Maybe there was something wrong with her. She'd enjoyed their dates, but she'd never been wildly attracted to him, and had never been completely excited about the relationship. She couldn't put her finger on it, exactly, except to think there was some kind of chemistry disconnect that had only grown more apparent after she'd met Flynn. It seemed she couldn't stop herself from mentally comparing the two men, and Seth always came up short.

"I think Seth thought I'd be grateful," she muttered. "Afterward, when we were alone, he actually told me I didn't need to worry about a career because he would always take care of me."

"How sweet," Rachel murmured without conviction.

Lori cast her a baleful look. "It was condescending. He knows how much I wanted that job. He actually said I could join him on his business trips—imagine the gall. Inviting me to accompany him on trips that should have been mine to arrange in the first place. I still can't believe he actually proposed."

"Maybe he really does love you."

Lori dropped her face into her hands and groaned. "Who knows? He's never said so. Not even when he proposed. He said the company was like his family and nothing would make him happier than officially becoming part of the Woods family." She lifted her head and gave Rachel a bemused look. "What does that even mean? I swear he's more interested in romancing my dad than he is me. He's only after the company and thinks I'm the way to get it."

"Do you love him?"

Seth Bieler was good-looking in an affluent, Ivy League sort of way. He was polished and charming, and her entire family liked him. Even her older brothers approved. Honestly, she had a hard time finding any fault with him as he'd always been a perfect gentleman. He called when he said he would, responded to texts right away, and took her on dates to interesting places. Most women would be thrilled to be seen with him. But did she love him?

"No."

He'd never made her pulse quicken, never made her feel anxious about what he might be thinking, never made her ache to feel his lips against hers. In fact, his kisses had been pretty ho-hum and not once had she ever had the urge to tear off his clothes and do more. Not the way she had with—

She abruptly shut down the treacherous thought. She

wouldn't think of Flynn O'Rourke.

"Okay," Rachel was saying, bringing her back to the present. "So you did the right thing in refusing him." When Lori remained silent, Rachel's eyes widened. "You did refuse him, right?"

"Not at first," Lori admitted. "He proposed in front of every director and manager in the company, and if you could have seen the expression on my father's face . . . he was practically bursting with pride. How could I embarrass him or Seth like that?"

"So you told him later, in private, that you couldn't marry him?"

"Of course I did," Lori said, indignant. "I was very clear that we were not engaged and there was no way I could marry him. But he wouldn't take no for an answer." She shook her head in bemusement. "He was very, very persistent. He didn't even seem to hear me when I told him I wouldn't marry him."

"So where's the ring?" She grabbed Lori's bare hand. "Did you give it back?"

Lori gave her cousin a tolerant look. "Why would I keep it? Besides, it didn't fit. It was loose, so Seth said he would have it resized. I told him I wasn't ready to get married, but nothing I said could dissuade him. He said once the ring is resized he'll propose again and it will be so romantic that I won't be able to refuse, but I have a bottomless supply of no, no, and hell no."

"So he thinks he still has a chance?" Rachel asked in disbelief. "You know once he finds out where you are, he's going to come over here."

"I doubt it. He'll be too busy trying to impress my father to take any time off."

Rachel considered her for a long moment. "It doesn't sound like he's going to give up easily. Honestly, I've never been a huge Seth Bieler fan, but at least he has the intelligence to know a good thing when he sees it, and you, my dear, are a very good thing."

"Tell that to my father," Lori grumbled. "I would have made a great commodities manager."

She'd worked at Lakeside Industries for six years, mostly as her father's assistant, doing whatever tasks he assigned to her. She'd come to Ireland the previous month to make a business assessment of McDermott Mills and lay the groundwork for a partnership with the Irish textile company. Lori had been certain it was a test. Her father had wanted to determine if she was ready to move into a position with greater responsibility. But she'd been wrong, as evidenced by the fact he'd gone and given the job to Seth instead.

"I don't think he doubts your abilities," Rachel said. "I just think he worries more about you than he does your brothers. You're his only daughter—his baby girl. He wants to keep you safe."

What Rachel had said was true—as the only daughter among five children, Lori's parents had always treated her differently than her brothers. It didn't help that she was also the youngest child by six years. Her mother had desperately wanted a baby girl and had all but given up when Lori had arrived. The result was her parents had spoiled and indulged her—she could readily admit it—but they had also restricted her activities to those they considered *safe*. They had shielded and safeguarded her as if she was a precious treasure, while her brothers had been allowed to backpack through Europe, disappear for days on end, take up exhilarating and dangerous hobbies, and basically do whatever they'd wanted.

"It's just not fair," she grumbled, knowing she sounded like the child she insisted she wasn't.

"Listen, you've had a stressful day and a long flight," Rachel said, rubbing a hand over Lori's back. "Why don't you go up to my room and get some sleep? I'll check with Mrs. O'Leary and see if she has any vacant rooms. If not, I'll go over to the hotel and ask there. You'll feel better after you've had some sleep."

Lori nodded. "Thanks. I know I shouldn't have come over without letting you know first, but I had to see you. I had to get away."

"I understand," Rachel said, her tone sympathetic. "I'm glad you're here. I just hope we can find you somewhere to stay. With the Festival of Fire starting in just a few days, I'm worried there won't be anything available."

"What *is* the Festival of Fire? I saw the signs coming into town."

"Only the biggest festival in this part of County Donegal, apparently. Conall said it's their version of a May Day festival, to celebrate Beltane."

Conall McDermott, the owner of a local running shop and nephew of the man who owned McDermott Mills, was the true reason Rachel had chosen to stay in Ireland. Bad enough she'd fallen into a boghole while out walking during her first day in Ballylahane, but after Conall had rescued her, she'd fallen for him too. She could have returned to Chicago and accepted a position as lead textile designer at Lakeside Industries, but had opted to remain in Ballylahane and design tweed for McDermott Mills instead. With his bright-ginger hair, intense blue eyes, and ready smile, Lori acknowledged Conall McDermott was the complete package. More importantly, he and Rachel were perfect together. Lori couldn't blame her cousin for wanting to stay in Ireland with him.

"Beltane," Lori repeated. "As in, the pagan ritual where people dance naked around a bonfire?"

Rachel laughed. "Well, I don't know about the dancing-naked part, but apparently there *will* be a bonfire at the top of Carraig O'rga, which means Hill of Gold. Conall said it's the highest hill in the area."

"And that's it? That's the Festival of Fire?" Lori gave a snort of laughter. "No offense, but I hardly think a bonfire in the tiny little town of Ballylahane is going to attract hordes of people. I'm not worried about finding a place to stay— I'm sure there'll be plenty of rooms available at the hotel."

# Chapter Three

"SERIOUSLY? THERE ISN'T a single room to be had in the entire town?" Lori stared at her cousin in disbelief. Rachel had been gone when Lori awakened the following morning, but had left a note to meet her in town later. They were having a late breakfast at The Yarn Spinner's Café above the McDermott Mills retail shop.

Rachel liberally slathered a scone with butter and strawberry jam before looking across the table at Lori. "Nope. I told you the festival might make it difficult to find something."

"But did you check the other B&Bs in town?" Lori persisted.

"Of course I did. Mrs. O'Leary was nice enough to make some calls and even Seamus did what he could, but there's nothing within twenty miles of town. Even the self-catered cottages are all taken." She bit into her scone and considered Lori as she ate. "I'm sure you could find something in Donegal town, but you're more than welcome to stay in my room with me."

Lori swallowed her frustration. "That's very sweet of you,

but I don't want to stay in Donegal. It's a forty-minute drive from here. I want to stay in Ballylahane—in my own room. In case nobody has told you, you're a bed hog. You stole all the blankets last night and I nearly froze to death."

"Sorry," Rachel said, sounding anything but contrite.

Lori took a sip of her coffee and considered her cousin over the rim of her mug. "So what do we do now?"

"What about staying with Seamus and his wife? Their daughter, Mary-Kate, is back at school so I could ask if you could use her room, at least until the festival is over and things get back to normal."

Seamus McDermott owned the local weaving mill and, besides being Rachel's boss, had recently gone into business with Lori's father at Lakeside Industries, providing luxury Irish tweeds for the Chicago-based home textile company. He and his wife lived in a large manor house overlooking Ballylahane harbor. While they were nice enough, Lori couldn't envision herself staying with them.

"No, thanks," she said. "They barely know me, and I'd hate to impose on them. Besides, Seamus knows I'm looking for a room and he didn't offer for me to stay with him and his wife, so I think that's your answer."

"You're right. I seem to recall they have family staying with them from out of town for the festival."

"You could always stay with Conall, and I could take your room," Lori suggested slyly.

She watched in amused surprise as Rachel's face turned

rosy. "Oh, I couldn't. What would his parents think?"

Lori couldn't contain her astonished laugh. "Really? That's your concern?"

"We're taking things slow," Rachel said, defensive.

Lori raised her hands. "Okay, sorry. It was just a thought."

"We'll keep looking. I'm sure something will turn up. Maybe the hotel will have a cancelation."

But she didn't sound very optimistic and Lori acknowledged she had nobody but herself to blame since she'd chosen to arrive unannounced, without any prior reservations. She sighed and picked at her bowl of porridge, the aroma of hot-buttered cinnamon apples not enough to tempt her, given the dismal outlook regarding accommodations.

"Did you call your dad?" Rachel asked, rousing her from her thoughts.

"Yes. He didn't answer, but I left a message and told him I arrived safely and not to worry about me."

Rachel nodded. "Okay. You know, I've been thinking about what happened with you and Seth. Just because his proposal wasn't as romantic as you wanted doesn't mean he doesn't genuinely care for you. Maybe he's just one of those guys who finds it hard to express his feelings."

Lori narrowed her eyes in disbelief. "Really? He proposed to me in the company boardroom. There was nothing romantic about it at all. Like I said, he's more interested in becoming Jack Woods's son-in-law than he is in becoming my husband. He's not in love with me any more than I am with him. And when did you become such a Seth Bieler fan, anyway?" She pushed her bowl away. "You know what? I'm not actually hungry right now. Maybe I'll just get a muffin or something for later. Do you want anything else?"

Rachel shook her head. "No, thanks."

Pushing to her feet, Lori crossed the café to peruse the baked goods behind the glass counter. Torn between a chocolate stout cupcake and a Danish cheese pastry, she stilled at the sound of masculine voices on the staircase behind her.

No, it couldn't be.

Cautiously, she turned her head as two men entered the café. They paused at the top of the wide stairs to search for a vacant table. They didn't see her and for a moment, Lori was able to drink in the sight without restraint. How was it that in the space of mere weeks, Flynn O'Rourke had gotten even bigger and hotter than she remembered? He was a towering bulwark of steaming masculinity. His wavy black hair was longer, falling over his forehead and his collar, while his shoulders seemed broader and his arms thicker. He wore a blue jersey with the local football logo on the chest, and a pair of dark-gray running pants that clung lovingly to the hard muscles of his butt and thighs.

All the strength seemed to leech from her limbs and her heart began to pound, making her feel light-headed. For a moment, Lori thought she might need to sit down before she passed out. She'd known she would likely see Flynn again, but hadn't thought it would be so soon, or that she would have this kind of reaction to him. She wasn't ready. She hadn't mentally prepared herself.

He was with Conall, and now they were making their way toward the table where Rachel sat by herself, her gaze flicking quickly to where Lori stood rooted to the floor. Conall leaned down to kiss Rachel, and Lori knew the precise instant when Rachel told them she was there. She watched, mute, as Flynn's back stiffened, and then both men swiveled in her direction. Lori was only aware of Flynn, of how his silver-gray eyes widened in surprise and—was that pleasure?—before his expression turned to one of mocking humor.

"Well," he said softly as she approached, "that didn't take long. What's it been—four weeks? Missed me something fierce, did you?"

"Like the sheep misses the sheepdog," she retorted, grateful he had resorted to his usual habit of needling her. If he'd said something kind or if she'd seen any softness in his expression, she might have flung herself into his arms, which would have been the absolute worst thing to do. She turned toward Conall with a genuine smile, her arms outstretched. "How are you?"

Conall pulled her into a swift embrace. "Doing well. It's good to see you again."

As Lori stepped away, Flynn spread his arms wide.

"What, no hug for me? I'm hurt, truly."

Lori cast him an assessing look, hoping her face didn't betray how much she actually did want to feel all that rugged virility pressed against her. "No way. You're all sweaty."

*And big, and muscular, and completely gorgeous.*

"Ah, c'mon, sweetheart, bring it in. You know you want to," Flynn said with a taunting grin.

Before she could protest, he hauled her against the solid brick of his chest, nearly lifting her onto her tiptoes as he enfolded her in his arms. In the brief seconds before he released her, Lori was aware of the heat that emanated from him, as if he'd soaked up the sun's rays and stored them beneath his skin, and now let them seep into her. How else to explain the melting sensation that swamped her limbs? Beyond that, she became aware of how delicious he smelled—like woods and spice and clean laundry, and not at all like sweat, despite the fact his black hair was damp and there was a sheen of moisture on his neck.

She actually swayed a little as he set her back on her feet. She swiftly sat down at the table, hoping he hadn't noticed. Her heart was racing and she took some deep, calming breaths, willing herself to stay calm.

"Mind if we join you?" Conall asked.

"Of course not." Rachel smiled, moving her backpack from the empty chair beside her. "We're just finishing up, but we have no plans and I don't need to be back at work for another hour."

Without asking permission, Flynn lifted Lori's large handbag from the empty chair next to hers and hung it on the back before sitting down beside her. He angled his head toward her and Lori knew his silver gaze missed nothing, not the shadows under her eyes or her hair, hastily pulled into a messy bun at the top of her head, or her ancient college sweatshirt that had seen better days.

"When did you get in? You look terrible."

"Gee, thanks." Lori shrugged. "I got in yesterday. I'm still a little jet-lagged, and I didn't get much sleep last night."

"She stayed with me in my room," Rachel added. "We had to share the bed, so both of us are a little off this morning. I'll apologize in advance if we're not in a great mood."

Flynn gave Lori an amused look. "With you, how would I tell the difference?"

"Ha-ha." Lori narrowed her eyes at him. "Maybe you just bring out the worst in me."

*Liar.*

She wouldn't think of that day by the waterfall, just over a month earlier, when she'd allowed Flynn O'Rourke to see a side of her she rarely revealed. When for once, in the short time they'd known each other, neither had been interested in insulting or teasing the other. No, that day had been all about the pleasure they'd made each other feel. Just thinking about that heat-drenched afternoon caused warmth to crawl up her neck and into her face. She didn't miss how Flynn's gaze seemed suddenly riveted on her, or how his mouth curved in the barest hint of a smile, as if he knew exactly what she was thinking about.

Conall rose abruptly to his feet. "I'm going to take a look at the baked goods. Anybody want anything?"

"I'll take a bottled water," Flynn said, his eyes never leaving Lori's.

"I'll come with you," Rachel said.

After they left, Flynn leaned toward Lori and lowered his voice. "Are you going to just ignore what's right in front of you?"

Bemused, she could only stare at him. "What?"

He dropped his gaze briefly to her untouched bowl of oatmeal. "The porridge. Are you going to eat it?"

She blew out an aggravated breath and pushed the bowl toward him. "No. If you want it, go for it."

She watched as he lifted the bowl in one big hand and began to eat.

"Delicious," he confirmed. "They make the best porridge here."

He offered her a spoonful, but she shook her head. Lifting her coffee mug, she took a sip and watched surreptitiously as he ate with gusto, making appreciative noises as he polished off her breakfast. How could he make even the simple act of eating oatmeal look—and sound—sexy?

"Didn't you eat before you left the farm?" she asked, irritated that he could distract her so easily.

Pushing the empty bowl away, he leaned back in his chair and rubbed a hand over his stomach, drawing her attention to the flatness of his abs, visible beneath the stretchy athletic jersey. "I did, yeah, but that was nearly five hours ago."

Lori glanced at her watch. It was ten thirty, which meant he'd been up since sunrise. "What brings you into town, anyway?"

He leveled a steady look at her. "I might ask you the same thing."

The last thing Lori wanted was to tell him the truth, but something in his clear, gray eyes—a gentle understanding—caused words to tumble out of her mouth before she could stop them. "My father chose Seth Bieler for the position I wanted and then Seth proposed to me in front of the entire company and I was so furious, I came here."

Flynn nodded as if he understood. "That was a shite thing to do."

Lori didn't know which part of her babbled explanation he referred to, but then decided maybe all of it. Before she could say anything more, Rachel and Conall returned. Conall placed a sweating bottle of water and a steaming mug of coffee in front of Flynn.

"Thanks, mate," Flynn said, and twisted the cap from the bottle. He proceeded to drain nearly the entire thing in one long swallow, and Lori was helpless to look away, fascinated by the working of his strong throat. Finally, he set the bottle down and wiped the back of his hand across his mouth. Collecting herself, Lori tore her gaze away and looked instead at Conall, who was eating the chocolate stout cupcake she had admired just minutes earlier.

"Were you out for a run?" she asked, her question including both men.

"Well, sort of," Conall said, his gaze flicking to Flynn. "We're part of the relay to carry the torch through town to Carraig O'rga for the Festival of Fire—"

"So we did a practice run this morning with the other torchbearers," Flynn finished.

"How long is the relay?" Rachel asked.

"It starts in the center of town and follows the bike path along the river and into the hills, before coming back into town by the mill, and then up to Carraig O'rga," Conall said. "It's only about ten kilometers and we have five runners, so none of us is going to exert ourselves overly much."

"Says you," Flynn grumbled. "I have to carry the torch up that monster of a hill, which is no walk in the park."

"Ah, but you get the honor of passing the torch to the May Queen." Conall grinned. "The festival can't start without you."

But Flynn only shrugged, as if unconvinced, and a brief silence settled over the table.

"So how long are you planning to stay?" Conall asked Lori.

"I'm not sure. I thought—"

"Until her fiancé comes and fetches her home again," Flynn said, sounding annoyed.

"Wow," Rachel said, her eyebrows shooting upward. "That didn't take long. I guess we were gone longer than I realized if that conversation's already happened."

"Wait." Conall stared at Lori in confusion. "You're engaged?"

"No." She glared at Flynn. "*No*. I mean, Seth Bieler *did* propose, but—it's complicated."

"Keeping him dangling, eh?" Flynn muttered, lifting his coffee mug. "Nice."

"For your information," Lori said hotly, "I refused his offer. It's not my fault if he won't take no for an answer." She turned her attention to Conall, determined to ignore the big, surly man beside her. "I don't know how long I'll be here, to be honest. There don't seem to be any rooms at the inn, so to speak. Because of the festival, everything is booked. As much as I don't want to, I may have to stay in Donegal."

There was silence for a moment as they each considered her words.

"You could stay at my place."

For a moment, Lori thought she'd misheard, and turned to stare at Flynn. He didn't look at her, just cradled his coffee mug in his big hands and considered the contents.

"What did you say?" Surely she'd imagined that Flynn O'Rourke had just invited her to stay with him. Even as her pulse leaped at the suggestion, she knew it wasn't possible for so many reasons. Despite the fact he exasperated her as no other man ever had, he also had the ability to tempt her and make her want things she had no business wanting. And since she had no intention of remaining in Ballylahane, she couldn't allow herself to want Flynn.

He swiveled his head to look at her, pinioning her with his mercury gaze. "My grandmother's cottage is empty. We just finished renovating it with the intention of renting it. Nobody would mind if you stayed there."

"Oh." For a moment, Lori was too surprised to speak. And if she felt any disappointment he was not, in fact, inviting her to stay under the same roof with him, she hoped it didn't show in her expression. "Where is the cottage, exactly?"

"On the farm, about one hundred meters from the main house. It's the original farmhouse, but like I said—it hasn't been occupied since my gram passed away a few years ago. But it's clean and comfortable and we just installed new windows and fixtures."

"Are you sure your family won't object?"

"I can't see why they would, it's just sitting empty," Flynn said with a shrug. "If you want it, it's yours."

Lori had visited the O'Rourke sheep farm the previous month with Rachel and Conall, which was when she'd first met Flynn. He'd provided a sheepdog demonstration, had let them bottle-feed some lambs, and had shown them how to cut blocks of peat from a nearby peat bog. The farm was located on the outskirts of town on a beautiful, windswept bluff overlooking a deep saltwater inlet. While the scenery had been breathtaking, the real attraction that day had been Flynn himself, as he'd provided a guided tour of the farm.

Her gaze slid unwillingly over him, noting the broad shoulders and impressive bulge of muscles beneath the nylon jersey he wore. He was classically handsome, with his strong cheekbones, proud nose, and a square jaw that boasted a cleft in the center of his chin. But combined with his thick, unruly hair and his winter-sky eyes, Lori thought him extraordinary. Right now, his expression was impassive, as if he couldn't care less whether she accepted his offer.

"You have a car," Rachel reminded her, pulling Lori's attention away from Flynn. "And it's only a ten-minute drive into town. Once the festival is over, you can easily find a room at the hotel for the rest of your stay."

"I don't know." She hesitated, torn between the lure of seeing Flynn every day and the reality of living—even temporarily—on a working sheep farm. She couldn't even begin to fool herself into thinking it would be like staying at O'Leary's B&B. Lori didn't miss the silent encouragement on Rachel's face. Still, she hesitated. The thought of living in such close proximity to Flynn O'Rourke caused all kinds of alarms to go off in her head. What if he came on to her?

*What if he didn't?*

"I would hate to impose."

"I doubt that's true," Flynn said, a half smile curving his

mouth. "But I wouldn't have made the offer if it was an imposition."

"Okay," she said, before she could change her mind. "If you really don't mind, I accept, but only if I can pay you whatever the going rate is for a cottage rental. I won't accept if it's free."

"Whatever makes you comfortable," Flynn said with a decisive nod. "That's settled, then. You can move in this afternoon."

# Chapter Four

He'd lost his flipping mind.

There was no other explanation for why he'd offered the cottage to Lori Woods, except he'd been completely floored to see her standing there in The Yarn Spinner's Café, staring at him as if he was one of those sugary pastries on display in the cabinet behind her. For a moment, he'd been too stunned to react. Only one thought had reverberated through his befuddled brain.

*She'd come back.*

He'd known their paths would eventually cross again, since she and her cousin were like sisters, and Rachel had made the decision to remain in Ballylahane and continue working at the woolen mill. It made sense that Lori would want to visit occasionally. But he hadn't expected to see her again so soon. He hadn't been prepared.

He especially had not been ready to hear that her absolutely useless gobshite of a lad back in Chicago had proposed to her. He'd known about him, of course, but Lori had led Flynn to believe the relationship wasn't serious, at least on her part. Obviously, it hadn't been serious on his part either.

Because if it had been, the idiot would have already arrived in Ballylahane, having caught the very next flight to Ireland in order to convince her they belonged together.

At least, that's what he would have done.

He glanced into the rearview mirror. Behind him, Lori drove a full-sized sedan along the narrow, bramble-hemmed road that led to the O'Rourke farm. Rachel was beside her in the passenger seat. He had a small satisfaction in knowing the road was too tight for Lori to turn around and drive back into town. She'd have to follow him all the way to the farm before she could find a spot wide enough, and he was confident he could talk her out of it if she had, in fact, changed her mind about staying at the cottage.

The hedges gave way to low stone walls topped with wire fencing and on either side of the road, dozens of black-faced sheep grazed lazily in the fields. Soon, the farm itself came into view, dominated by a large whitewashed barn with a metal roof, and several cottages and outbuildings. Despite having lived on the farm his entire life, Flynn never tired of the dramatic views. He never took for granted how lucky his family was to have settled this particular bit of earth, which had belonged to the O'Rourkes for five generations. Situated at the top of a steep hill, the property swept down to a narrow, sparkling blue inlet that led to the ocean. The long stretches of meadow that sloped down to the water were a lush green, bisected by stone walls and dotted with sturdy sycamore trees. Clusters of white sheep meandered along the hills, or sought shade beneath the spreading branches of the trees.

Pulling his work van to a stop beside the barn, Flynn killed the engine and climbed out, waiting as Lori parked her car. He heard barking and turned to see his two border collies, Rob and Brody, round the corner of the barn and streak toward him. They swarmed around his legs, tails wagging as they gazed adoringly up at him.

"Good lads," he murmured, bending down to give each of them a rub behind the ears.

"I see some things never change." Lori got out of the vehicle and watched as Flynn greeted the dogs, a smile curving her mouth. "Still as devoted to you as ever."

Flynn straightened, unable to suppress a grin. "Jealous?"

"Confused," she retorted.

She looked around as if seeing the farm for the first time. Near the barn were several fenced enclosures where they brought sheep for shearing and exams. The narrow, private road that led to the farm continued past the barn to a large farmhouse, set back a bit from the drive and overlooking the water. His older brother's house sat just over the rise, with only the roof and chimney stack visible from where they stood. "So which one is it?"

Turning, Flynn indicated a small, whitewashed cottage perched on a knoll behind them. Partially hidden by a hedge of flowering rhododendrons, the cottage was nearly invisible from the road. "That's it there. Come along. I'll give you the tour."

With a word for the dogs to stay, he made his way along a gravel walkway that led to the cottage. He opened the door and stepped back to allow the two women to enter.

"Oh, this is wonderful," Rachel said, looking around.

Flynn followed them inside, leaving the door open. The main living space was a long, high-ceilinged room with a cozy sitting area and a smoke-blackened stone fireplace at one end and a large kitchen at the other, with an enameled Aga cooker. The walls were whitewashed stone, and the floors were dark wood, covered with warm, red-patterned carpets. The furnishings were understated and comfortable. A flatscreen television sat on a small table in the corner.

"This is nice," Lori murmured, her gaze lingering on the Aga. "I don't think I'll do much cooking, though. I would have no clue how to use that stove."

"It's a cinch once you know how," Flynn assured her. "I can show you."

She cast him a swift smile. "Thanks."

"Sure." He gestured to a door tucked into the wall beside the fireplace. "The bedroom is through there. You can have a look if you'd like. There's an en suite bathroom as well."

He waited in the living room as the two women examined the bedroom. He could hear their soft murmurings, and when they reappeared in the doorway, Lori seemed pleased.

"The bedroom is very comfortable," she acknowledged. "I love the iron bedframe, and the bathroom looks as if it's been renovated recently."

"It has, yeah," Flynn agreed. "The appliances are new, as is the mattress and bedding. You should find everything you need in the linen press." He indicated another door in the corner of the kitchen. "There's a second bedroom through there. It's smaller and there's only a half bath, but if you wanted to stay with her, Rachel, there's plenty of room. You'd be more than welcome."

"Thanks, that's very generous of you, but I enjoy being spoiled at Mrs. O'Leary's," Rachel said, laughing. "She's a great cook. Besides, I'm just a short walk from work, and if I stayed here, Lori would have to get up early every morning to drive me into town."

"Yeah, forget that," Lori retorted, but her quick smile took any sting out of the words. Stepping around Flynn, she moved to the doorway and peered outside. "Where do you live, exactly?"

"Me?" He hesitated before indicating the larger house farther down the road, beyond the barn. "I live in the main house with my folks and my brother, Declan."

"Oh." Lori was silent for a moment before she turned to face him. "Why don't you live here? It seems perfect for a single guy like yourself."

Flynn hesitated, not wanting to tell her the house *was* his, and the plan had always been for him to live in the cottage; it was what his grandmother had wanted—what he had wanted too. He and his dad had spent the better part of a year renovating the building, tearing out and rebuilding interior walls and modernizing the kitchen, repairing the exterior mortar and replacing the roof and windows, upgrading the plumbing and electrical and installing new appliances, all while managing the day-to-day operation of the farm. When they'd finished, the cottage was exactly as Flynn had envisioned.

Then his dad had fallen sick.

At first they'd thought he just had a bad case of flu that he couldn't shake, but when he didn't improve, he'd gone to see his doctor. A battery of tests had followed, and within weeks, they realized it was worse—much worse than a bout of flu. He'd been diagnosed with an aggressive form of leukemia, which required equally aggressive—and expensive—treatment. The farm barely sustained itself, so there wasn't any extra money to cover the medical bills. That's when his mother had asked if he would consider renting the cottage, just until his father's health improved. The income would be nominal, but every bit helped.

Flynn had agreed without hesitation, but he'd never imagined it would be Lori Woods staying in the cottage. He tried to imagine her living in the space he'd designed for himself, preparing a meal on his enameled cooker or curled up on his sofa as a peat fire sputtered in the hearth.

Sleeping in his bed.

He blew out a hard breath and pushed the images aside.

"Oh," Lori said carefully, her brow creasing. "This *is*

your house, isn't it?"

"No," he said quickly, lest she decide not to stay. "At least, not at the moment. We'd already planned to rent it as a self-catered vacation cottage. Just hadn't gotten around to posting it."

"Are you sure?" She chewed her lower lip and looked adorably concerned. "I'd hate to think I was putting you out of your own home."

"You're not, truly. I'm happy where I am," he replied. "Renting it will help me recoup some of the renovation costs."

"Well then, that's good news for both of us, right?"

"Absolutely," Flynn agreed, relieved. "Very good news."

"I'll just bring my suitcases in, if that's okay?" Lori said, moving past him and down the walkway to where her car was parked.

"I'll get them for you." Flynn followed her, but before she could open the trunk, her cell phone rang. She pulled the device out of her pocket and looked at the display. Her brow puckered into a small frown.

"I'm sorry," she said, stepping away. "I need to take this."

Flynn didn't need to guess the caller's identity.

"Hello, Seth," she said in greeting as she glanced over her shoulder at Flynn. "Yes, it's true. I'm in Ireland. No, I just needed to get away for a bit."

Flynn leaned against the car and crossed his arms over his

chest, watching her. She walked a short distance up the road and lowered her voice so that he could no longer make out their conversation. It took all his restraint not to yell to her to end it with Seth, to tell him in no uncertain terms that she didn't love him and would never marry him, no matter how many times he proposed. His hands itched to snatch the phone from her fingers and grind it beneath his heel in the dirt.

He did neither.

Rachel came out of the cottage and stood beside him.

"Who is she talking to?"

Flynn scowled. "One guess."

"Oh. Well, you can't begrudge him a phone call."

"Are they engaged or not?" he asked. "I'm a little confused on the issue."

"She only said yes initially because she didn't want to embarrass him," Rachel explained, "but once they were alone, she returned his ring and told him she wouldn't marry him. My understanding is he refuses to accept no as an answer. He told her not to make any decisions until after he gets the ring resized and has a chance to propose to her again, this time in a private, romantic way."

"Will it make a difference?"

"I don't think so."

Flynn grunted. "Thick as a plank, is he?"

Rachel leaned against the car next to him. "Just very persistent, but I'm not sure he could make her happy." She turned her head to look at him, her expression sympathetic. "But, in all fairness, neither can I see her staying here."

Meaning he could never make her happy either.

Flynn felt his scowl deepen. "Why not? Stranger things have happened." He gave Rachel a pointed look. "Take you and Conall, for instance."

Before Rachel could respond, Lori turned back toward them, shoving the phone into the pocket of her jeans. Her expression was carefully neutral, but her cheeks were splotchy with emotion. Flynn pushed himself away from the car so she could open the trunk.

"Everything settled, then?" he asked.

"There's nothing to settle. He knows my feelings on the matter, and that's the end of it." She gave an irritable shrug. "I can't help it if he wants to delude himself."

"The lad needs to understand you're not going to marry him, or even date him ever again."

Lori stared at him in wide-eyed astonishment.

"In fact," he continued, holding her gaze, "give me your phone. I'll call him back and let him know it too."

"Flynn, you wouldn't," Rachel said, sounding both appalled and impressed.

"Thanks, but I have it under control," Lori said stiffly. Reaching into the trunk, she struggled with her baggage.

"Sure you do." Gently pushing her aside, Flynn took hold of the oversized suitcase and smaller carry-on bag. Lifting them out, he pretended to stagger. "Sweet Mary and

Joseph, what have you got in here?"

"Just the essentials," Lori said with a sweet smile. "If it's too much for you, just say the word and I'll take them."

Flynn grunted and, ignoring her comment, carried the bags into the cottage, moving through the living area to the bedroom. He set the suitcases on the floor and cast a quick glance around the room to ensure all was tidy. The iron bedframe had belonged to his grandmother and looked fine with a new coat of black paint. The red-and-white star-patterned quilt had been stitched by her as well. The linen press, an antique cabinet designed for storing linens and clothing, stood against one wall. When the decision had been made to rent the cottage, his mother had added some feminine touches to the room, including heaps of pillows on the bed, lace doilies on every surface, framed photos of border collies and sheep on the walls, an antique dresser with attached mirror, and a pretty carved chest at the foot of the bed. The final result was warm and inviting.

Lori entered the room and lowered a backpack onto the carved chest. She'd pulled her hair out of the topknot and now it hung in tousled waves around her face. Standing on the opposite side of the bed, the room seemed suddenly small and very intimate. Worse, all Flynn could think about was her, spread across his bed like a pagan offering. He had no business envisioning her like that—hadn't she'd told him all the reasons why they were completely wrong for each other? Yet here she was, in his house.

In his bedroom.

He knew a deep satisfaction that when Bieler had proposed, she'd fled to Ballylahane.

*To him.*

Well, technically, to her cousin, but she had to have known she would eventually run into him again. Nothing had changed, at least for him. She still managed to arouse and aggravate him in equal measures. It didn't help that she was even lovelier than he remembered, her dark-brown hair framing her face, her wide, hazel eyes fringed with thick lashes, and her mouth as pink and tempting as the raspberries that grew wild along the hedgerows. But the underlying vulnerability he sensed in her was new—attributable, no doubt, to the loss of the coveted position within her father's company and her inability to control the narrative. He tried to dredge up some sympathy, but all he felt was triumph.

"Well, I'll leave you to it," he said, his voice gruff. "Let me know if there's anything you need."

"And where exactly would I find you if I need you?"

"I'm always around."

Lori glanced toward the living room, where Rachel was pretending interest in a stack of magazines about rural farming, and lowered her voice. "Flynn, about that day at the waterfall and what I said to you later, the night before I left . . ."

Flynn stilled. He hadn't forgotten that afternoon at the waterfall. In fact, he thought about it too often for comfort—about how she'd made him feel. She'd also crushed any hope he'd had of maintaining a relationship when, a week later, he'd suggested he might fly over to Chicago for an extended visit. She'd seemed almost panicky at the thought.

*Face it, Flynn—it was fun, but we both knew it couldn't last. We come from different worlds.*

"It's forgotten," he said, because she was here now. Reason suggested if she felt that strongly about keeping her distance, she would never have agreed to stay at the farm.

He watched as she traced a finger along the stitching on the quilt, not looking at him. "I never meant to lead you on."

Flynn didn't believe her for a second. She'd teased and tantalized him at every opportunity, and he hadn't been able to resist. He wasn't sure he could now. He gave a self-deprecating laugh. "Don't torture yourself. I'm easily led."

He got as far as the bedroom door when she said his name, so softly he almost didn't hear. He paused without turning.

"I'm sorry. For everything."

Without acknowledging her words, he strode through the living room, ignoring Rachel's sympathetic gaze. He needed to get out of the cottage. He needed to put distance between himself and Lori because seeing her again had made him realize one thing—he still wanted her.

And by inviting her to stay at the farm, even for a few days, he risked everything, including his heart.

# Chapter Five

"I'LL STAY OVERNIGHT," Rachel said. "It will mean you having to drive me into town in the morning, but I don't like leaving you alone."

They stood in the kitchen unpacking the groceries they had purchased in town. Lori hadn't bought much—just enough to see her through the weekend, when the Festival of Fire would end and she could relocate to the Grand Arms Hotel.

"I'll be fine," she assured her cousin. "I'll probably just go to bed early anyway. No point in you staying when I won't be very good company, and you could be enjoying the evening with Conall."

"I'll at least stay for dinner," Rachel said, eyeing the Aga cooker. "I'm dying to see how this thing works."

"It's like a relic from the iron age." The enameled oven was unlike anything Lori had ever seen, with two large, round covers on the top and three heavy, cast-iron doors on the front. Lifting one of the covers, she felt heat radiating from the surface of the metal plate. "Someone left it on!"

"You're right," Rachel agreed. "I think that's the secret to an Aga—they're always on, so it helps keep the house warm during the colder months. Conall has one in his house."

"But there aren't any temperature controls," Lori said. "Maybe I should find Flynn and ask him to give us a quick tutorial."

She didn't miss Rachel's knowing smile. "In that case, maybe I should leave."

"Somehow, I don't think Flynn has any desire to be alone with me." Lori was quiet for a moment. "I think I may have bruised his ego the last time I was here."

Rachel paused in the act of pulling a quart of milk from the bag. "Really? Because Flynn has never struck me as the kind of guy with a big ego. Pride? Sure. But not ego. What happened?"

Lori shrugged and took the carton of milk from her and put it in the fridge. "The day I left, he said he wanted us to stay in touch and even suggested coming to Chicago to visit me."

"Oh. I didn't realize . . . I thought it was all just flirting and fun. More of a holiday fling."

"Well, it was. Sort of."

Lori didn't want to admit to Rachel that it had started out that way, but had unexpectedly become more than that. But when Flynn had suggested visiting her in Chicago, she'd panicked. She was already dating Seth, even if the relationship was unsatisfying and teetering on the brink of a breakup. How would he react if a big, hunky Irishman showed up on her doorstep? He'd run straight to her father, who would think she was too frivolous to handle the position of commodities manager. He'd sent her to Ballylahane to do a specific task, and if he thought she'd spent that time fooling around with one of the locals, he'd be more than just disappointed—he'd be convinced she was too irresponsible for the job. So she had crushed Flynn's suggestion, not wanting anyone back home to know about him.

Considering how things had turned out, Lori wished she'd done things differently. Instead of alienating Flynn, she should have stayed longer in Ireland. She should have ended things with Seth then and invited Flynn to come to Chicago. She should have agreed to a long-distance romance and indulged in late-night, sexy video chats with him.

So many *should-haves*.

Now it was too late.

She gave Rachel a helpless look. "I managed to mess everything up."

Rachel gave her a hug, her expression sympathetic. "Well, you're here now. And you're staying on his farm, so that should count for something. If he didn't feel *anything* for you, he never would have made the offer." She dipped her head and looked into Lori's eyes. "The real question is, how do you feel about him?"

Before Lori could answer, there was a light rapping at the front door.

"That could be him," Lori said, hating how hopeful she

sounded.

But it was not Flynn. An older woman stood on the doorstep, a covered dish in her hands. Seeing Lori, she smiled.

"Good afternoon, I'm Maureen O'Rourke."

She had a lovely, lilting accent and a smile that immediately put Lori at ease.

"Oh." Then, noting the silver eyes and shoulder-length, black hair liberally sprinkled with gray, Lori realized this must be Flynn's mother, and she hastily opened the door wide. "*Oh!* Please, come in."

"I don't want to intrude," Maureen said, stepping inside, "but I wanted to be certain you're settled and have everything you need."

"That's very kind of you," Lori said, before turning toward Rachel, who had come forward to say hello. "I'm Lori Woods, and this is my cousin, Rachel Woods. She works at McDermott Mills, so I thought I'd fly over and visit her."

"Hello, Rachel. I've heard so much about you." Her smile was warm and genuine. "All nice things, of course."

"Thank you," Rachel murmured.

There was an awkward silence as Lori noted how Maureen did not mention hearing anything—good, bad, or otherwise—about her. Had Flynn bad-mouthed her to his own mother? If so, what had he said? Or had he never mentioned her at all?

"I didn't realize there was a festival going on, or that all the accommodations in town would be booked," Lori blurted, feeling the need to fill the sudden silence, and also explain her reasons for being here, on the O'Rourke farm. "Flynn said you were renting the cottage, so I'm feeling very fortunate and grateful that it's available. It's absolutely charming, by the way."

"Well, that would be Flynn's doing. You're our first guest, so I'll be counting on you to let me know if anything is amiss." She held out the dish as if she'd almost forgotten she still carried it. "Oh, I made an apple tart this morning and thought you might enjoy it with your tea, or even for breakfast."

Lori took the dish and peeked beneath the checkered hand towel to see an apple pie, baked on a shallow plate instead of a deep dish. She breathed in the aromas of baked apples and cinnamon. "Mm, this looks and smells delicious. Thank you so much."

"Would you like to stay for tea?" Rachel asked, flicking a quick, meaningful glance at Lori. "We were just going to put on some water, weren't we?"

"Oh, yes," Lori enthused, although there had been no such plan. "Please stay, and maybe you can show us how to use the stove. It's not like anything we're familiar with back home."

Maureen laughed. "Very well, thank you. The cooker is quite simple, really. This one only looks old, but it's a newer model modified to run on propane. Let me show you how it works."

After she had provided a quick tutorial on the various hot plates and ovens, Lori filled a kettle and set it on the boiling plate, while Rachel cleared away the groceries and gathered together teacups and dishes and arranged them on the table. Lori found an airtight container of tea on the counter near the stove and, when the kettle began to whistle, filled a teapot with steaming water.

"So you're here in time for the festival," Maureen said after they were seated at the small table in the kitchen. "Did Flynn tell you he's carrying the torch to the bonfire?"

"He did," Lori said. "Just how big is the festival? It sounds like it draws a lot of people."

"Oh, it does. Ballylahane has celebrated Beltane for nearly two hundred years, but it's only been in the last twenty years or so that the festival has really taken off." She waited as Lori poured them each a cup of tea. "There's a street fair that includes food and crafts vendors, and of course, the shops all run discount sales. There's a petting zoo, with lambs and goats and donkeys, for the children. The pubs will be quite full, and different musical groups will play throughout the weekend, and the local girls will weave ribbons around the Maypole. Then, of course, there are the Beltane fire dancers."

Lori watched as Maureen cut the apple tart and placed a generous slice on each plate. "Those are the ones who dance naked around the bonfire?"

Maureen's eyes widened, and then she laughed. "Oh, now that would be something to see, wouldn't it? There may be some naked revelry in other locations during Beltane, but there's none of that here in Ballylahane, at least not that I know of." She gave Lori a cheeky wink. "No, these fire dancers are a professional dance troupe. The fire dance is an interpretive dance, and it's quite beautiful, really."

"I can't wait to see it," Lori said, smiling. She took a forkful of apple tart and popped it into her mouth, savoring the tart sweetness of the apples and the flaky crust. "Oh, this is delicious, Mrs. O'Rourke."

"I'm so glad you like it, and you must call me Maureen," she said, looking pleased. "How long will you be in Ireland, Lori?"

Carefully wiping her mouth with a napkin, Lori hesitated. "I'm not sure. That is, I haven't bought a return ticket yet." Seeing Maureen's surprise, she felt compelled to explain. "I came over on impulse, without a real plan. I had no idea about the festival."

"Well, it's lucky we had the cottage ready."

"I'm surprised it wasn't already rented, especially with the festival going on," Rachel said.

"We've only recently completed the renovations and hadn't yet gotten around to advertising it," Maureen said. "As I said, you're the first. I'm sure the hotel will have rooms available once the festivities are over, but you're more than welcome to stay on here for as long as you'd like."

Lori looked at her in surprise. "Thank you. I'll think about it and let you know."

When they'd finished their tea, Maureen stood up to leave. "It's been lovely meeting you both. Lori, if you need anything at all, come up to the main house. Otherwise, feel free to ask one of the lads. They're always about the place. You can't miss them. It's going to be chilly tonight, so I'll ask one of them to bring you some peat for a fire."

"Do all your sons work on the farm?" Lori asked. While she knew Flynn had two brothers, they had never talked much about his siblings or what they each did for a living.

"Flynn and Declan manage the farm and my oldest son, Shane, raises mussels down in the bay, although he helps out on the farm during the busy season." She paused. "They're good, hardworking men. I can't for the life of me understand why they're still single, especially Flynn. He's always been popular with the ladies."

"It must be by choice," Rachel said, her eyes dancing. "Otherwise, some smart girl would have snapped him up long ago."

After Maureen left, Lori rounded on her cousin. "Really?"

"What?" Rachel asked, eyes wide.

"You and I both know why some *smart girl* hasn't snatched him up—because he's a thirty-year-old sheep farmer who still lives with his mother. Maybe if he had his own place, like Conall, he'd have a better shot at finding

Mrs. Right."

"That's not fair. He still lives with his parents because they *need* him, not to mention he has his own place and he's letting you rent it. It's a family farm, after all. At least you know he's probably not bringing girls home after a night out at the pub."

Lori gave Rachel a speculative look. "Did you notice how his mother said she'd heard good things about you, but she didn't say anything about me?"

"Honestly, I think that's a point in Flynn's favor. No girl wants to think a guy shares details about his romances with his mother."

"Except she said he's popular with the ladies," Lori grumbled. "How would she know that? What does that even mean?"

But Rachel only laughed, which made Lori feel even grumpier. She reminded herself she had no interest in Flynn, and therefore, his love life didn't matter to her. But the thought of him with other women caused an uncomfortable knot to form in the pit of her stomach.

"C'mon," Rachel said, pulling her toward the kitchen. "I think tonight calls for comfort food. Would you rather have homemade mac and cheese or a pint of rocky road ice cream?"

Lori gave her a reluctant smile. "Can't we do both?"

"Honey, you're on vacation—you can do whatever you want."

DARKNESS HAD FALLEN by the time Lori drove her cousin back to town and then returned to the farm. Mist had settled over the fields as she negotiated the long gravel road that led to the O'Rourke property. A half-full moon had risen over the distant hills, lending an eerie beauty to the rural landscape. As she parked the car near the cottage, she could see lights on in the barn. She was tempted to see if Flynn was still working but, hearing mysterious noises and rustlings in the nearby hedges, decided against it and quickly made her way up the path to the cottage. On the front step was a sturdy wicker basket filled with peat logs. Had Flynn put it there? Or one of his brothers? Unlocking the door, Lori lifted the basket. The night air was chilly, and once inside, she set the basket beside the fireplace, turned on the lights, and stood for a moment near the Aga cooker to absorb its radiant heat.

Without any company, the cottage felt a little bleak, and yet it was too early to turn in, despite her lingering jet lag. Instead, she washed and put away the dinner dishes and then went into the bedroom and changed into a comfortable pair of flannel lounge pants and a long-sleeved cotton jersey, before rummaging through her carry-on bag for the paperback novel she'd started reading on the airplane. She glanced through the window that faced the barn. The lights were still on inside. Was it Flynn? If so, what was he doing? After a moment, she dropped the curtain and returned to the living room. She considered making her way to the barn to thank him for delivering the peat, and then remembered the mysterious noises she'd heard in the nearby hedgerow. No, better to wait until morning.

Tossing her book onto the coffee table, she crouched beside the fireplace and examined it. A stack of newspapers sat near the hearth and a container of long matches stood on the mantel. She crumpled several sheets of newspaper into balls and shoved them beneath the grate and then stacked four peat logs on top before applying a match to the paper. The resulting flame was both bright and gratifying, and Lori rocked back on her heels with a smile. She would make a cup of tea and read her book by the cozy fire until bedtime. She was just pushing herself to her feet when the newspaper burned itself out and the flame died, leaving nothing but an acrid plume of smoke behind.

"Oh, no," she muttered, and grabbed several more sheets of paper and balled them up before pushing them beneath the logs and lighting them. But again, the newspaper burned without fully catching the peat. Worse, residual smoke began to fill the room. Coughing, Lori went to the door and flung it open, waving it back and forth in an effort to coax the smoke out of the cottage.

"Need a hand?"

The deep voice came out of the nearby shadows, startling Lori so that she jumped, and then put a hand to her chest as

Flynn stepped forward.

"Oh, you scared me," she gasped. "What are you doing out here?"

"I was heading back to the house and saw your light on, and came by to see if you wanted to start a fire."

*Oh, did she ever.*

She cleared her throat. "I can't seem to get the peat to catch. I don't think it's dried out enough."

She heard his soft chuckle and then he was making his way up the walkway until he stood at her door, big and masculine and reassuringly capable. "I'll get it sorted, shall I?"

Lori pressed herself against the narrow doorjamb to allow him to enter, and couldn't prevent her small intake of breath as his arm brushed against her breasts. If he noticed her reaction, he gave no indication. He dropped to his knees in front of the fireplace and grabbed a stack of the newspaper.

"Did you leave the basket of peat logs?" she asked, closing the door and leaning against it.

He angled his head to look at her. "I did, yeah, while you were out."

"Thank you." She gestured toward the fireplace. "I actually have no idea what I'm doing."

"No problem. Lighting a peat fire can be tricky." He began rolling the paper lengthwise on the floor before twisting it into a tight knot. "The peat needs a sustained flame before it can catch, but loosely crumpled paper burns too quick.

These paper knots will take longer to burn through, allowing time for the peat to catch." Leaning forward, he reached into the firebox and manipulated a lever. "It also helps to have the flue open. That should draw the smoke out."

"Sorry. I've never actually made a fire in a fireplace before." Crossing the room, Lori lowered herself to the floor beside him. He threw her a quick look and handed her a small pile of newspapers. Eyeballing his method, she did the same, and soon they had a dozen newspaper knots heaped on the floor between them.

Leaning forward, Flynn pushed the knots beneath the grate and between the peat logs before lighting them. "That should do," he said and stood up before extending a hand to Lori and effortlessly pulling her to her feet.

"Thanks." Lori crossed her arms over her breasts, suddenly self-conscious. "I was just going to make some tea. Would you like some?"

"Sure."

He followed her into the small kitchen as she filled the kettle and placed it on the boiling plate. He leaned against the counter, hands pushed into his front pockets as he watched her. "How are you settling in?"

"Fine. I met your mother earlier." She indicated the remaining apple tart on the counter behind him. "She dropped by and brought that. Would you like a slice?"

"You know me," he said softly, one side of his mouth curving upward to reveal an irresistible dimple. "I'm never going to say no to something sweet, even when I know it's bad for me."

Lori looked sharply at him, suspecting his words held a double meaning. "Then I should probably tell you this one is more tart than sweet."

"Excellent." Pushing away from the counter, he took a step toward her. "I happen to like tart. In fact, I prefer tart."

Lori stared at him, mesmerized by the expression in his silver eyes and the way he watched her—focused and intent. Without conscious thought, she swayed toward him but was startled by the high, keening whistle of the teakettle. Moving quickly away, she busied herself preparing the tea and pulling cups down from the cupboard. She watched as Flynn cut a slice of apple tart and placed it on a plate.

"Will you have some?" he asked.

Lori shook her head. "No, thanks. I had a big dinner, and then Rachel and I killed a pint of ice cream."

"Ah," he said with a grin. "Not so tart, after all."

Casting him a meaningful look, Lori arranged the tea and cups on a tray and carried it over to the coffee table. Flynn followed and sat down smack in the middle of the sofa, leaving Lori no choice but to sit uncomfortably close to him. So close, she caught enticing whiffs of spicy soap and the earthy scents of hay and peat. She perched on the edge of the cushion and poured them each a cup of tea, adding sugar and milk the way she knew Flynn liked it. The guy might say he preferred things tart, but she knew for a fact he had a serious sweet tooth.

Just as he'd promised, the peat was now burning steadily, casting a warm glow across the room. "Thanks for getting the fire started. You make it look easy."

"It is easy when you've had years of practice."

He finished eating the tart and placed the empty plate on the tray before leaning back and stretching an arm along the back of the sofa. It would be so easy for Lori to sit back and lean into him, and she was more than tempted. Being this close to him reminded her of how it had felt to be held in his arms, to have all that strength and heat surrounding her. Instead, she perched on the edge of the cushion and balanced her teacup on her knee and pretended she wasn't affected by his nearness.

"Did you know he was going to propose?"

Lori's teacup clattered on the saucer, and she hastily set it on the table next to Flynn's empty plate.

"No." She turned to look at him and found him nearer than she realized. Up close, his irises were the same color as the gray mist that had settled over the fields beyond the cottage. "Trust me when I say it came as a complete surprise."

"Really." His dry tone told her he was unconvinced. "And yet a man doesn't typically propose marriage unless he has a fairly good idea he'll be accepted."

Lori resisted the urge to squirm beneath his skeptical gaze. "I think he knew—" She broke off, realizing what she had been about to say.

*I think he knew I'd met someone else. Someone significant.*

"What?" Flynn asked, suddenly intent. "What did he know?"

"Only that we'd reached a make-or-break point, and proposing was a last-ditch effort to save the relationship," she amended weakly.

"Well, I can't fault the guy for trying, but he should know he doesn't have a chance with you." The words were spoken softly, but the tone was one of complete certainty. He'd spoken with that same confidence earlier, when he'd told her he would call Seth himself and tell him Lori wouldn't marry him.

"You've never even met him, so what makes you say that?"

He smiled then, his eyes glinting in a way that caused awareness to gather beneath her clothes. "Because now you're here—with me."

# Chapter Six

FLYNN COULDN'T SLEEP that night, tortured by thoughts of the woman who slept in the cottage just a hundred meters away. He lay in bed with his arms bent behind his head and stared at the ceiling, replaying his visit with Lori over and over again in his head. He'd left as soon as they'd finished their tea, knowing he was only tempting fate if he stayed. He'd recognized the expression in her eyes, had known she wouldn't push him away if he reached for her.

But he hadn't.

As much as he'd been tempted, he'd realized he didn't want something casual. Not with Lori. He didn't know how long she planned to stay in Ballylahane—only knew she hadn't yet made any return flight reservations—but that could change in a heartbeat. If there was one thing he could count on with Lori Woods, it was her unpredictability. But this time, he wouldn't let her leave without a fight. He'd given up too easily before, letting her bolt without telling her how he felt about her. Seeing her again, he realized his feelings hadn't changed.

She still drove him crazy.

He flung an arm over his eyes. If someone had told him six weeks ago that he'd fall fast and hard for a woman who was about as attainable as the stars in the sky, he'd have laughed himself silly. Turning his head, he glanced at the illuminated clock on the bedside table. It was barely four o'clock in the morning. He could stay in bed for another hour, but he knew he wouldn't sleep. He heard a noise from down the hall, a creaking of a door being opened, and the murmur of voices. Sitting up, he listened for a moment before climbing out of bed and opening his door. Seeing his parents in the hallway, he moved quickly to put a supporting arm around his father, taking the brunt of his weight.

"I've got this, Mam," he said softly. "Go back to bed."

Even in the darkness, he could see the concern that etched her face. "Are you sure? He's had another nosebleed."

"Yeah, yeah, no sense in all of us being up." He grinned at his father, who held a hand towel against his face. "This is your way of exacting revenge on me, isn't it? All those years as a teenager, when I refused to get out of bed before sunup."

His father chuckled, but it sounded weak. Flynn tried not to notice how thin his father's once-robust frame felt beneath the bulk of his bathrobe. "Hell of a way to get back at you, son."

"No worries," Flynn said as they made their way to the bathroom. "I've gotten a little behind in working the peat bog for next winter. Saving that fun chore for you, Dad, so don't think a little nosebleed is going to get you out of it."

His father gave a noncommittal grunt.

Flicking on the bathroom light, Flynn helped his father to sit and then ran a washcloth under cool water, before handing it to him and taking the soiled towel and tossing it into the hamper. Since his grim diagnosis, nosebleeds had become a common occurrence with John O'Rourke, but he took it in stride with stoicism and good-natured humor.

"Your mam tells me you have a girl staying in the cottage," John said from behind the washcloth. "Is she pretty?"

"Keep your head back, Dad." Flynn leaned against the sink. "She's only renting the cottage for a few days. And yes, I think she's very pretty."

That was an understatement.

He thought again of Lori's hazel eyes, fringed with the thickest lashes he'd ever seen on a woman, and her pert mouth, usually curved in a teasing smile. With her lush figure and slumbrous eyes, she reminded him of a 1940s-era starlet. But there was an innocence about her, as well, as if she had no idea the world could be cruel and unforgiving. Her natural optimism made her believe everything would always work out in her favor, and when it didn't—she ran.

"You'll have to bring her over to the house to say hello," John said, his voice muffled. "When I'm feeling a bit better."

"Sure, Dad." Flynn scrubbed a hand over his face. Despite the months of chemotherapy, followed by a strict regimen of expensive medications, he could see his father was failing. Over the past several weeks, there had been fewer and fewer good days, and more days when he preferred to just recline on the sofa by the fireplace and sleep. His appetite was almost nonexistent, and although Flynn could see he tried to stay positive, his father's hope for a full recovery was dwindling as fast as his strength. Flynn reached for the washcloth. "Here, let me see. Yeah, that looks better. Back to bed?"

John glanced at the dark windows. "I'd say so. You too, son. Sorry to wake you at this hour."

Flynn chuckled. "Never thought I'd hear you say that to me, Dad. Admit it—you relished every morning you had to drag my sorry arse out of bed."

"Yeah, I did," John agreed with a grin. "And now look at you—a proper farmer, up before the birds."

Leaning down, he helped his father to his feet, and they made their way slowly back to the bedroom. Downstairs, he could hear his mother moving around in the kitchen. When his father was back in bed, he softly closed the door and then returned to the bathroom to shower and brush his teeth before dressing quickly in the predawn chill. As he headed downstairs, he passed Declan's door, knowing he wouldn't see his younger brother for at least another couple of hours. He didn't begrudge him the extra sleep, since he'd taken the first shift with Dad and had bottle-fed the lambs around midnight. He likely hadn't gone to bed before one a.m.

In contrast to the rest of the house, the kitchen was warm and bright. Seeing him, Rob and Brody rose eagerly from their beds near the cookstove and came over to greet him, tails wagging furiously.

"Good morning, boys," he said, bending down to rub their heads. "Looking for breakfast, are you?"

"They've been fed, the wee scamps." His mother had made a pot of coffee and was unwrapping a package of puff pastry. Beside her on the counter stood a leftover ham roast and a block of cheddar. "Now they're hoping for a handout, the cheeky little beggars."

"Ah, ham and cheese jambons," he said, pouring himself a mug of coffee. "Dad's favorite."

"The man is wasting away before my eyes," she muttered. "I have to do something to make him eat. I cannot understand it. He should be responding to the medicine by now."

Flynn glanced at his mother, seeing the worry and exhaustion that etched her features. Despite the excellent care his father received, there was no doubt he was steadily getting worse. Flynn didn't know how much longer they could hold on, financially or emotionally. His father was the heart and soul of the farm, the rock to which they each clung. He couldn't bring himself to think of a world without him in it.

"You know the medicine can't cure him, Mam," he said quietly. "There's only one way to do that."

His mother stopped what she had been doing and her shoulders slumped. But when she turned to look at him, her face betrayed none of her inner turmoil. "I know you mean well, son, but you're not a strong enough match. Even if you were, the doctors said there's no guarantee that a bone marrow transplant would work. There's only a slim chance of success, and I cannot ask him to do it."

"What about Uncle David? Have you been able to reach him?" Flynn's father was one of five sons, and they had initially hoped one of his siblings might be a good match for a bone marrow transplant. Three of his four brothers had been tested, but none of them had been deemed a close enough match to go through the process. Only the youngest of the five brothers, Uncle David, remained untested, but he lived in California, and they hadn't seen him in several years.

"We haven't heard anything from him," his mother replied. "It's unlikely he'd be a good match, at any rate. The doctors said there's only a twenty-five percent likelihood he could be."

"So let me try," Flynn urged. "I can start the injections next week, and the doctors said it would only be another week or so before they could harvest enough stem cells to start the process. He's growing weaker every day, Mam. If we don't do something soon, he won't be strong enough to do it at all." Setting his coffee mug down on the counter, Flynn pulled his mother into an embrace. "Just think about it, okay? You're not asking me to do it—I'm offering. I want to. But we need to decide soon."

She nodded against his shoulder and then pulled away.

She turned quickly back to the counter, but not before Flynn saw the moisture in her eyes. "We'll wait until after the festival to decide, shall we?"

Flynn blew out a hard breath. The festival began in earnest the following day, and then they would be into the weekend. He didn't want to wait another four days to make a decision. Inaction had never suited him, and it was all he could do not to protest.

"Yeah, fine," he said, his tone grudging. "I'm headed to the barn."

"Take the rest of the coffee with you," she said, nodding toward the nearly full pot. "Your brother won't be up for hours yet. Be back for breakfast at seven."

Flynn poured the steaming brew into a thermos and, carrying his coffee mug in his other hand, slipped out of the house with the dogs at his heels and made his way up the road toward the barn. The moon had nearly slipped below the horizon, and in the east, he could just see the beginnings of a pink glow heralding the sunrise. On the low hill beyond the barn, the cottage was dark, and Flynn envisioned Lori snug beneath the blankets.

In his bed.

She likely wouldn't be awake for hours yet.

Opening the wide doors to the barn, he flipped on the lights and breathed in the familiar scents of sweet hay, wood shavings, grain, and manure, all mixed with the warm smell of the animals themselves. In the small pens, the lambs stirred and came to poke their heads through the rails, bleating in hopeful anticipation of breakfast.

"Good morning," he greeted them. "Keep your wool on. Your breakfast is coming."

In the small ante room that he used as a makeshift office and where he stored medicines and other supplies, he set down his coffee and thermos and began preparing the formula for the lambs. The dogs lay down and watched him. The task of feeding a half dozen lambs didn't take long, with the bulk of the work comprised of mixing the milk replacement with warm water. But once he'd filled the bottles, he took them two at a time into the pens, where they quickly guzzled the contents. He was preparing the last two bottles when a shadow fell across the open door and the dogs bolted to their feet. Looking up, he was surprised to see Lori standing there. He turned his attention back to the bottles so she wouldn't see how pleased he was to see her.

"You're up early."

She shrugged and stepped inside, bending down to greet the dogs as they flocked around her legs. Pushing her hair back from her face, she glanced around, looking anywhere but at him. "Jet lag. I couldn't sleep, and then I saw the lights on in the barn and figured it was you."

"Yeah, well, you're just in time. I've fed all but these last two. Feel like lending a hand?"

Her face brightened. "Yes! I was hoping you might still have some lambs. You didn't have this many the last time I was here."

"Yeah, that was the beginning of the season. All the lambs have now been born. These guys are between three and five weeks old." He handed her a bottle. "The ones in this pen, over here, are between six and eight weeks old."

Stepping into the pen, they crouched in the straw as the two remaining lambs jostled each other for access to the two bottles.

"Whoa, someone is hungry. Strong little things, aren't they?" Lori laughed, nearly falling over as the lambs pushed against her. Reaching out, Flynn supported her with a hand at her back.

"They're small, but they're determined," he agreed. "There you go, all finished." Standing, he scooped the two lambs up and deposited them in the neighboring pen with the other lambs that had already been fed.

"You do this every morning?" Lori asked.

"Yeah, every four to six hours."

"By yourself? That seems like a lot of work."

"Nah, it goes quickly, and I don't mind. Besides which, my brother does the midnight feeding."

"What will happen to these little guys after they're weaned?" she asked, cuddling one of the lambs in her arms.

"The females will be placed back into the flock and we sell the males when they reach four or five months old."

"Who buys them?"

Flynn narrowed his eyes, certain she was being deliberately obtuse, but then realized she truly had no idea.

"Maybe it's better you don't know." He nodded with his chin toward the animal she was holding. "In fact, probably best you don't get too attached. That's a male you're holding."

He knew the precise instant Lori figured out his meaning. Her mouth fell open, and her eyes reflected her dismay. "No! Please tell me this little guy is not going to end up on someone's dinner plate. I've already given him a name. How could you even think about sacrificing this sweet boy to such a horrible fate?"

"How do you think we earn a living?" he asked drily.

"Well, maybe you could make an exception for this one lamb," she begged, her expression earnest. "If you're just going to sell him, I'll pay you whatever the going rate is and he can just stay here as a—a mascot!"

Flynn only barely suppressed a smile. "We don't need a mascot. Besides, who would bear the cost of his maintenance? You?"

"Yes." She leaned forward, the lamb squirming to be released. "Please?"

Flynn gave her his fiercest frown. Not that she seemed the tiniest bit impressed or intimidated. "No. Absolutely not. If I make an exception for him, they'll all want special treatment."

She squeezed the lamb a little tighter. "Don't worry, Woolly Wonka, I'll find a way to save you."

"Woolly Wonka?"

"Because he's so sweet, like candy," Lori crooned, and kissed the lamb's nose. Reluctantly, she set the animal down and watched as it bounded away.

Flynn shook his head in bemusement, grateful when she didn't pursue the topic further. "Now comes the part that's not as much fun."

"Which part is that?"

"Washing out the buckets and bottles. And cleaning the pens."

"Oh. Well, I can help you with that," Lori said, eyeing the large, industrial-sized sink, now filled with dirty bottles. "In return, you can give me a discount on renting the cottage."

"Not a chance," Flynn retorted, knowing she wasn't serious. As the daughter of the man who owned Lakeside Industries, he knew the last thing Lori Woods lacked was money. He'd charged her a fair price for the cottage. His mother might have argued he'd given her too fair a price. "There are people who would pay good money to bottle-feed lambs."

"Really?"

"Well, not here," Flynn acknowledged, plugging the drain in the sink and turning on the hot water. "This is a working farm, and we don't have time to pander to tourists. But I know of other farms that charge a fee for visitors to bottle-feed lambs, see a sheepdog demonstration, or try their hand at shearing."

Lori leaned against the pen and watched him, an amused glint in her eyes. "Oh, you mean like we did when we came out to see the farm the last time I was here? When you and I first met?"

Flynn recalled the day when Lori and Rachel had accompanied Conall to the farm to see the inner workings of a sheep farm. He hadn't been all that keen on the idea of visitors until he'd seen Lori, and despite the fact she'd aggravated and annoyed him during the visit, he'd enjoyed every minute of it.

"Yeah, I expect it's very much like that day," he agreed.

"Why wouldn't you do that here? I thought it was fun."

She smiled at him, her eyes warm with the memory of that day. Her hair was loose and fell in unruly waves around her face. She'd applied a coat of red lipstick to her full lips, which made his rampant imagination hurtle down roads it had no business traveling. She wore a cream-colored turtleneck under a black down vest, paired with slim brown slacks that flattered her shape. She looked rested, and the stress he'd seen in her face the previous day was gone.

Realizing he was staring at her, he turned abruptly away. Removing the nipples from the bottles, he submerged everything in the hot, soapy water. "That's not how I remember it. As I recall, you were opinionated and critical of everything." He cast her a meaningful glance. "As usual."

She came and stood beside him, watching as he shoved

the sleeves of his sweater over his forearms and began scrubbing the bottles with a soft wire brush. Flynn caught whiffs of her soap or shampoo . . . something floral and feminine. He resisted the urge to bend closer and inhale her fragrance more deeply.

"I only wondered why you don't capitalize on what you have here," she said, seeming oblivious to the effect her nearness had on him. "You could invite tourists in, and even have a small shop selling farm-fresh products like soap or cheese made from sheep's milk. City people would love that." She leaned closer, angling herself so that she leaned back against the sink and could look into his face. "Not to mention you could have all the free labor you want for your turf bog. Trust me when I tell you people would pay good money to cut your peat."

He glanced at her, a reluctant smile pulling at his mouth. He was sure there must be a joke in there somewhere. "Oh, yeah? How much money?"

She shrugged. "I don't know—fifteen euros per person? I'd have to check and see what the going rate is."

"Forget it." Flynn rinsed the bottles and put them on pegs to dry. "I'm not interested. If you really want to help, you can grab that shovel and muck out the pens."

She blew out a hard breath, clearly disappointed. "Okay, fine. It was just a thought."

Flynn watched, surprised, as she grabbed a shovel and used it to scoop up the soiled straw in the lamb enclosure and transfer it into a nearby wheelbarrow. She wasn't dressed for barn work and when a clod of wet sheep dung landed on her pristine pant leg, she grimaced and gingerly tried to swipe it off.

"Here," Flynn said, taking pity on her. He wiped his damp hands on the seat of his jeans and vaulted easily over the railing and into the pen. "Give me that; I didn't actually mean for you to do this. I was hoping it might get rid of you."

Her mouth fell open, and she stared at him in mock outrage. "Oh, you—you—" Tossing the shovel away, she tried to shove him backward, probably hoping he would land on his backside in the straw. But her efforts were puny in comparison to his size and strength. Laughing, he caught her and pulled her against his chest.

"You're no match for me, Lori Woods," he teased, letting his gaze drift over her face. "The sooner you realize that, the easier it will be for you."

"Oh, really?" She stared up at him, a glint of challenge in her eyes.

Before he could guess her intent, she reached up and pulled his head down and pressed her mouth against his. For a moment, Flynn was too stunned to react. But when she wreathed her arms around his neck and softened her lips, testing the seam of his mouth with her tongue, he couldn't prevent his helpless response. With a soft groan, he gathered her close, fusing his lips with hers in gentle, biting kisses.

The heat and taste of her was unbearably decadent, the feel of her in his arms a sweet torture. He coaxed her mouth open, sweeping his tongue inside as he slid his hands over the curve of her hips and lifted her against him. She made a sound of pleasure and pushed her fingers into his hair, angling his head for better access as she plundered his mouth like a small, sensual pirate. Long minutes passed, and when she finally released him and stepped out of his arms, Flynn nearly toppled over. He felt slightly dazed by the force of his own response to her.

Lori stepped quickly back, as if she half expected him to reach for her again. He might have, if he'd been able to think clearly. Her cheeks were flushed and her breath came in soft pants. She gave him a satisfied, triumphant smile. "Who says I'm no match for the great Flynn O'Rourke?"

Then she opened the gate of the enclosure and sauntered out of the barn, leaving Flynn to gape after her, wondering what the hell had just happened.

# Chapter Seven

THE MAIN ROAD that ran through Ballylahane had been transformed into a festive street fair with colorful tents and vendor booths occupying the green space in the center of town, and a tall, beribboned Maypole at the center of it all. The local shops brought their goods out to the sidewalks, and restaurants set up tables and chairs beneath bright umbrellas, cordoned off from the street with enormous pots of flowers and greenery. Traffic had been temporarily diverted to the back roads, and the main street had become a dedicated pedestrian zone for the duration of the weekend, and already the small town teemed with people.

The local weaving mill had closed at noon to give the employees an opportunity to enjoy the festivities, so Lori had driven into town to meet Rachel for lunch. After leaving her car in the parking lot of the mill, they walked into town and spent a pleasurable hour perusing the vendor booths. Lori purchased Irish-knit sweaters for each of her brothers, and a hand-thrown stoneware tea set for her mother, glazed in shades of green and blue that reminded her of the Irish hills sweeping down to the ocean.

"Very pretty," Rachel approved as the artist carefully wrapped the pieces and packed them into a sturdy box.

"We'll come back for it after lunch," Lori promised the woman.

"You're going to need a bigger suitcase for when you go home," Rachel teased as they continued through the fair.

Lori was silent, thinking about what awaited her back in Chicago. "Maybe I won't go back," she mused.

"Of course you'll go back," Rachel said, sounding surprised. "Where else would you go? Even if Uncle Jack didn't select you for the commodities manager position, you still have a job waiting for you. Your father needs you."

"No, he doesn't. Now that I think about it, all the things he had me do were just busy things, not essential things. I don't think he trusts me enough to handle a job with real responsibility."

"I'm sorry, but I disagree," Rachel said. "What about the year he asked you to manage the retail store? You were responsible for everything and you did a fantastic job. You could have foisted the bulk of the duties off to someone else, but you owned that job. You even expanded the company's online offerings and helped set up the drop-ship order fulfillment center. In fact, if I recall correctly, that job was what got you interested in the commodities manager position in the first place, because you loved sourcing the products."

"That's true," Lori acknowledged. "But working in retail

is not the same as being part of the company management team."

"As I recall, you were crazy busy, and yet, I'd never seen you so happy. You were so proud about expanding the store." She gave Lori a pointed look. "And so was Uncle Jack."

Lakeside Industries operated a retail store on the ground level of the textile factory, where they sold fabrics and an extensive line of luxury home goods. Lori had done all the sourcing and purchasing for the shop, had supervised the employees, and had also been responsible for the floor layout and product displays. But her real pride had been working with local artisans and incorporating their products into the store displays. She'd also created an online site for the store and had worked with the IT department to set up a method of shipping items directly from the various vendors.

"That was a lot of fun," Lori admitted. "I enjoyed meeting the vendors, and I liked creating the displays and changing out the products to reflect the seasons or the holidays." She shrugged. "But anyone could have done it. My father only put me in the position to keep me entertained, like a small child. Keep me happy. Keep me quiet. But don't give me anything with real responsibility or meaning."

"That's not true that anyone could have done it." Putting an arm around her shoulders, Rachel gave her a sympathetic hug. "You did it, and just because you enjoyed it doesn't mean it was easy or insignificant. I don't think you give yourself enough credit. Even if you can't see it now, the retail store gave you valuable experience and really sparked your creativity. I distinctly remember your father celebrating your success because you tripled the revenue in less than a year." She paused. "If you don't go back to Lakeside Industries, what else would you do?"

Lori shrugged. "I'm sure I'll find something. I have a degree in marketing, and Lakeside Industries can't be the only company looking to hire a commodities manager."

"You're chasing a job title when you should be looking for something that excites and fulfills you," Rachel said.

Lori glanced at her cousin, envying her for having always known where her passion lay. For as long as Lori could recall, Rachel had wanted to design fabric, and now, here she was, designing tweed for one of the most respected names in Ireland. Her entire future looked bright and shiny. By comparison, Lori felt as if she was floundering in dark and choppy waters with no direction and nothing to guide her.

She was completely adrift. Lost.

But she wouldn't share any of that with Rachel, who would only worry and then try to fix it, probably by calling Lori's father. So instead, she smiled brightly, as if losing the commodities manager position was the best thing that could have happened to her, the silver lining in the storm cloud.

"I've been thinking about that, and I have enough money saved to take some time off. Not much, just a few months, but I could do some traveling. Reassess my life and my priorities. I thought maybe I'd explore Ireland and then travel through England."

"By yourself?" Rachel sounded less than impressed. "That doesn't sound like much fun."

"You could come with me," Lori suggested hopefully.

"Oh, well, I'd like to, but I still have to complete my internship and present my thesis to my department committee at the end of the semester. I'm sorry, but I just don't see how I can take any time off right now." She gave Lori an apologetic smile. "Maybe next year?"

"Forget it," Lori said morosely. "By next year, you and Conall will be married and expecting your fifth child."

Rachel laughed. "Since he hasn't proposed, I doubt that very much. Besides, we're taking things slow."

"So you said."

"He did ask me to move in with him," Rachel admitted. "But I think it's too soon. Honestly, we're still getting to know each other. I'd love to move in with him, and at some point, I probably will, but not yet. I don't want to rush anything and ruin it."

Lori stopped walking and turned to face her cousin. "Rachel, anyone can see the guy is crazy about you. I don't think you could ruin anything, even if you tried. The man is completely in love with you."

She watched as Rachel's expression grew soft. "I still can't quite believe it. To think, I almost stayed on that bus as it pulled out of Ballylahane; I almost went back to Chicago."

"My dad says *almost* only counts with horseshoes and hand grenades," Lori said as they resumed walking. "Even if you had left, I don't think you would have stayed away. Whatever you and Conall have, it's the real deal. Anyone can see that."

"It's what I want for you too," Rachel said. "If Seth didn't make you feel happy down to your bones, he wasn't the right guy."

"Forget about bones. What if he makes the rest of your body happy? What if, when he touches you, every strand of your DNA stands up and begs for more?"

Rachel looked sharply at her. "I take it we're no longer talking about Seth."

She was too perceptive, but she always had been. Lori had never been able to keep anything secret from Rachel for very long. Even when she'd been in Ballylahane previously, to secretly assess the viability of a partnership with McDermott Mills, Rachel had somehow known.

"I may have run into Flynn earlier this morning, in the barn."

"And . . .?"

"And I may have kissed him." She risked a glance at her cousin, who was staring at her in open-mouthed surprise.

"Well, that didn't take long," she finally replied. "I figured it would take at least a week before one of you made a move on the other. So, who kissed who?"

Remembering the heat and intensity of that intimate moment in the barn, Lori felt renewed warmth gather beneath her skin. "I may have initiated it, but trust me when I say he was all in."

"I don't doubt that," Rachel murmured. "The guy looks at you as if he wants to devour you. So what now?"

"What do you mean?"

"Well, you just said you'd like to do some traveling and reassess your life. But I think we both know you'll eventually return to Chicago. I know he's gorgeous, but if you're not serious about Flynn, don't lead him on. He's a decent guy, and he doesn't deserve to be toyed with."

Lori suppressed a quick surge of annoyance. "Says the woman who took every opportunity to be with Conall, while telling him all the reasons why a serious relationship would never work."

"It was unfair," Rachel agreed. "Which is why I don't want you to do that to Flynn. We both know you'd never be happy on a sheep farm, and Flynn could never be happy in Chicago. How could he, after living where he does? Nothing could ever match the beauty of that farm."

"Well, maybe neither of us is looking for a happily-ever-after," Lori retorted, feeling defensive. "Maybe we're only interested in a short-term fling."

Rachel put her hands up in surrender. "Okay, okay. I get it—it's none of my business. All I'll say is you've never been the casual type, and I can't see you starting now."

"Well, I'm sure I *can* be the casual type," Lori snapped. "For once in my life, I'm going to do something for *me* and damn the consequences."

"I'm sorry," Rachel said, her expression contrite. "I didn't mean to upset you, but you're like a sister to me. I love you, and I just don't want to see you—or Flynn—get hurt."

Lori's irritation evaporated. She linked her arm through Rachel's. "I know. I'm sorry I bit your head off. I'm just so tired of people telling me what to do all the time, and of trying to meet other people's expectations."

"Maybe you're right—this is a good time to reevaluate your life and decide what it is *you* want. Not your father, not Seth. *You*."

*She wanted Flynn.*

The realization was alarming. She couldn't recall any other time in her life when a guy had had this kind of impact on her. But she knew better than to let Rachel know the direction of her thoughts. Instead, she smiled and pulled her cousin to a stop on the sidewalk. "Right now, I want lunch. Preferably a big plate of fish and chips with a pint of Guinness. I'm starving."

Rachel laughed. "Sounds perfect."

They had reached Mallone's Pub and, since the outdoor tables were full, made their way inside where the atmosphere was old-world, cozy, and dark. Lively music filled the pub through hidden speakers, and most of the tables in the dining area were occupied. They found seats at the bar and each ordered a pint of beer as they browsed the menu.

"Maybe I'll have the fish and chips too," Rachel murmured.

Before they could order, the door opened and a group of men entered, laughing and talking loudly enough that Lori and Rachel both looked up. There were five of them, and even as Lori turned, she recognized Flynn and Conall among them. Seeing her, Flynn stopped laughing, and his expression turned serious. Lori fought the urge to squirm beneath that laser gaze. There were more than enough seats at the far end of the bar for the guys to sit together, but Flynn spoke quietly in Conall's ear and came to sit on the empty stool next to Lori, while Conall and the others took the stools on the other side of Rachel.

"Are you stalking me?" Lori asked lightly, eyeing him over the rim of her pint glass.

Flynn bent his arms on the surface of the bar and leaned toward her, lowering his voice so that only she could hear him. "Maybe I've come back for round two of the O'Rourke challenge."

Lori's heart skipped a beat at his reference to what had happened that morning in the barn. How would he react if he knew it had taken every ounce of willpower she'd had not to drag him down to the soft, fresh hay? Pushing the uncomfortable thoughts aside, she slanted him an amused glance. "Maybe there is no round two. Maybe it's a one-and-done deal. No rematch. Sorry, you lose."

To her consternation, Flynn gave her a slow smile, as if he knew every explicit thought going through her mind. The look in his eyes sent her pulse into overdrive, and her breath got stuck in her lungs.

"Scared to take me on, sweetheart?"

"No, just smart." She gave him a deliberate look. "We both know all the reasons why we shouldn't get involved."

"Define *involved*."

Before Lori could reply, the bartender came over to take their orders. After he'd placed a pint of beer in front of Flynn and had moved away, Lori glanced at her cousin to ensure she wasn't listening to their conversation. But Rachel was turned toward Conall as he and his friends related a story from their run that morning, making her laugh.

Lori returned her attention to Flynn. He'd changed out of the work clothes he'd worn that morning in the barn, and now wore a soft cotton jersey in a blue-gray that made his eyes look even more intense. A thick lock of wavy, black hair fell over his forehead, and she watched as he pushed it impatiently back.

"You need a haircut," she observed.

"Don't change the subject."

"I'm just stating the obvious. I'm surprised you can see anything through that mop."

"Are you offering?"

Lori looked at him in surprise. "You'd trust me to cut

your hair?"

He shrugged and lifted his glass. "Sure, why not?"

"What if I did a terrible job?" She smiled. "I could shear you like one of your sheep, and then the ladies of Ballylahane might not be so enamored of you."

"I'm not that narcissistic, and it would grow out, eventually."

"Hmm." Reaching out, she threaded her fingers through his hair on the pretext of measuring its length, when she really just wanted to feel the heavy, silken texture of it against her fingers again. "I used to give my brothers haircuts. I could do yours, if you'd like."

He made a noise, something between a sigh and a groan, and Lori realized she was still stroking his hair, the feel of his scalp beneath her fingertips warm in contrast to the cool strands. She snatched her hand back.

His eyes gleamed as he watched her. "I'll bring the shears."

Lori shuddered, picturing herself trying to cut his hair with the same shears he used on his ewes. "Thanks, but I think I'll borrow a pair from Rachel—they keep the scissors at the mill nice and sharp."

"On second thought, maybe I'll take a raincheck," Flynn said with a quick laugh.

"Oh, no. You're committed now."

"Speaking of which—"

They were interrupted as Conall leaned forward to catch

their attention. "Hey, we're getting a group together at my house tonight, if you're interested. Just drinks around the firepit, but it should be a nice night for it."

"Yeah, sure, sounds good," Flynn said, and then glanced at Lori. "I can drive us both over."

"I haven't said I'll go."

"But you will." Flynn looked annoyingly confident. "What else would you do?"

She gave him a tolerant look. "*If* I decide to go, I'll drive myself, thanks."

"Do you even know where Conall lives?"

"Somewhere near the water." She gestured vaguely. "I'll ask Rachel."

"Let me drive you," he said softly. "I'll come by the cottage around six thirty. You can give me a quick haircut, and then we'll head over to Conall's."

She would let him, of course. When he looked at her like that, with his expression almost gentle, she didn't think there was much she would refuse him. Besides, he trusted her to trim his hair, which in some ways felt even more intimate than a kiss.

"Fine."

Their meals arrived, and then there was little opportunity for further discussion as the conversation expanded to include the entire group, who apparently were all planning to be at Conall's house that night, some with their girlfriends.

"So what are your plans for while you're here?" Flynn

asked as the bartender cleared away their empty plates.

Lori shrugged. "I don't really have any plans to speak of. Rachel will be working, so I thought I might venture out and explore the area."

"On your own?"

"I have a car, so why not?"

"Doesn't sound like much fun, all by yourself." He angled his head toward her. "I could show you around, if you'd like."

Rachel had said the same thing about traveling alone, and if Lori was being honest, the thought of sightseeing by herself did feel a little bleak. Flynn's casual suggestion caused all kinds of bright sparks to explode inside her as she recalled what had happened the last time he'd played the role of tour guide to her tourist. "That's nice of you to offer, but you have a farm to run. I doubt you have the luxury of jaunting around the countryside whenever you want."

"I don't manage the farm on my own," he said, looking amused. "I do have two brothers who help out. As long as I can get the lambs fed first thing and take care of the morning chores, I think I could manage a few hours away, here and there."

"I could help you feed the lambs," Lori offered on impulse. "I mean, if you trust me to do that. You'd have to show me how to mix the formula, but I would actually love to feed them."

"Really?" His expression was doubtful. "It means getting

up early."

"I don't mind, since I'll get to spend time with Woolly Wonka." She grinned when Flynn gave her a disbelieving look. "But if I agreed to do all that, what would you be doing?" She pictured him lounging on a haybale, watching her through those astonishing eyes.

"I'll be right beside you, doing what we did this morning."

*They'd been kissing that morning.*

Her alarm must have shown on her face, because Flynn laughed softly. "You can mix the formula and feed the lambs. I'll wash the bottles and clean out the pens. The dogs and I will do a quick inventory of the flock, and that's pretty much it until the next feeding, which Declan can manage."

"Really?" Lori looked at him in surprise. "So you just feed the lambs and check on the ewes and then you're done for the day?" She made a light scoffing sound. "Doesn't sound like such a hard life."

"No, I'm saying I could curtail my other chores in order to spend time with you. There are plenty of other things to do on the farm, but nothing that can't wait."

She slanted a cautious look at him. "You'd really take time off to spend it with me?"

She recalled the last time they'd gone sightseeing together, a shimmering memory that was never far from her thoughts. He'd brought her to the Assaranca waterfalls and there, surrounded by lush greenery and the thundering sound of falling water, he'd kissed her. That kiss had been unlike any she'd experienced before—as breathtaking and powerful as the waterfall itself, drowning her in sensation until she'd lost all sense of where they were or how long they'd stood there, drinking each other in. Now, as he offered to take her out again, she half thought he might make some romantic reference to that day, but she couldn't have been more wrong.

"I've seen the way you drive," he said, his dimples deepening. "I think my fellow countrymen are safer if you're not allowed on the roads unaccompanied. Best let me drive you."

She narrowed her eyes at him. "Very funny. You do realize I drove here all the way from Dublin?"

"Miracles really do exist."

"Ha." She feigned an air of indifference. "Fine. Offer accepted."

"Good. Let me know if there's anything special you'd like to see; otherwise, I can make some recommendations."

Rachel leaned toward them. "What are you two cooking up?"

"I've just offered to take Lori sightseeing," Flynn said. "Safer than her heading out on her own."

"Oh. Are you sure you can spare the time?" Rachel's eyes reflected her concern, and Lori didn't miss the quick warning glance she threw her way. She heard the unspoken message in Rachel's tone: *Did you forget what we talked about?*

No, she had not forgotten. She knew Rachel was right—

LOVE ME BENEATH THE IRISH MOON

she had no business flirting with Flynn. She shouldn't enjoy teasing him as much as she did either.

And she definitely shouldn't kiss him.

But whenever he was near, she had a hard time remembering he was off-limits and an even harder time maintaining any distance. He was too distracting, too aggravating, and altogether too tempting. In her heart, she knew what Rachel had said was true—she had no business leading him on. They could never have a serious relationship, because there was no future for Lori in Ireland, and she was pretty sure Flynn would never leave the farm. But what was the harm in a light romance? A spring fling? Maybe Rachel was right. Maybe it *was* time for her to do something just for herself.

She looked expectantly at Flynn, waiting for him to respond to Rachel's question. "Well? Are you sure you can spare the time?"

But Flynn only smiled. "Absolutely, *mo chailín*. I have all the time in the world."

# Chapter Eight

F LYNN HAD NEVER whipped through his evening chores so fast before returning to the main house to help get his father settled for the night. A glance at his phone showed he was already late. He tried to curb his impatience as his father turned off the water in the shower and extended a hand for a towel. Flynn passed him one and waited as the older man dried himself and then pushed the shower curtain aside, the bath towel wrapped around his hips.

"I can manage, son," he said, gripping the towel rack on the nearby wall.

"I know you can," Flynn assured him, "but Mam won't be happy if you lose your balance and I'm not here to pick you up. She'll refuse to feed me for at least a week."

His father chuckled and obligingly took Flynn's arm, leaning on him as they made their way across the hall to the bedroom. Without a shirt, Flynn could see how thin his father had become, his bones protruding sharply beneath his skin. The chemo port that had been inserted in his chest was a grim reminder of his dire health situation. Flynn's mother had left a clean pair of night clothes on the bed, and after

100

ensuring his father was safely seated, Flynn moved to the window to give him some privacy.

"Dad, we need to think about a bone marrow transplant," he said over his shoulder. "The chemo isn't working. I've been tested. Maybe I'm not a perfect match, but right now, I'm the best chance you have for recovery."

When he glanced at his father, he had finished dressing and was sitting in silence, studying his hands.

"There are risks involved," the older man finally said. "And I'd need to be isolated for at least three months following the procedure. It's a lot to ask of your mother, to drive back and forth to Letterkenny for weeks on end. She's also convinced it will finish me."

It didn't surprise Flynn that his father's first concern was for his wife. His family had always been his first priority, never himself. He would rather die than ask a member of his family to sacrifice anything on his behalf. But Flynn couldn't accept that. His father was only sixty-two, and he had so much more to offer. Flynn refused to let him just check out without a fight.

"It's not a lot to ask," he protested. He crossed the room and crouched on the balls of his feet in front of his father. "I'll drive Mam back and forth if that's what she wants, or she can stay with Aunt Sheila. She's only ten minutes from the hospital. But the decision has to be yours, Dad. If you say you're ready, then Mam will agree. Otherwise, she won't even discuss it."

John raised his head, and Flynn's heart clenched hard at the conflict in his father's eyes. "It's also a lot of money, son, with no guarantee it will work. I'm not sure we can afford it."

"Screw the cost. We'll figure it out. The only thing that matters is getting you healthy again, and this is your best chance. But if we wait much longer, the doctors will say you're too weak. If we're going to do a bone marrow transplant, we have to do it now."

After a moment, his father nodded. "Okay. I'll talk to your mother tonight and call the doctor first thing on Monday morning."

For the first time since his father's diagnosis, Flynn felt a sense of hope. Finally, after weeks of watching his dad suffer and waste away, they were doing something proactive. Reaching out, he gripped his father's hands in his own.

"That's good, Dad," he managed past the lump in his throat. "This is going to work. I just know it."

His father gave him an amused look. "Don't say it—you can feel it in your bones?"

Flynn laughed. "Something like that."

When his father was seated in a comfortable chair in front of the television, Flynn grabbed a coat and paused in the kitchen, where his mother was preparing supper.

"I'll be at Conall's," he said. "Declan will help Dad to bed, so don't wait up for me."

His mother laughed. "I stopped doing that years ago,

son. Have fun."

Flynn hesitated, wanting to give his mother a heads-up regarding the conversation that awaited her, but then decided it might give her the opportunity to come up with possible arguments against the transplant procedure. She was terrified that with his weakened immune system, he wouldn't survive the procedure and no amount of reassurance could dissuade her.

"Yeah," he said instead. "Have a good night."

It was still light outside as he crossed the yard and made his way past the barn to the cottage. Lori answered the door on his first knock, stepping quickly aside to let him pass. She looked good in a pair of jeans and a shimmery gold top beneath a soft, champagne-colored cardigan that fell nearly to her knees. Her hair had been swept back and secured with a large clip, but curling tendrils fell around her face and neck.

"Hi," she said, closing the door behind him. "You're late. I thought you might have changed your mind."

"Not a chance," he assured her.

She gestured awkwardly. "I have everything ready for you in the kitchen."

Was it just his imagination, or did she actually seem nervous? The thought amused him as much as it steadied him. At least he wasn't the only one. Tossing his jacket over the back of the sofa, he followed her to the kitchen, where she had pulled a chair into the center of the room. On the counter, neatly arranged on a hand towel, were a pair of scissors, a comb, and a small spray bottle. Next to those stood a bottle of wine and a wineglass, nearly half full.

"Do you want something to drink?" she asked. "I have beer or wine."

"No, I'm fine."

"Okay, then." She gave him a bright smile and gestured toward the chair. "Have a seat."

He did, watching as she picked up the wineglass and drained the contents in one long swallow.

"Er, maybe you shouldn't be wielding a pair of scissors if you've been drinking," he said, unable to keep his mouth from quirking into a smile.

She made a sound of dismissal. "Don't be such a baby. This is going to be a cinch." She draped a towel across his neck and shoulders, tucking it into his collar and ensuring his shirt was protected. "This is just to protect your clothes—don't want to get the collar wet."

"Would you like me to take my shirt off?" He couldn't resist asking, enjoying the swift flush of color that came into her cheeks. For a second, he actually thought she'd say yes.

"No, no, definitely not," she said instead. "But I think I'll take off my sweater—would that be alright? It's cashmere, and I'd hate to get it covered in hair."

Flynn shrugged, but had to swallow hard when she slipped out of the cardigan, revealing the gold top was, in fact, a camisole that left her arms, shoulders, and upper planes of her chest and back completely bare. Beneath the silky material, her breasts were a sweet, rounded temptation that made the palms of his hands itch. When she stood behind him and began to work the comb through his hair, he could actually feel the soft heat of her pressed against his shoulder. She lifted a section of hair and spritzed it with the spray bottle.

"What is that?" he asked, instantly suspicious.

"Relax. It's only water."

"Just tell me you haven't infused it with lavender or rose water or some other girly stuff."

Resting one hand on his shoulder, she leaned forward far enough to smile into his eyes. "No girly stuff, I promise."

But she lied because as she leaned forward, the front of her camisole gaped away just enough that he caught a swift, unsettling glimpse of all her gorgeous, very girly stuff. Stifling a groan, he closed his eyes and prayed that he would get through the next few minutes without doing something he'd regret, like hauling her across his lap and kissing her until she couldn't breathe. Instead, he tried to think about anything that would keep his libido in check—mucking stalls, or administering maggot treatments to the ewes. Meanwhile, his heightened senses were aware of every tiny movement she made as she snipped and spritzed and threaded her fingers through his hair in a way that made him want to groan in pleasure. He could feel the warmth of her breath against the back of his neck as she worked.

"Your hair is very thick. I doubt you'll ever need to worry about going bald." She paused. "Not that it would matter."

"Why wouldn't it matter?"

"Seriously?" She gave him a resigned look. "I doubt there's a woman alive who could turn you away, baldheaded or not."

For a moment, Flynn couldn't speak. He was under no illusions about his looks, but it had been a long time since he'd had anything resembling a relationship, mostly because the farm consumed so much of his time. He'd had more than his share of girlfriends in college and in the years immediately following graduation, when he'd lived in Galway and played Gaelic football for the county league. Since he'd returned to Ballylahane, however, he'd hardly dated. Not that there weren't attractive women in the countryside, but most of them were already spoken for. Not to mention, it wasn't easy to have an intimate relationship with someone when you still lived with your parents. It was just one of the reasons he'd opted to fix up his gram's cottage—he hoped to meet someone, eventually. But he'd never dreamed that *someone* would literally turn up on his doorstep. And now that she had, there was no way he was letting her get away.

"Does that include you?" he dared ask in response to her observation.

She paused, and when she finally spoke, he could hear the wry self-deprecation in her tone. "I think you already know the answer to that."

Flynn was glad she was standing behind him and couldn't see his pleased grin.

"There," she said, giving his hair a final comb-through before gently mussing it with her fingers. She came around to stand in front of him and surveyed him through critical eyes before smiling. "Perfect."

Out of habit, Flynn pushed his hand through his hair, gratified when it didn't immediately tumble back over his eyes. He stood up and pulled the towel away from his neck. The floor was littered with curling snippets of dark hair, and he felt a moment of alarm.

"Did you leave any on my head?"

But Lori only laughed. "Go check the mirror."

He ducked into the guest bedroom and examined her handiwork in the bathroom mirror, surprised by what he saw. She'd done a good job. Better than good, actually. Turning his head side to side, he admired the cut.

"Thanks," he said when he returned to the kitchen.

Lori paused in the act of sweeping up the remnants and looked at him in expectation. "No complaints?"

"Only that I won't get half as good from the barber in Ballylahane after you're gone," he replied, only half joking.

"Well, don't think I'm flying over here every six weeks just to keep you looking good for the ladies," Lori retorted, turning away.

"Yeah, because right now you're averaging every five

weeks. How long are you planning to stay this time?"

He thought she would come back with some smart response, but instead, she set the broom aside, braced her arms on the counter, and hung her head. When she spoke, she sounded desolate. "I don't know. I told HR to put me in for three weeks of vacation, and after that . . . I don't know. There's no way I can go back to Chicago, but I can't stay here. What am I going to do?"

"Hey," he said, alarmed by the uncharacteristic despondency in her voice. "Look at me."

She shook her head, and Flynn stepped forward to take her by the shoulders and turn her gently to face him. She kept her eyes averted, but her chin trembled, and Flynn knew she was barely holding it together.

"Listen to me," he said quietly. "You don't have to do anything right now. Stay here for as long as you need to—until you get things sorted. You can't solve anything when you're stressed, and rushing to a solution could just make the problem worse or even prolong it." He dipped his head down to look directly into her eyes. "Sometimes all you need is some distance in order to gain a new perspective."

She looked at him then, and the misery in her eyes just about gutted Flynn. "I've certainly accomplished the distance part, coming to Ireland. I just feel as if I've let everyone down, including myself."

"Come here," he said gruffly, and pulled her into his arms. She buried her face against his chest and curled her fingers into his shirtfront. Flynn circled a hand between her shoulder blades, part of his brain registering how soft and smooth her bare skin felt beneath his fingers. "I promise you haven't let anyone down. Neither the job nor the lad back in Chicago are meant for you, *mo chailín*."

"That's the second time you've called me that." She lifted her head to look at him. "What does it mean?"

Flynn let his gaze drift over her face, noting the tiny mole at the corner of her left eye and the way her pulse visibly throbbed along the side of her smooth throat. "It's Irish for *sweetheart*."

"Oh." Her glance flicked from his eyes to his mouth and back again. "Do you always call women you hardly know *sweetheart*?"

Flynn knew he was treading dangerous ground, but was helpless to resist. She was in his arms, looking at him in a way that made his own pulse surge on an unexpected tide of longing. "Only you," he murmured, and drew her closer.

Her lips parted on a soft *oh*, and Flynn was a goner. Lowering his head, he let his lips graze hers, hearing her softly indrawn breath. But when she turned her face upward, searching for more, he fitted his mouth against hers in a deep, slow kiss. She shifted closer, lifting her arms to encircle his neck, her fingers sifting through his hair and holding him fast. She tasted like sweet wine, and her mouth felt like hot silk. Her tongue tangled with his, drawing him deeper. Hardly aware of his actions, he lifted her easily onto the edge of the counter and pressed into the splayed vee of her thighs. Dragging his mouth softly from hers, he worked his way down her throat, kissing and nibbling the tender skin. Her breath came in warm pants, and she clutched his shoulders, her head falling back to allow him better access. When he flicked aside the fragile strap of her camisole and tugged the fabric downward to release one perfect, rose-tipped breast, she drew her breath in sharply, but didn't stop him.

"So beautiful." He stroked the backs of his fingers over her, watching as her nipple tightened into a tempting bud. He wanted badly to taste her, but the sight of his own hand, so big and work-roughened, next to the soft paleness of her breast, brought him abruptly back to his senses. Reluctantly, he pulled her top back into place and stepped away, pushing a hand through his newly cropped hair. "We should get going or we'll be late."

He didn't miss the disappointment in her expression before she nodded and lowered herself to the floor. She pulled her sweater on and wrapped it close, folding her arms across her middle as if to protect herself from him.

"Lori—"

She put a hand up. "No, don't say anything, and whatever you do, don't you dare apologize. If this was your attempt at a rematch, fine. You win."

Despite his own frustration, Flynn couldn't suppress a smile. "I don't plan to apologize. But you should know we were never going to leave the cottage if I hadn't stopped."

He didn't miss the slight widening of her eyes, but when she spoke, her voice was even. "So I'm supposed to thank you?"

"No, sweetheart," he said, gathering his jacket and opening the cottage door to let her precede him outside. "That comes later."

# Chapter Nine

L ORI WOKE UP the following morning feeling restless and out of sorts. She'd hardly slept. She'd lain awake for hours thinking about the kitchen kiss, knowing she was in real trouble. If she was smart, she'd book a return ticket home and get as far away from Flynn O'Rourke as fast as she could, because the man was seriously messing with her head. That kiss had been *hot*. He'd been right—if he hadn't ended things by stepping away from her, who knew how far she would have let it go?

A tiny voice told her, *All the way*.

She didn't pretend to misunderstand what he'd said about thanking him either. The implicit promise in his voice had only confirmed what she'd already suspected—if and when they finally came together, it was going to be off-the-charts amazing.

It would also be a colossal mistake.

The evening at Conall's house had been fun and relaxed, sitting around the firepit on his patio. Conall's friends had been nice too. Flynn had reverted to his usual self, doing his best to tease or aggravate her, but Lori sensed a change in him, as if his heart wasn't really in it. He'd sat across from her on the terrace and several times she'd glanced his way to find him watching her through brooding eyes. But each time their eyes met, he'd looked away. They'd ordered pizza for the entire group and had watched the sun set over the ocean, but there had been no opportunity to speak privately. When the evening had finally ended and they'd driven back to the farm, Lori had found herself hoping he might walk her to her door, maybe even kiss her again.

Maybe stay.

Instead, he'd pulled his car to a stop at the bottom of the knoll and had said good-night as if they were no more than acquaintances. As if the kitchen kiss had never happened. But Lori hadn't missed how he gripped the steering wheel with both hands, as if he couldn't trust himself to let go.

"Would you like to come in?" she'd asked, refusing to be put off by his manner.

He slid a pewter glance in her direction before he turned to stare resolutely through the windshield at the darkness beyond. "If I go into that house with you, everything will change."

"Will it?"

He gave her a warning look. "Go to bed, Lori. You're tired, and you're not thinking straight."

"Fine. You don't need to take me sightseeing tomorrow, since you so obviously don't want to be with me."

He swiveled his head toward her, his eyes gleaming dangerously in the dash light. "Is that what you really think?" His voice was low and tense. "That I don't want to be with you?"

She stared at him, mute, her heart fluttering with both apprehension and excitement because she'd never seen this side of Flynn before. His usual humor was gone. He looked intense and even a little threatening, his entire body tightly coiled, as if he might pounce on her at any second. Later, she wasn't sure who moved first, only that they were suddenly in each other's arms, straining over the center console as their lips met in a searing kiss, charged with all the urgency and pent-up need from their earlier encounter. Flynn's hands were in her hair, angling her face for better access. She gave him everything he demanded. Lori didn't know how long the heated kiss went on, only knew that at some point, Flynn's touch became gentler, his hands soothing, before he finally broke the kiss. He bent his forehead to hers, his fingers still buried in her hair. Their breath mingled in soft, hot pants.

"I hope that settles the issue of my wanting to be with you," he murmured against her mouth.

She nodded, unable to speak.

"Go to bed. I'll see you in the morning, *mo chailín*."

Lori nodded again and fled into the cottage, feeling equal amounts of disappointment and relief. Disappointment because her body had thrummed with need, and relief because she had known he was right—if he had come inside, everything would have changed.

Now, glancing at her phone, she realized it was six thirty. She'd told Flynn she would feed the lambs, but she was already late. Scrambling out of bed, she pulled on a pair of jeans, boots, and a sweater before brushing her teeth and letting herself out of the cottage. It had rained overnight and the surrounding hills were shrouded in mist. The sun had risen over the horizon but struggled to penetrate the fog. At the doorway to the barn, the lights were on and Flynn stood at the sink, elbow-deep in sudsy water.

Suddenly shy and uncertain, she hesitated. He looked ridiculously handsome and virile in a white T-shirt that strained over his shoulders and impressive biceps, and clung lovingly to the long muscles on either side of his spine. He was gorgeous and smart and hardworking, and any woman would consider herself lucky to have a man like him by her side.

"Good morning," she called out as she stepped into the warmth of the barn. "What can I do?"

"There's coffee there," he said, indicating a thermos and two mugs on the worktable, where he kept a laptop and ledgers. "Help yourself."

"I'll clean out the pens," she offered as she poured them each a mug of steaming coffee. "After I say hello to my little Woolly Wonka."

"No worries. It's already been done."

He didn't sound annoyed, but neither did he look at her

as she set his coffee down beside the sink. Lori wondered if he regretted what had happened last night.

"I couldn't sleep last night," she offered, crouching next to the pen so that she could reach in and pet Woolly Wonka. "As a result, I overslept. Sorry."

Flynn shot her a sharp glance, and Lori knew he *was* thinking about the kiss, but as if by tacit agreement, neither of them made any mention of what had happened.

"It's fine. I couldn't sleep either," he acknowledged, his tone rueful. "I've been up for hours, which means all the chores have already been taken care of."

"Wow. So counting sheep doesn't work, after all," she mused in feigned astonishment. "I mean, if there's any truth to that cliché, you would know. Right?"

He gave her a tolerant look, but Lori was pleased to see the barest hint of a smile curve his mouth. He nodded his head toward her cup. "Drink your coffee before it gets cold."

With a last caress for the lamb, Lori stood and curled her fingers around her mug and watched him, intrigued. What had kept him awake? She was vain enough to hope it had been thoughts of her, but sensed it was more than that. Something was bothering him. Despite his assurances that he did want to be with her, was he regretting what had happened? Maybe he did want to put some distance between them, after all. She found the thought depressing.

"Is everything okay?" she asked, all traces of humor gone. "Can I do anything?"

He glanced at her, and for just an instant, the bleakness in his eyes startled her. It was gone so quickly she wondered if she had imagined it. "Ah, no," he said with a quick smile. "It's a family matter. But thanks just the same."

His dismissal was polite, but firm. She nodded, telling herself she had no reason to feel hurt because he chose not share a family issue with her. It was none of her business. "Okay. Well, I do feel badly about letting you do all the work when I said I would help out. Let me make it up to you and cook us both breakfast."

Flynn looked at her then. "You don't need to do anything, Lori. If you're worried that I'll change my mind about taking you sightseeing, I won't."

"I'm not worried," she fibbed.

"Good." He glanced at his watch. "Since you haven't eaten yet, you might as well come up to the house and have breakfast. Mam will have it ready by now."

"Oh, I don't know . . ." She balked, suddenly uncertain.

"What's wrong?"

"Won't your mother mind?"

"Why would she?"

"Well, she's not expecting an additional mouth," Lori reasoned. "Besides which, she might not be in the mood for company at this early hour."

"Trust me, she always cooks too much." He reached for a sweater that lay on the worktable and pulled it over his head before tugging it into place. Even the thickly cabled wool couldn't conceal his strong physique. If anything, it made him look bigger and more powerfully built. "She'll be happy to see you."

She walked with him to the farmhouse, feeling a little apprehensive about what sort of welcome she might receive, but Flynn had been right—his mother seemed genuinely pleased to see her.

"Good morning, Lori," she said, smiling. "Sit down and help yourself to whatever you like. But be quick—my boys don't believe in leftovers."

Thanking her, Lori sat in the chair Flynn pulled out for her, scanning the platters of food on the table. Flynn hadn't exaggerated—there were scrambled eggs still in the skillet, thick cuts of bacon and a plate of sausages, shredded potatoes cooked to a golden brown, grilled tomatoes, and a rack of toast beside a jar of homemade jam. The kitchen was warm and bright, and smelled delicious, and Lori found herself scooping eggs and hash browns onto her plate with anticipation.

"No bacon or sausage for you?" Maureen asked as she placed a pitcher of orange juice on the table.

"Oh, no, thank you," Lori said.

"She doesn't eat meat," Flynn added as he piled his own plate high with eggs, bacon, and sausage.

"Everyone is entitled to their own choices," Maureen said as she put together a plate that included a little bit of everything. "She's likely healthier for it."

"And the lambs are too," Lori quipped, sliding a mutinous glance toward Flynn.

"Do I need to worry about you staging a revolt, cutting the fences, and driving my flock to freedom?" he asked, a dimple appearing in his cheek.

Lori grinned in return. "No, I wouldn't dream of *fleecing* you like that."

Flynn laughed, setting off tiny explosions of delight in Lori's heart. He had a great laugh, deep and genuine and utterly contagious, and she found herself laughing in return.

"Well, while you two laugh yourselves silly, I'll just take this upstairs to your father," Maureen said, lifting a breakfast tray laden with food, juice, and coffee. Seeing the question in Lori's eyes, she shrugged. "My husband's feeling poorly today, so I'm going to spoil him a bit with breakfast in bed."

"I hope it's nothing serious."

"Not at all," Maureen replied brightly. "He'll be right as rain in no time."

But Lori thought her tone sounded falsely cheerful, and she didn't miss how Flynn grew silent and hunkered over his breakfast.

"Just how sick is he?" she asked after Maureen had left.

Flynn raised his head. "He's not doing well, actually. Mam wouldn't want you to know, but he was diagnosed with leukemia just after Christmas."

Lori recalled how distracted Flynn had seemed the previous night at Conall's house and how just that morning, when she'd asked if he was okay, he'd told her it was a family matter. A wave of guilt washed over her at own selfishness in wanting his attention for herself.

"I'm so sorry," she said now. "Will he be okay?"

"I hope so, but only time will tell."

Before Lori could say more, she heard heavy footsteps in the hall and a young man entered the kitchen, stopping abruptly when he saw Lori at the table. He looked to be in his early twenties and judging by the way his black hair stood up in all directions, he'd no idea she would be there, in his kitchen. Now his face turned ruddy with embarrassment and he tried to smooth his hair with one hand.

"Sorry," he muttered. "I just woke up. Didn't know we had company."

"Yeah, no worries, Declan. This is Lori Woods. She's staying at the cottage." Flynn glanced at Lori. "This is my brother Declan."

While he was as tall as his older brother, he lacked Flynn's broad shoulders and thick muscles. Still, Lori was sure the local girls probably went a little weak in the knees when they saw him—sort of the way Lori felt whenever she found herself near Flynn.

"Morning," Declan mumbled, and sat down without looking at her. He poured himself coffee and began helping himself to eggs, hash browns, and bacon. He glanced at his brother. "I'm working with Shane today, dropping spat collectors."

"Great," Flynn said. "Will you be going to the festival later?"

"Dunno," Declan said. "Don't worry about Dad; I'll see him settled."

"Thanks."

Lori glanced between the two men. "I'm sorry—what are spat collectors?"

"We grow mussels down in the bay," Declan explained between mouthfuls. "Spat are just mussel larvae. We drop ropes—spat collectors—into the water and the larvae attach themselves to the rope, where they continue to grow. In a couple of years, the mussels will be mature enough to harvest."

"There's a decent market for mussels?"

Flynn threw her an amused glance. "Huge, actually."

"It's a competitive market," Declan confirmed. "We sell our mussels internationally as well as locally. Have you ever had Guinness and cream mussels?"

Lori suppressed a grimace. "Not that I can recall."

"I'll bring you to Mallone's Pub for lunch one day," Flynn said. "They do a decent job of it."

"Well, you'd better go today," Declan added with a wink. "It's the last day of April and the last day you can eat mussels until September."

"Really?" Lori looked at Flynn for confirmation, but he only shrugged.

"Some people believe you can only eat mussels during

months with the letter *r* in them. I don't believe that, though."

"Yeah, it's not actually true," Declan said. "Probably just a way to ensure people don't harvest mussels during the hot summer months, when there's a risk of them going bad before they get to your plate."

"Does Ireland actually have hot summer months?" Lori teased.

"Guess you'll just have to stick around and find out," Flynn replied, his tone lightly challenging.

"Hmm," she mused, pretending to consider. "I'm not sure you can handle me hanging around for the entire summer."

To her surprise, Flynn leaned toward her, his expression oddly intent. "Try me."

Unsettled, Lori bent her head and focused on her food, not wanting Flynn to see how his words affected her. She wanted to believe he meant them—that he'd like for her to stay longer than just a few weeks, but the very idea was as scary as it was thrilling.

She couldn't stay.

She and Flynn had little in common beyond their combustible chemistry. This whole trip was a dream, but reality would eventually intrude. Her family would demand she return. Seth would want her to return, too, although she felt zero inclination to cater to his wishes.

Declan stood up and crammed a last bite of toast into his

mouth. "I have to run, sorry. Nice to meet you, Lori. Maybe I'll see you at the bonfire."

She nodded and threw him a swift smile as he left the room. She and Flynn ate in silence before she stood up and took her plate to the sink. Behind her, she heard Flynn gathering up the dishes from the table before he came to stand beside her. He stacked the plates and bowls on the counter.

"Are you okay?"

"Yes, of course," she assured him, keeping her tone light. "I just thought I'd wash these up so your mother doesn't have to."

"Let me help you." Pushing back the sleeves of his sweater, he turned on the water and squirted detergent onto a sponge. "I'll wash, you dry."

He handled the dish deftly as he swirled the wet, soapy sponge across the surface, and Lori found herself staring stupidly at his strong hands and wrists. When he handed her the first slippery plate, she almost fumbled it onto the floor.

"Careful there," he said, grinning. "Sure you've done this before, princess?"

"Ha-ha. Where do these go?"

Flynn indicated a shelf over her head. "Up there."

"What a gloomy day for the festival," she commented, looking through the window at the mist that still floated over the hills and water.

"This will clear up by lunch," Flynn said. "We'll have a

fine afternoon, and tonight is supposed to be clear and dry."

"When will you head into town? Since you're carrying the torch?"

"Not until just before the Festival of Fire begins. In fact, I thought maybe we could take a drive this morning."

"Oh." She glanced at him, but he was focused on rinsing a coffee mug. "Where to?"

"Well, you said you wanted to see some of the sights while you're here, and I have a place in mind that I think you'll enjoy."

Memories of their day at the waterfall swamped her, and heat collected and pooled low in her womb. She didn't dare look at Flynn and concentrated instead on drying the last dish and placing it carefully in the cupboard.

"Is it far?" she finally asked.

"Not at all. We'll only be gone a few hours at most."

Maureen chose that moment to reenter the kitchen. "Where is it you're going?"

"Fort Doon," Flynn replied, drying his hands.

"Oh. I thought the site is closed to tourists, due to the repairs being made," she said, setting the breakfast tray on the counter.

But Flynn only smiled. "Then it's a good thing I'm not a tourist."

Maureen gave her son a tolerant look. "You're a charming lad, I'll give you that, but I doubt even you can sweet-talk old Mrs. McHugh into loaning you one of her rowboats."

"We need a boat to get there?" Lori asked, her curiosity piqued.

"The fort is located in the middle of Loughadoon," Maureen said.

"What is Lock-a-Doon, exactly?"

Flynn chuckled. "Loughadoon is a lake, and Fort Doon is an ancient ring fort situated on an island in the middle of the lake. Hardly anyone goes out there or even knows about it, aside from the locals."

"The McHughs are the guardians of Fort Doon, and they're fiercely protective," Maureen said darkly. "I doubt you'll get past them easily."

"Ooh," Lori said, resisting the urge to rub her hands together. "A secret island? Guardians of an ancient ring fort? It all sounds very *Lord of the Rings*. I can't wait."

"I thought it might appeal to you," Flynn said with a laugh. "We can head out whenever you're ready." He looked at his mother. "Provided you don't need anything from me before we go."

"No, your father is resting comfortably. Go and have fun."

Lori watched as Flynn pressed a swift kiss against his mother's cheek. "Thanks for breakfast, Mam."

"Yes, thank you," Lori said. "It was delicious."

"You're welcome to join us anytime," Maureen replied. "I mean that."

As she followed Flynn out of the house and across the yard toward the cottage, he surprised her by slinging an arm casually around her shoulders. Caught off guard, Lori didn't know whether to shrug him off or move in closer. Instead, she gave him a deliberately pointed look.

"What?" he asked, feigning innocence.

"Your mother could be watching from the window. I'd hate to give her the wrong idea about us."

But Flynn only laughed and hugged her against his side. "Sweetheart," he said, grinning down at her, "if my mam invites you to come for breakfast anytime you wish, it's because she definitely has the wrong idea about us. You may as well marry me now, because as far as she's concerned, you're already part of the family."

# Chapter Ten

L ORI FELT AS if she'd been prodded with a stun gun for the five minutes it took her to gather her jacket and handbag from the cottage, while Flynn mercifully waited for her by the car.

Had he really suggested she *marry him*? Even knowing the comment had been made in fun, his words had rendered her speechless and robbed her of the ability to put him down with a few well-chosen words.

*Marry him.*

She had a sudden image of herself cooking a traditional Irish breakfast at the enameled Aga cookstove in the cottage, while Flynn deftly herded a small flock of black-haired children to the kitchen table, making them squeal in delight as he tossed them over his head before settling them in their chairs.

*No.*

She pushed the enticing image out of her head. She had absolutely no business fantasizing about a life with the big, hunky Irishman. She wasn't cut out for life on a sheep farm, no matter how gorgeous and irresistible the farmer might be.

Even if it meant she could kiss said farmer anytime she wanted and spend every night wrapped in his muscular arms.

*No.*

She refused to dream about a future with Flynn. What she felt was nothing more than physical attraction. He was handsome and even charming when he put his mind to it. But once she returned to the States, she'd forget all about him, just as he would no doubt forget all about her.

With a groan, she threw a raincoat and handbag over her arm and stepped out of the cottage. Flynn waited for her at the bottom of the path. He was crouched on the balls of his feet, petting Brody and crooning soft words of approval as the border collie's tongue lolled out of his mouth and he fixed Flynn with a gaze of utter canine adoration.

"God, it's disgusting," Lori muttered, stomping past him. "Even the dogs have no dignity around you."

Laughing, Flynn rose to his feet. "You're just jealous."

Lori made a scoffing sound. "Hardly."

But the word lacked conviction. Worse, it brought to mind images of his big hands cupping her face as he feasted on her lips. Climbing into the driver's seat of the rental car, she slammed the door with slightly more force than necessary and switched on the engine, revving the gas as Flynn folded his big frame into the passenger seat. Pushing the seat back as far as it would go, he threw her an amused glance.

"You seem a little . . . agitated."

"I'm fine," she said sweetly. "Buckle up."

*Rev, rev.*

"Am I safe with you?"

Lori reversed out of the parking spot, her tires churning up dirt and gravel. "We'll see, won't we?"

But in the end, she was too fearful of hitting a sheep in the mist to do more than drive at a snail's pace. They reached the main road, and she followed Flynn's directions, driving away from town and into the surrounding countryside.

"You're actually doing a fair job of driving, all things considered," he said, watching as she shifted into fourth gear.

"Thanks. Four hours of driving from Dublin, with a gazillion roundabouts, gave me plenty of practice." Lori peered through the windshield at the surrounding landscape, not seeing many houses or even areas of interest. "Just where are we going, anyway?"

"Turn into the driveway of that house on the left," he said, indicating a small farmhouse up ahead. Despite the fact it was the only house in sight, Lori gave him a doubtful look. They had been driving for less than ten minutes.

"Here?"

"This is the place."

Lori parked the car. "Now what?"

"Wait here."

She watched as he climbed out of the car and approached the house. Before he could knock, the door opened and an elderly woman stood in the entry. Seeing Flynn, she reached up to hug him, her face wreathed in a smile. They spoke for several minutes, and then Flynn turned and beckoned to Lori.

"This is Mrs. McHugh," he said as she approached the doorstep. "I've known her since I was a small, wee lad."

This sweet woman was the same person Maureen had warned them about? She looked like everyone's favorite granny. Lori couldn't imagine her guarding anything, except perhaps a pot of tea and a basket of knitting. Lori smiled and extended her hand to the older woman. "It's a pleasure to meet you, Mrs. McHugh. I'm Lori Woods."

"Happy to meet you as well," she replied. "Wait here a moment, and I'll get the key to the boat lock."

She vanished inside the house, and Lori slid Flynn an appraising look. "Small and wee, were you?"

"Yeah. Once upon a time."

"I'm having a hard time picturing it."

Mrs. McHugh returned and handed a large iron key ring to Flynn. "Take whichever boat you like and mind the walls."

Accepting the key, Flynn bent and pressed a kiss against the woman's soft, weathered cheek. "Thank you. We'll be careful. I promise you, Josie won't find a single stone out of place."

Mrs. McHugh chuckled and patted his arm. "Go on now, before he returns."

Lori followed Flynn across the road to where a small

footpath led into the scrubby wilderness. "Who is Josie?"

"Josie McHugh is her husband, the true guardian of Fort Doon, along with his brother. If he'd been home, we likely wouldn't have had much success in getting the boat key. But I know for a fact he goes to Ardara on Saturday mornings to meet with the local heritage council. After the meeting, they head over to the local pub for a pint. He won't be back for hours."

"How do you know all this?" she asked, laughing.

"Their grandson, Michael McHugh, is a close pal of mine. When we were lads, we'd take the boat out to the island to drink his dad's whiskey and smoke cigarettes."

Lori liked to imagine Flynn as a boy, all lanky limbs and mischievous grins.

"Ah, so you were a bad boy. I should have guessed."

Flynn laughed. "Not so much bad as brainless. We couldn't have been more than twelve or thirteen at the time. I actually haven't been out here in years."

"So just where is this secret island? I don't see anything."

Flynn caught her hand in his and helped her climb a particularly steep, rocky part of the trail. "Well, it wouldn't be much of a secret if everyone could see it plain as day, now would it?"

The path wound its way through marsh and bogland, and Lori had to stop several times to catch her breath, as the terrain was steep. At some point, she realized they were steadily climbing downward, until suddenly they rounded a bend in the trail and a long lake, shrouded in mist, appeared in front of them. Small, green islands dotted the water and steep, wooded hills edged the shoreline. From where she stood, there were no houses or buildings and, except for the footpath, no sign of civilization.

"How beautiful," Lori breathed as Flynn helped her navigate the last part of the path, which dipped sharply to the water's edge. Gazing out over the lake, she couldn't see any sign of an ancient fort. Even the small islands that were visible seemed too small to support any type of man-made structure. "Where is the fort, exactly?"

"Once we row past that small outcrop, you'll see it."

She followed Flynn to where two rowboats lay upside down on the shore, chained to a stone post that had been driven into the ground. He used the key to unlock and loosen the chain and then flipped one of the boats over and retrieved two oars from where they were stored under the seats. Dragging the boat to the water, he held it steady with one hand and extended the other toward Lori.

"My lady, your journey through time awaits you."

"If only I'd worn my flowing white gown and crown of flowers," she said, only partly teasing.

"You look grand." He swept her with a look that missed nothing, and in that instant, Lori forgot she was wearing jeans, boots, and a raincoat. He made her feel beautiful, and her face grew warm beneath his steady regard.

With a sense of anticipation, Lori took his hand and

stepped into the boat, clutching his fingers when it rocked sharply. She sat abruptly down on the bench seat as Flynn fitted the oars into the oarlocks and then gave the boat a mighty push before nimbly jumping in and settling himself on the seat across from her. They were so close that their knees bumped. Flynn took the oars and expertly maneuvered the boat into deeper water.

"You've done this before."

"Plenty of times, and not just here. My brothers and I grew up rowing on the water below the farm."

His muscles bunched and flexed with each long stroke until the shoreline grew more distant. They drifted past the small islands, disturbing a flock of nesting birds who took flight above their heads.

"Why is the fort closed to tourists?" she asked, leaning over to trail her fingers through the clear, cold water.

"The walls have begun to crumble in places, as one would expect after fifteen hundred years. The local heritage council has been working to restore the site and they want to keep it closed to visitors until the work is complete."

"Should we be out here, then? I'd hate for you to get in trouble."

Flynn grinned at her. "You do care! Seriously, though, it's not a problem. We have Mrs. McHugh's permission, and we'll treat the walls with respect."

"But not each other?" she teased.

Flynn pinioned her with a look turned suddenly intent.

"Is that what you want? Because the things I'd like to do with you probably wouldn't pass the respectability test."

Lori swallowed hard and found she couldn't drag her gaze away. Her heart pounded hard behind her breastbone. The attraction was always there between them, simmering just below the surface, but even on the few occasions when they'd given in to temptation, Flynn had never crossed a line or demanded more than she was willing to give. He'd always been in control and had never once pushed her to do more than kiss. And until this moment, neither of them had spoken of the raw need they both felt. The knowledge that he thought about doing more—wanted to do more—caused her bones to go a little weak.

"Well," she finally managed, her voice weak. "How nice."

Flynn's mouth curved in the barest hint of a smile, as if he knew exactly what his words did to her.

"Oh, there it is!" she exclaimed as the boat glided silently past an outcrop of land and into a larger section of lake hidden beyond the trees. There, rising out of the water like a mythical creature, was a circular stone fortress with high walls. Vapors of mist swirled around the base of the fort, and thick ropes of ivy clung to the rock. As they drew closer, an opening appeared in the stones, half hidden behind a curtain of vines. Lori caught glimpses of lush greenery inside.

"Is this a portal to the fairy realm?" she asked, only half teasing. The place had an ancient, otherworldly feel to it, and she wouldn't have been at all surprised to see a sprite or a water nymph cavorting among the stones.

"Could be," Flynn said. "This is Ireland, after all. Ancient standing stones and cairns could be fairy portals." The boat scraped softly against the shore. Flynn jumped out and pulled the dinghy onto a sweep of green grass at the base of the wall and then held out a hand to Lori. "'Come away, O human child! / To the waters and the wild / With a faery, hand in hand, / For the world's more full of weeping than you can understand.'"

Lori stared at him, surprised and impressed. He was such a contradiction, and she wondered if anyone truly knew the real Flynn O'Rourke. She recalled how, during her previous visit to Ballylahane, Flynn had recited another poem by the famous Irish poet. "Have you memorized all of Yeats's poems?"

Flynn looked embarrassed. "I only remember that part, actually. Yeats spent his childhood in Sligo, so his poetry was required reading in school, but I've forgotten more than I remember."

Taking his hand, Lori stepped out of the boat and gazed up at the ancient wall. "Well, I think he would approve of your reciting that particular poem in this particular place. It really does feel mystical."

The massive walls of the fort towered over them, covered in lichen and dripping with moisture as they made their way toward the opening in the rock. Flynn pushed aside the thick sweep of vines that obscured the interior, and Lori stepped through. The walls themselves were at least twelve feet thick, giving her the sensation that she had walked into a tunnel.

"Here, look at this," Flynn said, stopping her in the middle of the passageway. There, in the center of the wall, was a rectangular opening—a gaping black hole that descended into nothingness.

"What is it?" she asked.

"We call it a *creep*, because it's small and difficult to negotiate."

"I'd call it a *creep* for an entirely different reason," Lori said, shivering. "What's down there?"

He withdrew a small penlight from his pocket and shined it into the opening. Peering closer, Lori could make out a narrow, low-ceilinged tunnel that ran inside the wall and descended downward via a steep stone staircase. It looked dark and dank, and she instinctively drew closer to Flynn's protective bulk.

"You couldn't pay me enough money to go in there," she muttered. Forget about fairies; she could easily imagine something sinister lurking in those dank shadows.

"It only goes in about twenty feet and then dead-ends. There's nothing in there to be afraid of, except maybe slipping and cracking your skull."

"I'm surprised you could actually fit. It looks very tight."

"It is," Flynn said. "But I was only a lad at the time and a lot smaller than I am now."

"What do you think it was used for?"

"Legend has it there's a secret tunnel beneath the lake, connecting the fort to the mainland. If this is the entrance, it's been sealed up, maybe for centuries."

"Probably for a very good reason," Lori said, eyeing the dark tunnel. "Who knows what they might have trapped down there? I wouldn't want to find out."

Flynn laughed. "My thoughts exactly. C'mon."

They emerged into the interior of the fort, and Lori wouldn't have been at all surprised if they had been greeted by the Fae King himself. Inside the circular space, everything was eerily quiet, as if the thick walls prevented any sound from the outside world from penetrating. Beneath her feet, the ground was soft with damp grass, and the surrounding walls were covered in ivy and moss and thick lichen. A section of wall near the back of the stone circle had begun to collapse beneath the dense ivy. Scaffolding had been erected near the wall, the only sign of the ongoing repair work that Maureen had mentioned. There were trees inside the fort, as well, standing in overgrown rows on one side of the open space.

"Is that an orchard?"

"It is, yeah. The fort has been used as a garden over the years because the soil is so rich."

"A secret garden," she mused, smiling. "Inside a secret fort, hidden on a secret lake."

They spent an hour exploring the fort, searching for other passages but avoiding the stone staircases that had been built into the walls, which would have brought to them to the top of the fort.

"We wouldn't have great views at any rate," Flynn reasoned, seeing her disappointment. "Not with the mist. In fact, we should probably head back if you're ready."

Lori followed Flynn back toward the entrance, reluctant for the morning to end. Flynn had been a fun and informative guide, recounting stories of ancient gold torques found in the nearby fields, and of mysterious lights seen on the lake and the surrounding bogland on misty nights. She liked having him all to herself, had enjoyed being the focus of his attention, and had delighted in making him laugh at her stupid quips.

"Thank you for bringing me here," she said as they made their way back toward the opening in the wall. "I never would have seen or even known about this place if it weren't for you."

"I'm glad you enjoyed it. At least the weather held out."

As if to mock his words, the skies suddenly opened and released a torrent of rain so heavy that they both gave a surprised shout and sprinted toward the exit. Once in the passage between the thick walls, Flynn pulled her into the narrow tunnel and pressed her against the stones as he hunched over her in an effort to protect her from the deluge.

"Where did that come from?" Lori gasped.

"It's just a cloudburst. It'll soon pass."

His big body pressed against hers in the cramped space as rain sluiced down outside, and Lori breathed in the familiar scents of wool, peat, and spicy soap that she'd come to associate with him. He was so close, she could see the way his thick eyelashes spiked over his silver eyes, and droplets of water beaded on his skin and trickled down the strong planes of his cheekbones. Raindrops glistened in his dark hair and settled like tiny diamonds on the rough wool of his sweater. He stared at her, his gaze soft and hot, and prickles of awareness chased themselves across Lori's skin. Lifting a hand, he used one finger to gently push a damp tendril of hair back from her face and wipe a drop of moisture from her cheek.

"I want to kiss you," he said in a low voice, his accent more pronounced.

Later, Lori couldn't remember if she'd nodded or made a sound or said anything at all. She could have pushed him away with a witty rebuff, but she didn't. She wanted that kiss.

Badly.

Without conscious thought, she reached up to catch his face in her hands and urge him down until his mouth covered hers. He gave a soft groan and pulled her against his body, his lips slanting over hers in a hot, open-mouthed kiss that dissolved her self-control. The raw sensuality of the kiss undid her. Flynn made a leisurely exploration, alternately biting and licking into her mouth as the delicious contact went on and on. Lori felt dizzy with the pleasure of it. Her hands clutched his shoulders, her entire existence reduced to the sweet, hot sensation of his lips against hers. One big hand cradled the back of her skull while his other arm curved behind her shoulders, shielding her from the cold stones and pressing her into his hard warmth. When, finally, he lifted his head, Lori leaned against him, curling her fingers into his sweater.

"The rain has stopped," he murmured. His breath was warm against her face.

"You did say it was only a cloudburst." Her voice trembled.

"I did, yeah," he agreed, his silver gaze boring into her. "They're intense, but they never last."

Lori stared at him for a long moment, feeling certain he wasn't talking about the weather. "Well," she finally managed. "That's lucky for us, isn't it?"

# Chapter Eleven

FLYNN DIDN'T KNOW what had possessed him to kiss Lori the way he had, but he couldn't bring himself to regret it, even knowing it likely meant little to her. He'd been an idiot to think he could spend the morning with her and *not* kiss her. Every time they were alone together, he ended up kissing her. It was like a biological imperative. She'd never know what it had cost him not to accept her invitation the previous night. Only the knowledge of where it would end had made him remain in the car. Maybe the best thing for both of them would be for her to leave the cottage and find a place to stay in town for the remainder of her visit. Having her on the farm was messing with his head.

Maybe more than just his head.

He wasn't sure he could spend another couple of weeks with her around, only to watch her leave again. But the thought of not seeing her caused an ache to settle in the center of his chest.

He'd never felt so conflicted in his life.

By the time they returned to the farm, the sun had made a heroic appearance, burning away the last vestiges of mist that clung to the surrounding hills and fields.

"Look there," he said as he parked the car near the cottage. "A rainbow."

The translucent arch of color stretched over the narrow inlet of water below the farm, and he smiled at Lori's indrawn gasp of delight.

"When Rachel first came over here, she called me in Chicago and tried to describe this place. I envisioned green fields full of sheep and rainbows around every corner." She laughed softly. "I wasn't wrong."

"We do have our share of sheep," he agreed, unable to suppress a grin as they watched a flock graze on the hillside. After climbing out of the car, he walked around to her side and opened her door, and they stood for a moment, admiring the dramatic scenery.

"Have you ever wanted to do something else?" Lori asked, turning to look at him. "I mean, I realize the farm has been in your family for generations, but I do know something about the pressures of working for the family business. It's not always everything it's cracked up to be."

"Did you always want to work for your father's company?" Flynn countered, leaning back against the car and pushing his hands into the pockets of his jeans.

Lori gave him a pointed look that told him she wouldn't be put off by his tactic. "Let's just say I knew what was expected of me. My parents always assumed I'd work for Lakeside Industries, and I guess I did too."

"And now?"

Lori blew out a hard breath and leaned her hip against the car, facing him. "I'm not so sure, to be honest. I really thought the commodities manager position was meant for me. Not created for me, of course, but something I would be good at. Meeting people, sourcing new products, and managing inventory—it's something I enjoy doing. I ran the company retail store for a year and my favorite part was meeting the vendors and getting to know them. But after a year of managing the store, my father pulled me out in order to gain experience in a different area of the company. But he doesn't *need* me to work for him. He has a staff of business elites who come with all kinds of degrees and experience. I think it was just a way to keep me close. Keep me safe."

"Your family cares about you, Lori. That's not to be taken lightly."

"And I don't," she protested. "But I need some space, some room to figure out who I am and what I'm meant to do. I can't do that back in Chicago, with everyone else making decisions for me."

"That's fair. So what is it you *want* to do?"

For just a moment, she looked lost, and Flynn had to keep his hands firmly in his pockets to prevent himself from reaching for her. She turned and looked out over the landscape, but he knew she wasn't really seeing it, her expression faraway. A breeze stirred the hair at her temple.

"Honestly," she finally said, turning to look at him, "I

have no idea. I wanted that position so much I didn't really consider any other options. I have no backup plan. Maybe I'll go home and run the retail store again." She shrugged and gave him a half smile. "At least I enjoyed that."

"You could do that anywhere," Flynn reasoned. "Your father doesn't have the monopoly on retail."

"You're right. I've been thinking maybe I'll take some time and do some traveling. I have some money saved. I thought I'd start here and then work my way through the United Kingdom."

"By yourself?"

"Now you sound like Rachel. I don't mind my own company, and I've been cocooned by my family for too long. I'm ready to be on my own and figure out what I want to do with the rest of my life."

Flynn made a grunting sound, not enjoying the idea of Lori traveling alone, although he knew better than to voice his concerns. The quickest way to get Lori to do something was to tell her all the reasons why she shouldn't do it.

"What about you?" she asked again. "Are you happy working on the farm? Is it everything you've ever wanted?"

He glanced sharply at her, suspecting her of mocking him, but her expression was earnest, and he found himself relaxing. "I never wanted to live anywhere but here. Even as a boy, I recognized it was special. Don't get me wrong—I loved living in Galway during college, and I did my share of traveling, but I knew eventually I'd come back here and take over the farm. I truly can't imagine living anywhere else."

"Don't you ever get lonely, living out here?"

Flynn studied her, instinct telling him the question had more to do with her than it did with him. "Maybe when I was younger," he admitted. "Especially when I'd just returned from Galway, where there's always something happening. The farm seemed unbearably quiet by comparison, but I've learned to appreciate the simplicity of it. Ireland isn't very large. If I want excitement, it's just a short drive away."

Lori looked away for a moment. His response must not have been what she wanted to hear. But he wouldn't lie to her. He loved the farm, and he actually enjoyed seeing his family every day, even when they drove him crazy. His father's illness had driven home just how important family was—and how it could all change in a heartbeat.

"So you always wanted to be a sheep farmer?" she persisted.

"I did, yeah." Flynn shrugged. "I guess you could say it's in my blood. The problem is, you can't make a living solely through sheep farming. When I was a boy, there was money in wool. My dad was able to provide for us all by selling wool, but those days are gone. He turned the farm over to me several years ago, and I've been running it the same way it's been run for generations. I know I need to make some changes, though. Otherwise, the farm won't survive."

They were silent for several long moments, watching the

rainbow. "I guess we just need to find that pot of gold," Lori said.

Flynn gave a soft scoff and pushed himself away from the vehicle. "I stopped chasing rainbows a long time ago."

To his surprise, Lori stepped close to him and laid one hand on his chest. He couldn't prevent the sudden leap of his heart beneath her fingers. She searched his face, her hazel eyes soft with concern. "Don't say that. Anything is possible, Flynn."

He gave a noncommittal grunt and watched as she moved away and made her way up the walkway toward the cottage, because he knew some things *were* impossible . . . like hoping this time she might stay in Ballylahane.

LORI AND RACHEL trudged to the top of Carraig O'rga while it was still light, carrying picnic blankets, food, and thermoses of hot chocolate and coffee in their backpacks. The trail was marked with solar lights and stakes topped with colorful streamers. The sun had dropped low in the sky, bathing the hill in a buttery-golden wash, while the ocean was a sparkling blue ribbon in the distance.

"I understand why they call this hill *Carraig O'rga*—Hill of Gold," Lori said, squinting into the setting sun. "It's blinding."

"And beautiful. The town was smart to purchase this

land and prevent anyone from building on it. Now everyone can enjoy it."

The grassy hilltop was already crowded with people who had brought folding chairs and blankets. At the center of it all was an enormous pile of wood and pallets, which would be the source of the bonfire, ringed by a dozen ten-foot-high torches. Nearby, a quartet of musicians played lively Irish music while children danced and ran through the crowd, waving streamers.

"Look how many people are already here," Lori exclaimed as they picked their way through the throng, looking for somewhere to sit.

"Conall's mother said the Beltane festival draws people from all over Ireland, so it's bound to get crowded," Rachel reasoned. "But you're right, the actual Festival of Fire won't start until sunset, and it looks like half of Ireland is already here."

They found a spot at the outer edge of the crowd, beneath the twisted, windswept limbs of a hawthorn tree, but close enough to the marked trail that they would be able to see Flynn as he carried the torch up the hill. After spreading the picnic blankets and unpacking the food and thermoses, Rachel pulled out her phone.

"I'll let Conall know where we are so he can find us," she said. "It won't be long now."

As more people made their way to the hilltop, the sun sank below the horizon, and the sky turned a deep indigo.

The musicians began to play a pulse-pounding Celtic tune, and there was a sense of mounting anticipation as darkness fell. In the distance came the sound of drums.

"Look there," Lori said, and gripped Rachel's arm.

A torch could be seen near the bottom of the trail, bobbing in the darkness as it advanced toward them. As Lori's eyes adjusted to the gloom, she could make out the figure of a man running up the slope, a torch held aloft. Behind him followed dozens of people, many of them beating drums. As the group drew closer, Lori could see it was Flynn who carried the torch, and her heart stuttered in her chest. Wearing only a loincloth and a wreath of greenery around his head, his muscular body had been painted in ancient Celtic symbols. He carried the torch high over his head as he ran the last part of the trail and approached the bonfire. A murmur ran through the crowd, and both Lori and Rachel stood for a better view.

A woman, dressed in flowing white robes and wearing an elaborate headdress of flowers, with her face painted white, stood near the pyre. As Flynn approached her, the drummers fanned out to encircle the pyre and the tall torches. The rhythmic beating of the drums grew louder and so powerful that Lori could feel the percussion in her chest. As the crowd watched, Flynn dropped to one knee and extended the torch to the woman like an offering.

"That's the May Queen," came a low male voice. "The passing of the torch celebrates driving out the darkness of winter and the return of spring."

Lori and Rachel turned to see Conall had joined them. He wore a sweatshirt and jeans, but there were vestiges of paint on his face and neck.

"Where's your Beltane costume?" Rachel asked, smiling at him.

"You missed it," he teased, pressing a kiss against her mouth. "There's no way I'm sitting here in my altogether, not with the temperatures dropping." He indicated his backpack. "I've got Flynn's clothing in here."

"That's a shame," Lori murmured, and then laughed when Rachel gave her a knowing look. "What? Look at the man! It's a crime to cover that up with clothes."

As Flynn knelt before the queen, she accepted the torch from him and held it high, before she stepped forward and applied it to the stacked pile of timber. Almost immediately, flames began to lick at the base of the pyre before she passed the flame to her followers, who began to light the tall torches around the bonfire. The crowd cheered, and the drumming grew louder and more intense.

Lori lost sight of Flynn as the May Queen and her followers, dressed in fantastical costumes, began whirling and dancing around the bonfire, their gyrating forms silhouetted against the leaping flames. The drumming intensified, accompanied by throbbing Celtic music.

"So what do you think of our Beltane festival?"

Startled, Lori turned to see Flynn standing right behind

her, the flames of the bonfire reflected in his silver eyes.

"Flynn!" she exclaimed, devouring the sight of him. "I didn't see you arrive."

He had removed the crown of greenery, but he still wore the loincloth, which Lori could see was just a strip of white fabric wound around his hips. Beneath the cloth, he wore a pair of stretchy running shorts. Now he fished through the backpack Conall had brought with him and pulled out a sweatshirt and a pair of pull-on running pants. Beneath the paint that covered his body, his shoulders and arms looked powerful and his flat stomach was banded in muscle.

"Are you enjoying the show?" he asked, glancing at her as he shook out the pants.

"Oh, most definitely," she assured him, giving him her best leer.

Flynn laughed. "That's very nice. Sorry to put an end to your entertainment, but I'm freezing my arse off."

He dragged the sweatshirt down over his body, and Lori wanted to weep with disappointment. He bent to pull the running pants on, working the fabric over his running shoes before he flicked the loin cloth away and pulled the pants up. Before Lori realized what he was doing, he caught her around the waist and sat down on the blanket, pulling her with him. She landed in an untidy heap, falling heavily against him with a cry of surprise.

"Sorry," he said, sounding anything but apologetic.

Flustered, Lori tried to push herself away, but he curled

one big hand around her upper arm, holding her in place. "Stay," he said softly, sliding his hand downward to twine his fingers with hers. The expression in his eyes was gently challenging. Lori hesitated and then slowly relaxed into a sitting position, curling her legs beneath her.

"That's better," he said, extending his long legs and reclining back on one elbow, looking satisfied and indolent. The movement turned him slightly toward her. He didn't release her hand, but instead played lightly with her fingers. Despite the increasing chill of the evening, Lori felt flushed with heat and a little giddy with pleasure.

"Here, have something to drink," Rachel urged, and pressed a travel mug filled with hot chocolate into each of their hands. She and Conall sat down beside them, with Rachel positioned between Conall's legs so she could lean back against his chest. Lori envied their easy relationship and how comfortable they seemed in one another's company. In contrast, she was a bundle of nerves, acutely aware of the big man who lounged beside her, watching her. Firelight illuminated his face, casting his features in light and shadow.

"Can you see okay?" he asked.

Lori nodded, even though she was barely aware of the performance. "What about you?"

"I've got the best view right here," he replied, his gaze never leaving hers.

Lori bent her head to take a sip of her drink and hide the pleasure that warmed her cheeks. The hot cocoa was unexpectedly sweet and sharp with Irish liqueur.

"Oh," she murmured. "Delicious."

She was unprepared when Flynn leaned forward and pressed a swift kiss against her mouth. "You're right, it is," he agreed, drawing back with a roguish smile.

"Flynn," she protested shyly, glancing at Rachel and Conall. But they were watching the performers and seemed oblivious to the bonfire that was slowly igniting on the blanket next to them.

"It's Beltane, *mo chailín*," Flynn reminded her. "If a man can't kiss a beautiful girl tonight, when can he?"

Lori blushed again, but didn't object when he urged her even closer, so that she sat tucked against his shoulder. The evening was a feast for the senses, and Lori found herself beguiled by the golden flames of the bonfire, watching as the sparks leaped into the night sky. Even from a distance, she could feel the warmth of the blaze and hear the hiss and pop of the logs as they were consumed in the conflagration. The primal beat of the drums, accompanied by the chanting and whirling of the dancers, awakened something in Lori that made her feel a little untamed.

Pagan, even.

She could almost sense what the ancient Celts must have felt during this night of celebration, and why they might have slipped away from the fire for some uninhibited pleasure of their own.

"What are you thinking?" Flynn asked. He stroked the

palm of her hand with his thumb, the movement sending frissons of awareness through her.

"I think I understand the primal appeal of Beltane. I don't think I've ever felt so—so—" She broke off, half expecting him to make a crude joke, but his expression was somber.

"It's powerful, isn't it?" He turned her hand over and lifted it to his mouth, pressing his lips to the center of her palm. "It is a fertility celebration, after all, and it's meant to get the sap rising, so to speak."

His words evoked images that caused Lori's sap to rise and flow, and she almost giggled out loud at the corny analogy. As it was, all she could manage was a breathless, "Yes, well, mission accomplished."

Flynn's expression turned focused and intent. "Really?"

Lori blushed beneath his interested regard. "Please don't invite me to slip away into the dark with you. It's too cold, and my teeth are already chattering."

"Tempting as that sounds, I'm not that much of a pagan," he said, laughing softly. "Come here and let me keep you warm." He put his arm around her and urged her closer, letting her absorb his body heat. "Better?"

She nodded, because the truth was she *did* feel warm with him so close. "Yes, thanks." She forced herself to focus on the fire dancers and not the heat and strength of Flynn's body supporting hers, or the sexy way he watched her. "So what is the story of Beltane, anyway?"

"Beltane means *the fires of Bel*, referring to the Celtic sun god, Belenus. In ancient times, the day marked the beginning of summer, when the cattle would be driven to the summer pastures. Two bonfires would be lit and the herd would be driven between them in the belief that the smoke would purify the cattle and increase their fertility."

"So it's all about the cows?" she asked doubtfully.

"No, not just the cows," he murmured, sounding amused. "Beltane is also the celebration of the sacred union of the divine feminine and masculine, a surrendering to something bigger than ourselves."

Lori glanced at him in surprise. She suspected there were undiscovered layers to Flynn O'Rourke, and that he knew more and felt things more deeply than he let on. The fact that he could spontaneously quote poetry, or handle a tiny lamb with utter gentleness, told her he was so much more than his size and manner implied. The knowledge loosened something inside her and released a rush of affection for him. She inched closer. He made no comment, but his arm tightened around her. They watched the fire dancers as they twirled and writhed around the flames, until the bonfire began to subside and the night air grew too chilly to sit any longer. The moon had climbed into the night sky, illuminating them in silvery light.

"Ready to go?" Flynn murmured in her ear.

"Yes, that was amazing. I'm glad we came."

Flynn stood and extended a hand to Lori, pulling her

effortlessly to her feet. Rachel was already shaking out the blanket they had brought before folding it and pushing it into a backpack. Flynn tossed the last remnants of their hot chocolate into the grass and helped Lori fold their own blanket before shoving everything into the second backpack.

"I'll carry this," he said, and slung the pack over one shoulder before taking Lori's hand to help her over the uneven ground.

"What are we doing tomorrow?" Rachel asked as she and Conall fell into step beside them.

"I'll be at the shop," Conall said, "but I could get away for a few hours if you want to meet up."

"I'd like to see the Maypole dance," Lori said.

"Yeah, you and Rachel should definitely do that," Flynn agreed drily. "Call me when it's over."

Lori laughed and bumped her shoulder against his arm. "You don't want to join us?"

"I'm not keen on watching a bunch of little girls weave ribbons around a pole, no. I've seen it plenty of times, but you should go and enjoy it."

"We can plan to meet somewhere later, maybe grab a pint or a bite to eat," Conall suggested. "There should be some good music at the pub."

They reached the bottom of the hill and the road that led into the village and walked to where Lori had left her car, agreeing to meet the following afternoon at Mallone's Pub.

"Well, this is me," Lori said.

"Can I catch a ride back to the farm with you?" Flynn asked.

"Sure, but you're driving," Lori replied. "The narrow roads freak me out at night."

They made their farewells to Conall and Rachel, and Lori climbed into the passenger seat of the rental car, grateful when Flynn started the engine and switched on the heat, turning the vents toward her.

"Oh, wonderful," she breathed, holding her chilled fingers toward the warmth. "I know I shouldn't complain because there's still ice on the lake back home, and Ireland is warm by comparison, but I really hate being cold."

"I'll light a fire for you when we get back," Flynn said as he navigated the car onto the road.

"That sounds nice," she murmured. She couldn't look at him, because she was certain he didn't intend for there to be any double meaning in his offer, but his words conjured up all kinds of images in her head. When they finally reached the farm, Flynn took the backpack and gestured for Lori to precede him up the walkway to the cottage. Inside, she switched on some lights and took the backpack into the kitchen to unpack, while Flynn crouched near the fireplace.

"Do you want some tea?" she called to him. "Or something stronger, maybe?"

"Don't go to any trouble on my account. It's late and I've an early morning, so I won't stay."

"Oh." Deflated, Lori glanced at the clock, realizing it was

past eleven o'clock. Flynn was an early riser, but his refusal felt oddly—painfully—like a rejection. "In that case, you don't need to build a fire for me."

Flynn paused in the process of stacking peat logs on top of the newspaper knots he'd made. His brows pulled together in concern. "Are you sure? I don't mind."

"I'm sure. If you're not staying, then it doesn't matter. I'll just go to bed." She knew she sounded forlorn and pathetic, but she couldn't help herself.

Flynn rose to his feet in one fluid movement and crossed the room until he stood directly in front of her, so close that she could see the individual stubble of whiskers that shadowed his square jaw, and the remnants of a Celtic design that had been painted on his neck. She drew in a soft breath when he reached out and bracketed her face between his big hands, his expression both tender and serious.

"I can't stay, Lori. I want to, but as things stand—"

"It's fine." She tipped her chin up and smiled. "Really. I only asked to be polite."

He continued as if she hadn't spoken, his callused thumbs stroking across her cheeks like the soft rasp of a cat's tongue. "I want you more than I want my next breath. There's a part of me that would take you to bed now, and damn the consequences."

Lori's breath caught at the intensity in his voice and the heat in his silver eyes. "Well, it is Beltane," she reminded him softly, as if that was a good enough excuse for them to cast common sense aside.

"I want more than a single night. I can't be casual about this, Lori." He was quiet for a moment, searching her face. "Until you have your own life sorted, it would be a mistake for me to stay."

His words caused Lori's insides to liquefy. Flynn had never tried to hide the fact he found her attractive, but she'd almost managed to convince herself he wasn't interested in anything serious.

Almost.

Now, seeing the expression in his eyes, she didn't pretend to misunderstand. If he stayed, it would create a complication neither of them was ready for, not when she didn't know how long she would remain in Ireland. Flynn still cradled her face in his hands, so instead of trying to change his mind, she curled her fingers around his heavy wrists, wanting so much more than he was willing to give her. "Will you at least kiss me?"

"Is that what you want?" He spoke in a low voice.

Lori nodded.

"Well then, I'd hate to disappoint you."

He slid one big hand to the back of her head and urged her toward him, covering her mouth in a kiss so sweet and so thorough that Lori knew she would compare all other kisses to it for the rest of her life. When he finally stepped away, it took all her strength to remain upright, when her entire body felt boneless.

He left her standing in the middle of the cottage, adrift, knowing her mistake hadn't been in returning to Ireland, but in believing she could leave again with her heart still intact.

# Chapter Twelve

S UNLIGHT STREAMED IN through the window beside the bed, waking Lori from a troubled sleep. With a sigh, she slid out of bed and pulled on her bathrobe, and padded into the kitchen to put the kettle on for coffee. As she peered through the curtains, the farm seemed unusually quiet. Even the dogs, who could usually be spotted near the pens or the barn, were nowhere to be seen. Flynn's van was parked in its usual spot, which meant he was nearby. When the kettle whistled, she poured steaming water into the French press, and as she waited for the brew to steep, her thoughts returned to the previous night.

She'd lain awake for hours after he'd left, trying to solve the dilemma of what to do next. The only thing she was sure of was that she was falling for Flynn O'Rourke. She needed to decide if she had a viable future here in Ireland, or if returning to Chicago made more sense. If she was going to go home, she needed to go soon, before her heart was irrevocably lost. She had a feeling it might already be too late, and the thought of returning to her old job and seeing Seth every day made her feel a little queasy.

She couldn't do it.

But neither could she see herself staying in Ballylahane. What would she do for work? She'd always planned a career at Lakeside Industries, and the thought of doing something else was a little frightening. But something Flynn had said kept repeating itself in her head.

*Your father doesn't have the monopoly on retail. You could do that anywhere.*

But could she really? Supposing she did want to open a retail shop in Ireland, what would that entail? More importantly, what would she sell? Her only experience was with home goods and giftware and, to a lesser extent, items made by local artisans. Should she focus on having an online shop, or look for a brick-and-mortar storefront? So many things to consider, but the prospect of starting her own business—online or otherwise—excited her almost as much as it terrified her.

She poured coffee into a mug and wandered back into the bedroom to stand by the window, which afforded the best views of the barn, the farmhouse, and the long sweep of meadow down to the sea. The sky was a startling blue, reflected in the water below, and the lush green hills were dotted with sheep. Stone walls and brilliant yellow gorse shrubs edged the property and overhead, gulls swooped and glided on the air currents. She understood why Flynn loved this place so much. Chicago, with its gleaming skyline, bitter winters, and unrelenting urban sprawl, would be foreign to

Flynn. She couldn't imagine him there. There was no place better suited to Flynn than Ireland. Even if he agreed to come to Chicago with her, the city would slowly but surely crush him.

Lori groaned and put her forehead against the cool glass window. If someone had told her just three days ago that she would find herself seriously considering a life in Ireland, she would have laughed hysterically. Now, however, the prospect didn't seem so ridiculous. A movement by the barn caught her attention, and she glimpsed Flynn's tall shape opening the barn doors. She hastily set her coffee down, shedding her pajamas as she hurried into the adjoining bathroom. She showered and dressed quickly and made her way to the barn. Flynn would already have fed the lambs, but she hoped he might still be finishing up other chores. She needed to see him and reassure herself that what she was contemplating wasn't completely nuts.

The barn doors were open and the lights were on, and she was gratified to see his towering silhouette at the far end of the barn, using a pitchfork to drag fresh hay down from the haymow. The lambs were going crazy in their pens, bleating and clambering against the rails as if they hadn't yet been fed. Flynn wore an oiled canvas work coat and a knit hat that she didn't recognize, but there was no mistaking those wide shoulders.

"There you are," Lori said. "I hope you meant what you said last night, because I have something to tell you."

He turned, pitchfork in hand, and Lori took an involuntary step back. While the family resemblance was undeniable, the man staring at her was most definitely not Flynn.

"Who are you?" he demanded, his black eyebrows drawing together in a fierce scowl.

"Er, I'm Lori Woods," she stammered. "I'm renting the cottage. I'm sorry—I thought you were Flynn."

"Well, I'm not." His tone was flat. "I'm his brother, Shane."

"Oh." She tried to recall what she knew of the oldest O'Rourke brother. His weatherproof coat and his hat now made sense to her. "The fisherman."

"Mussel farmer." His expression didn't change.

"Right."

"What do you want Flynn for?"

*Everything.*

"I've been helping him bottle-feed the lambs, but I overslept this morning, so I just came down to see if I was too late, and obviously, I am, since he's not here." She was rambling, and she couldn't prevent the wash of heat that crawled up her cheeks as he continued to stare at her. "I'll just go now." She started to turn away when he spoke.

"Do you know how to mix the formula?"

She turned back toward him, cautious. "Yes."

"Good, then I'll leave you to it." He tossed the pitchfork away and stomped past her, heading for the doors.

"Do you mean the lambs haven't been fed yet?" she

asked in bewilderment.

"That's exactly what I mean." He paused in front of her, hands on his hips, his expression impatient. "If you can't do it, say so now; otherwise, I have more important things to do."

"No, it's fine." Lori swallowed hard, telling herself she was not intimidated by this big, scowling man. "I can absolutely feed the lambs and clean the pens."

"Good." He turned to go.

"Wait. Where is Flynn?"

Shane hesitated, as if debating. "He's not here," he finally said. "I doubt you'll see him at all today, so no need to hang around once you're finished. Thanks, by the way."

He was gone before Lori could think of a suitable rejoinder, which was so unlike her that she wondered if she might be coming down with something. She walked to the open doors and watched as Shane strode toward the farmhouse. But instead of going inside, he climbed into the work van and drove toward the main road without so much as a nod of acknowledgment as he passed the barn.

Frowning, Lori looked at the farmhouse. The lights were on and she wondered if Maureen was serving breakfast to Flynn and Declan and then discarded the thought. Flynn would never eat before he'd fed the animals. So what had prevented him from doing that? Her vivid imagination immediately conjured up all kinds of scenarios in which he'd been injured in a farm equipment accident and rushed to the hospital. But looking around the barn, nothing seemed out of place, and she knew Flynn well enough to know he was both capable and careful. Not for the first time, she wished she had his phone number so she could call him. After last night, she needed to hear his voice.

After spending a few minutes cuddling Woolly Wonka, she busied herself preparing warm bottles of formula for the lambs and feeding them two at a time, as Flynn had shown her. When all the lambs had been fed, she cleaned and swept the pens and put down fresh straw and hay, and then washed all the bottles and pots. She welcomed the distraction from her troubled thoughts, but once she had finished the chores, anxiety took over again.

Why had Shane told her she wouldn't see Flynn that day? He'd agreed to meet her and Rachel in town that afternoon, and she didn't believe he would go back on his word, at least not without good reason. Had his father taken a turn for the worse? Recalling Shane's grim expression, she decided that must be it. Either the older man's condition had deteriorated, or—even worse—maybe he'd passed during the night. That would explain Flynn's absence and his brother's attitude. The depressing explanation didn't make Lori feel any better. The thought of what he must be going through— what his family must be going through—made her heart ache for him.

With nothing left to do in the barn, Lori hefted the half-empty bag of powdered formula and carried it into the small anteroom where Flynn stored medicines and supplies, placing it alongside the other containers of formula and feed. There was a worktable and chair in the room, and as she turned to leave, her gaze fell on a logbook on the table. Curious, she flipped it open. It was a farm management logbook, and turning the pages, she could see carefully detailed livestock records, equipment cleanout and maintenance logs, and notes about the farm. There was also an account ledger, detailing income and expenses for the farm for the last several years, carefully penned in a neat hand. In an open file box beside the ledger was a stack of bills, everything from animal feed and medicine to veterinary bills and government payments.

Without thinking, she sat down at the desk and turned the pages, absorbing the information. Lori was no stranger to financial record keeping, having spent time in her father's accounting department and managing the retail shop at Lakeside Industries, and she could see Flynn hadn't exaggerated when he'd said the farm might not survive. They were barely breaking even. One bad year or an unexpected financial burden could mean disaster. Flynn was right— something needed to change if the O'Rourke family wanted to hold on to the farm for future generations.

Closing the book, she returned to the cottage to change her clothes, consumed with thoughts of what she now knew. There was a part of her that was selfish enough to hope the farm might go under, because maybe then Flynn might not feel obligated to stay. Almost immediately, however, she pushed those ungenerous thoughts out of her head. With or without the farm, Flynn would never leave Ireland. The problem was, she didn't trust her own feelings enough to stay.

She took care with her appearance, choosing a colorful coral-print dress with a swirly skirt, and layered it with a chunky cream sweater and a pair of suede booties, just in case Shane was wrong and she did see Flynn that afternoon. Pushing aside her growing misgivings, she drove into town and pulled the car to a stop in front of O'Leary's B&B. It was just past ten o'clock and her stomach rumbled, reminding her that she hadn't had breakfast. When Rachel opened the door, Lori gave her a bright smile.

"Good morning. I thought maybe we could grab a bite to eat at The Yarn Spinner's Café."

Rachel gave her a mildly accusing look. "Too busy with your new boyfriend to eat?"

Lori linked her arm through Rachel's as they walked into the village. "Don't be like that. Besides, he's not my boyfriend."

"You could have fooled me," Rachel said, but her tone was mild. "The two of you were cozy enough last night on the blanket."

"But it was *Beltane*," Lori said, as if that one word explained everything. "Besides, Flynn is a big boy. He knows where he stands with me."

"Does he?" Rachel sounded unconvinced.

"Of course. Flynn and I are both adults, Rachel. Don't make a fuss."

"I'm not making a fuss. I'm just worried someone is going to end up with their heart broken."

"Yes, well, that will probably be me," Lori said brightly.

"Why? Did something happen?"

"I'm not sure. When I woke up, I went down to the barn, thinking Flynn might be there. I ran into his brother Shane instead, who told me I wouldn't see Flynn at all today. He wouldn't say why."

"So something *did* happen. Flynn wouldn't break his plans with us unless something urgent had come up."

"Yes," Lori agreed. "I had breakfast at his house the other morning, and apparently, his father has leukemia and isn't doing well. Shane took off pretty quickly after I agreed to feed the lambs this morning, so I have to think something happened. Either their father took a turn for the worse, or . . . worse."

A frown knitted Rachel's brow. "Poor Flynn. I had no idea his father was ill. Conall never said anything. Wouldn't Flynn have told him? They're best friends."

"I got the sense they don't want people to know."

"Hopefully it's nothing serious." She gave Lori's arm a squeeze. "Try not to worry. Whatever it is, I'm sure it has nothing to do with anything you've done. He'd definitely want to see you if he could."

Lori nodded as they resumed walking. She wanted to confess to Rachel about her deepening feelings toward Flynn, but suspected her cousin would disapprove. How would she react if she knew Lori was reconsidering her return to Chicago?

Rachel glanced at her. "What are you thinking?"

"That I might stay?"

"What do you mean, *stay*?" Rachel sounded genuinely perplexed. "For how long?"

"I'm considering not going back to Chicago." Seeing Rachel's shock, she raised her hands. "I haven't made any final decisions. But I'm working on a plan."

"Care to share?"

"I haven't thought it all the way through yet." How to explain to Rachel, whose life had always been on a straight trajectory toward success, how unmoored she felt now that her own life plan had been torpedoed? Despite her college degree and her credentials, she had no idea what she would do for the rest of her life. She only knew that being in Ireland made her feel happy in a way she'd never felt in Chicago. There was something special about the country and the people that seemed to call to her, and she could feel her soul answering.

"Well, let me know if I can help," Rachel offered. "You know I'd like nothing better than for you to stay." She paused. "I'm sure Flynn wants that too."

Lori hoped she was right.

AFTER BREAKFAST, THEY walked to the village green, which was crowded with tourists and families who had gathered to watch the Maypole dance. A series of small grandstands had been erected on the green, and Lori and Rachel found a place to sit and watch. In the center of the green stood a tall, white pole bedecked at the top with a garland of flowers. A dozen brightly colored ribbons dangled from the top, long enough to pool on the grass. A string quartet sat nearby, playing lively Irish music.

"Oh, how sweet. Look at the little girls in fairy costumes!" Lori exclaimed, pointing to a group of toddlers wearing tulle skirts and fairy wings, who danced in uninhibited joy near the musicians beneath the watchful eyes of their mothers.

"Conall told me this is called the Fairy Festival by the locals," Rachel said, smiling. "Look there."

A line of young girls, no more than twelve or thirteen years old, began to skip their way onto the green, dancing to the lively music. They each wore a long, tulle ballet skirt and leotard in varying shades of pastel, and a pair of fairy wings. Barefoot, with garlands of flowers in their hair, they did look like delicate fairies. As Lori watched, they circled the pole, and then each skipped forward to pick up a ribbon. What followed was an intricate dance where they circled the pole and stepped between each other, alternately ducking beneath or skipping over each other's ribbons in a graceful ballet that was beautiful to watch. As the girls danced, the ribbons slowly wove a colorful pattern down the length of the pole until, finally, when the ribbons became too short to maneuver, the girls dropped the remaining lengths on the grass and bowed toward the crowd, to a burst of applause.

"That was wonderful!" Rachel exclaimed, clapping her hands. "I can't believe the guys missed it."

"Based on Flynn's reaction, I think they've both seen their share of Fairy Festivals," Lori said, laughing. "From their perspective, I can understand why they were willing to give it a pass."

"But look at all the men who are here," Rachel protested, indicating the nearby families.

"I think it's different when you're a dad and you have little girls of your own," Lori said, amused. They watched as the children swarmed around the dancers, admiring their fairy wings and talking over each other in their excitement.

"I suppose so," Rachel agreed. "It's hard for me to believe that if I stay here in Ballylahane, that could be my daughter participating in the Fairy Festival one day."

"*If* you stay here?" Lori asked in surprise. "I don't think there's any doubt about you staying. In fact, it's revolting how in love the two of you are."

Instead of looking affronted, Rachel only laughed and gave Lori a one-armed hug. "Says the woman who is thinking about staying here because of a man."

"I never said it was because of a man."

"Well, maybe not in so many words," Rachel said, smiling. "But I know you too well."

Lori was quiet, thinking of how Shane had rushed off the farm that morning, telling her she would likely not see Flynn that day. Something had happened, and not for the first time, she wished she had agreed to let Flynn give her his phone number. He'd wanted to during her last visit to Ballylahane, but she hadn't seen the point in maintaining a long-distance relationship, and had all but told him not to call her. She'd been an idiot, but she was determined not to make the same mistake again.

"C'mon," she said, standing up. "Let's go check out the vendor booths."

"You've already visited every vendor here. Twice. Do you really think you've missed anything?"

"No, but I have an idea that I'd like to explore." They stopped by a booth where Lori couldn't resist a collection of fragrant soaps scented with rose, lemon verbena, lavender, and lilac. She spoke to the young woman behind the table. "Do you make these yourself?"

"I do, yes. They're made from sheep's milk, which makes the soap very creamy and good for your skin. Each bar also contains olive oil, coconut oil, and shea butter." The woman held out a small bottle of hand lotion. "I also make this, which smells lovely."

Lori took an obedient sniff. "Mm, lavender. That is lovely." After chatting with the woman for several moments, she purchased an assortment of soaps, lotions, and lip balms, and took the woman's business card. "Thank you. I may reach out to you for more."

"I look forward to it." The woman beamed.

"I think I know what you're up to," Rachel said as they made their way to a table selling honey, homemade mead, and beeswax products. "You're going to start an export business."

"Close!" Lori said. "I've had an idea simmering on the back burner for a few days now. Do you remember the crafts village we visited near Galway during my last visit?"

"You mean Spiddal Craft Village? Of course, how could I forget?" Rachel asked. "That's when I found out my father had once been in love with Conall's aunt."

Rachel's late father, Roger Woods, had spent a college summer working at the McDermott weaving mill in Ballyla-hane, which had prompted Rachel to follow in his footsteps and do an internship at the mill. While researching the designs her father had created, Rachel had discovered a luxurious tweed pattern called "Eileen." No one seemed to know the identity of the mysterious Eileen, until Conall had brought them to the Spidall Craft Village, where his Aunt Isla ran a jewelry studio. During the visit, Isla had seen the gold Celtic knot that Rachel wore on a chain around her neck, and had immediately known she was Roger Woods's daughter. Although everyone called her Isla, her real name was Eileen, and she had met and fallen in love with Roger during the summer he'd spent in Ballylahane. He'd designed a tweed pattern and named it after her. In turn, she had cast a Celtic love knot out of solid gold, which he had worn on a chain around his neck for the remainder of his life. They'd never married, because at the end of the summer he'd returned to Chicago, while Isla remained in Ireland.

"She only sells her jewelry out of her Spiddal shop, right?" Lori asked.

"I believe so."

"What if I could showcase her work internationally?"

Rachel gave her a doubtful look. "You want to sell jewelry?"

"Among other things. How nice would it be to have a one-stop shop that showcases Irish artisans and provides them an opportunity to promote their products?" She gestured to the nearby vendors. "I've talked with nearly every crafter here, and it seems they depend primarily on festivals to sell their goods. But what if they had a way to display their products every day to customers around the world?"

"You're talking about an online shop. And you would organize this?"

"Why not? I could travel around Ireland to source new products, and maybe even expand and include products from other countries." She smiled, warming to her idea. "I'd actually love to do something like that. There's no reason why I couldn't have both a storefront and an online site."

"If you had a shop, would you want to be in Ballyla-hane?"

"Not necessarily, but somewhere nearby would be per-fect."

"Conall might have some ideas," Rachel mused, admir-ing a beeswax candle in the shape of a songbird. "He's lived here his entire life, and he's very involved with the local small business association. He might know if a shop front becomes available for rent." Rachel shook her head in bemusement and placed the candle down. "It's a little surreal to have this conversation with you. I was so sure you'd go back to Chicago."

"Well, nothing's set in stone. Everything depends on how much red tape is involved. I don't even know if I'd be allowed to open a business over here, since I don't have a visa and I'm not a resident." She pulled a face. "Am I crazy? Is it a stupid idea?"

"What? No!" Rachel exclaimed, looking genuinely sur-prised. "It's a great idea and honestly, I haven't seen you this excited about something in years. If anyone can make this work, it's you. You're smart and business-savvy, and you have a way with people. Besides, I've seen what you can do with a website."

"Thanks," Lori said, grateful for her cousin's positive re-sponse.

"Sometimes, you just need to take a leap of faith." She slid Lori a sly glance. "Marrying a local guy would certainly make it a lot easier. If only you knew a gorgeous, smart, family-oriented Irishman."

"Very funny," Lori drawled and rolled her eyes, glad her cousin couldn't know how her heart quickened at the thought of marrying Flynn.

"So, jewelry, soaps and lotions, honey, and candles . . . what else?" Rachel asked, getting into the spirit of Lori's idea.

"I'd like to stop by the woolen table and maybe speak with the woman who made the tea set I purchased the other day. Her pottery is gorgeous. There're also the two sisters who make those pretty greeting cards, the ones with the local landscapes."

"Those are nice," Rachel agreed. "I bought several to send home."

They spent the next several hours talking to the vendors and collecting business cards, and selecting various items for purchase until they finally had to acknowledge they couldn't carry anything more.

"So what are you going to do with all of this?" Rachel asked as they made their way back to the car. "You don't even have a storefront yet."

"I thought I'd bring everything back to the cottage and take a closer look at the items," Lori replied. "I want to visit each of the vendors' websites, if they have one, and make a list of the products I'd like to sell in the shop. I'll stage the items and take some photos to include as part of my business plan." She hefted a small bag of gourmet cheeses and spreads she had purchased. "But I could use some help eating this, if you're interested."

Rachel laughed. "Let me call Conall and find out what's going on. If Flynn really can't meet up with us today, I'll pick up some crackers and a bottle of wine and come over. I'll also ask Seamus to keep his ears open regarding any available retail space in the area. He's pretty well connected, so I wouldn't be at all surprised if he knows of something before it becomes available to the general public."

"I'll start researching what I need to do to get started. I was going to do that for Flynn, anyway."

"What do you mean?" Rachel asked. "Is he opening a shop too?"

"No, but I'm hoping to persuade him to open the farm to tourists." Seeing Rachel's expression, she hurried on. "I know he said he's not interested, but just think of it—a guided tour of a real, working sheep farm to include a sheepdog demonstration, a chance to hand cut peat, and, depending on the time of year, either feed a lamb or try your hand at shearing. Just like you and I did when we first visited the farm last month. The money would help sustain the farm and if he also had a little gift shop on-site, it would be perfect." She gave Rachel what she hoped was a winning smile.

"And you would run the farm shop as well?"

"Maybe. What do you think?"

"I think it's a stretch. What if the O'Rourkes say no?

What if they refuse to open the farm to visitors?"

"Well, it's ultimately their choice," Lori acknowledged. "But whatever Flynn says, I think he would enjoy showing people the farm. It's a beautiful piece of property, and he has every reason to be proud. Why not take the opportunity to show it off and make money at the same time?"

But Rachel looked less than convinced. "I'm not sure Flynn is going to go for it. He barely tolerated us when we first came out to visit the farm."

"He said himself that he needs to do something different if he's to keep the farm running," Lori countered. "Why not open it to tourists?"

"Because from what I know of Flynn and what you've told me, the O'Rourkes seem like a tight-knit family who value their privacy, that's why. Besides which, there's probably all kinds of permits and red tape involved."

"Don't be a spoilsport. I'll get him to agree." Lori paused on the sidewalk. "Flynn told me the farm is barely holding on. I did some research into other sheep farms in Ireland— ones that welcome tourists—and I'm convinced the O'Rourkes could do the same and make a decent profit."

Rachel looked doubtful. "Would it be enough to really make a difference?"

"With some marketing and a good website, I think it would."

"Well, if there's one thing you know, it's how to sell." She gave Lori a meaningful look. "Now let's see if you can sell your idea to Flynn."

# Chapter Thirteen

FLYNN SAT IN the waiting lounge of the hospital in Letterkenny and tried to control his mounting anxiety. He felt impotent, angry, and useless. Declan sat in a chair across the room while his older brother, Shane, having just arrived, paced back and forth.

"What's taking so long?" Shane growled, pausing by Flynn's chair. "Shouldn't the doctor have come out to speak to us by now?"

"They'll be running tests and getting him stabilized," Flynn said. "It could be a while yet."

"Tell me again what happened."

Flynn scrubbed both hands over his face in grim recollection. "Dad had a nosebleed that wouldn't stop. He tried to get himself to the bathroom and collapsed. Mam couldn't get him up."

Shane narrowed his gaze. "And where were you, exactly?"

Flynn looked away. "I'd just dropped Lori off at the cottage after the festival, and I was in the barn doing the midnight feeding. Mam woke Declan up and then came out to get me to help bring him to hospital."

Shane grunted. "Speaking of which, I met the tenant from the cottage this morning."

"You met Lori?"

"She came into the barn looking for you," Shane explained, his gaze speculative. "She said she knew how to feed the lambs, so I left her to it." He paused. "Was I wrong? I was in a hurry to get to the hospital after I got your call."

"No, no," Flynn assured him. "She knows what to do. The wee lambs will be fine. One of us will need to go back for their next feeding, though. Lori wouldn't mind doing it, but I don't want to ask her to."

"So is she a tenant, or have you hired her as a farmhand?"

Across the room, Declan gave a snort of laughter, and Flynn shot him a quelling look. "She's a *friend*."

"Yeah, right," Declan retorted. "Don't think Mam didn't notice your bed hadn't been slept in yet."

Flynn ignored him and looked at Shane. "What did you tell Lori?"

"Only that you weren't around and that she likely wouldn't see you today."

Flynn scowled. "You don't know that. Once they get Dad sorted, I'm headed home."

"Mam said you're going to donate bone marrow," Shane said.

"I offered," Flynn acknowledged. "I'm not a perfect match, but I'm close enough to give him a fighting chance. But even if the doctors agree, it would mean a week or more of injections to boost my stem cells. Mam and I were going to arrange it tomorrow, but even if the docs agree to take me, the soonest they could perform the procedure would be next week."

"I think we can do better than that."

They turned at the sound of the new voice. A man stood in the doorway of the waiting room. In his early fifties, his resemblance to John O'Rourke was striking. But where Flynn's father looked old and frail, this man glowed with good health.

"Uncle David!" Declan exclaimed, shooting to his feet.

"What are you doing here?" Flynn asked, astonished. He hadn't seen his uncle in almost ten years, but he would have recognized him anywhere.

"I caught a flight from California yesterday and landed this morning," he said, hugging each of them in turn. "What are they feeding you lads on that farm? You're like a cluster of giant redwoods!"

He was one to talk, Flynn thought, as they were very nearly the same size. "But you couldn't have known Dad would end up in hospital today," Flynn reasoned. "So what made you come over here now?"

They sat down, pulling their chairs close. "When I heard none of my other brothers were a potential match for donor cells, I didn't hold out much hope that I might be any different," David said. "But I registered with the global transplant network and a representative reached out to me two weeks ago." He gave a rueful smile. "Against all odds, I'm a nearly perfect match. I just hope I'm not too late."

For a moment, Flynn couldn't breathe. "You're a match? But that's fantastic!"

"It is, yeah."

"Does Mam know?" Shane asked.

David nodded. "I just spoke with her. I didn't call sooner because I didn't want to raise her hopes until I was sure I could get here in time."

"But why didn't you come earlier?" Shane asked. "Even if you're a match, it might be too late, especially if what Flynn says is true, and you'll need to get booster injections. Dad is so weak, I don't know how much longer he can hold on."

Shane's voice broke, and he cleared his throat and looked away. Reaching out, Flynn put a hand on his shoulder. Of the three brothers, Shane was the most stoic, seeming determined to keep people at arm's length. This crack in his otherwise stern façade was both unexpected and heartening, giving Flynn some hope that he might not be as unfeeling as he liked to pretend.

"I did the injections in California," David said. "The doctors said they can do the blood draw immediately, so I flew over to start the process."

Flynn dropped his head into his hands, feeling equal measures of relief and impotent anger. Why hadn't David let them know he was a match two weeks ago? He might have spared them all unnecessary anguish. But he also understood his uncle's reasoning—he didn't want to get their hopes up in case something went wrong. But he was here now, and Flynn's relief was so great, he actually felt weak. "Thank God."

He needed to call Lori, to let her know what happened, and to thank her for taking care of the lambs. He didn't have her mobile phone number, but the cottage had a landline. With luck, she would still be there.

"Excuse me," he said, standing. "I need to make a call. Does the hospital know you're here?"

"Yeah, I spoke with the doctor and your mam as soon as I arrived. I'm just waiting for them to prepare a room," David said.

They turned as a doctor appeared in the doorway. "Mr. O'Rourke," he said, looking at David. "We're ready for you now."

"When will my father actually receive the donor cells?" Shane asked.

"Unfortunately, he's not strong enough to withstand the conditioning treatment required, so we're going to do a reduced-intensity stem cell transplantation."

"What does that mean?" Flynn asked.

"It means we won't be subjecting him to high doses of chemotherapy and radiation prior to the transplantation. I'm optimistic that the lesser doses he's received in the past few months will be sufficient, and that the disease will respond to the transplant." The doctor indicated David should precede him from the room and then turned back to Shane and Flynn, lowering his voice. "I've spoken with your mother, but I'll tell you lads what I told her—stem cell transplantation is a very expensive procedure, but we do have staff members who can help answer questions concerning health insurance and financial assistance. If you'd like, you can speak to someone in the billing department, just down the hall."

"Thanks," Shane murmured.

After the doctor and David left, Shane rubbed a hand across his eyes. "I know we don't have any other choice, but this could mean the end of the farm."

"Would you rather we just give up?" Flynn stared at his brother in dismay. "This is our Hail Mary, you know that. We can figure the rest out later, once Dad is better."

The bleakness in his brother's expression was disheartening; he wouldn't deny it. Of course they would do whatever it took to save their father, and David's arrival felt like an unexpected miracle, but he wouldn't fool himself into believing everything would be okay.

They could still lose everything.

"WE MISSED YOU at the May Day festival yesterday."

Flynn turned at the sound of Lori's voice, surprised to

see her. She leaned against the open door of the barn, looking pretty in a cable-knit sweater and jeans with her hair swept back from her face by a wide cloth headband. He was happy to see her. She hadn't been at the cottage when he'd returned home from the hospital the previous day, but her light had been on when he'd gone out to feed the lambs that evening. He'd almost knocked on her door, but then he'd heard Rachel's laughter from inside the cottage and realized Lori wasn't alone. He'd been disappointed, but given his morose mood, he wouldn't have been great company. In the end, he'd gone down to the barn and taken care of some things before heading to bed. The result was that he'd woken earlier than usual. Having already fed the lambs and mucked out the enclosures, he was in the process of laying down fresh straw. Now he set the pitchfork aside and watched as Lori pushed away from the wall and walked toward him. He shoved his hands into the front pockets of his jeans to prevent himself from reaching for her.

"You're up early," he said.

She stopped directly in front of him and studied him for a moment, her expression soft with concern. "Are you okay?"

Her quiet compassion nearly undid him. Turning away, he reached for the pitchfork and resumed the task of spreading straw. "Yeah, of course. Sorry I couldn't meet up with you yesterday. We had a family emergency. I tried to call you at the cottage about midmorning, but you must have already left for town."

"Is it your dad?"

Flynn gave a curt nod. "He took a turn for the worse, but it's not all bad news."

Reaching out, she took hold of the pitchfork, preventing him from continuing with his chores. "Tell me."

Flynn allowed Lori to take the instrument and set it aside. "He needs a stem cell transplant, but we couldn't find a good match for him. I'd planned to be a donor, but it would be two weeks or more before they could actually harvest the cells, while my dad grows weaker every day."

"But you said there's good news," she prompted.

"My uncle, who lives in California, showed up unexpectedly yesterday. It seems he's a near-perfect donor match. He went through the required prepping procedures at a hospital in Los Angeles, so they're actually performing the transplant today." He blew out a hard breath. "We're hoping it works."

"That's wonderful," Lori enthused, smiling. "How soon will you know?"

"If things go well, he should begin responding fairly quickly, within a few weeks. It will mean keeping him in isolation, since he's susceptible to infections, but the doctors are optimistic."

"And yet, you don't seem happy. Are you sure everything is okay?"

Flynn shrugged, unwilling to reveal to her how precarious their financial situation had become. While his uncle David had provided the miracle they'd all prayed for, he wondered if the farm would survive the cost. But the last thing he wanted was Lori's pity, so he forced himself to smile. "Yeah, of course. Everything is grand."

"What can I do to help? You can assign chores to me if that would make it easier for you to be with your dad at the hospital. I'd actually welcome something to do."

"Does that mean you're going to stay on at the cottage?" Flynn looked sharply at her. "The Beltane festival has ended. You could easily get a room in town."

She was quiet for a moment, considering. "Is that what you want? For me to leave the farm?"

"Since when has it mattered what I want? You'll do as you please anyway."

She studied him, and for a panicked moment, Flynn was sure she saw through his feigned indifference to how desperately he wanted her to stay.

"Fine. I'll stay, but only because I'd miss my sweet little Woolly Wonka too much if I left." Her voice took on a silly, baby-talk pitch as she leaned over the enclosure to greet her favorite lamb, rubbing him fondly beneath his chin. "Wouldn't I? Wouldn't I miss you so much? Who's the sweetest little lamb?"

Flynn made a sound of disgust. "You won't think he's so sweet when he weighs one hundred and seventy-five pounds and only wants to eat and tup."

"Ha, that won't faze me a bit." With a final pat, Lori straightened, swiping her hand across the seat of her jeans as she turned to face him, her mouth curved in a wry smile. "I grew up with four older brothers." Suddenly, her face filled with hope. "Wait. Does that mean you're going to keep him?"

Flynn eyed the little animal, who had thrust his fleecy head through the metal rails in an effort to reach Lori. Reaching down, she rubbed between his ears, and Flynn could almost see his satisfied, sheepish smile. He told himself he definitely was not jealous of a lamb. "I haven't decided yet."

"Oh, please, please keep him. Wait, I know—I'll work for his room and board. Let me do something. Anything!" she begged. "I don't care how dirty it is."

Her words conjured up all kinds of explicit images of the things he could have her do, each dirtier than the last. His deliberately leering expression must have revealed the direction of his thoughts because hot color flooded her face before she stepped forward to punch him hard on the arm.

"Not that, you big oaf. Jeez, are all men so single-celled?"

"Yes." Flynn felt his mood lifting. "Since you offered, I did mean to bring the peat in from the field today and stack it in the peat shed. I could use an extra hand. You can drive the tractor if you'd like." He indicated the big farm rig parked just outside the barn used to haul farm equipment and move heavy loads. With a bucket loader on the front and a farm trailer hitched to the back, he knew it might look intimidating to a city girl.

Following his gaze, Lori's eyes widened. "You want me to drive *that*?"

"Why not? Think you can't manage something that size?"

She slid him a sideward look. "I can manage you, can't I?"

Flynn gave a noncommittal grunt, unwilling to admit he was clay in her hands. "Put on a pair of boots and then you can give it a lash."

"A what?"

"Give it a try," he clarified.

Once Lori had swapped out her shoes for a pair of knee-high rubber boots, they left the barn and crossed the small yard to where the tractor stood. His two dogs, curious, abandoned their post near the fence and came over to sniff at Lori's pant legs. Before she could become distracted by the animals, he lifted her easily up onto the seat, ignoring her squeal of surprise.

"Hey, no manhandling allowed!" She gripped the steering wheel and glanced around. "Whoa, this thing looks even bigger from up here. I'm not sure—"

"Relax. If you can drive a standard shift, you can manage this."

Flynn stood on the tractor's step, which brought him on eye level with Lori. She turned to look at him, close enough that he could see the striations of gold and green in her hazel eyes and feel the warm exhale of her breath. He dropped his gaze to her mouth and watched as she moistened her lips. He wanted badly to kiss her. Instead, he reached down and adjusted the seat so that she could reach the pedals and levers, explaining the purpose of each.

"Okay, I think I've got it," she said. "Where will you be?"

"I'll ride here in the cab beside you," he assured her. "Go ahead and start her up, and we'll head out to the bog."

Flynn didn't miss the quick flare of excitement in her eyes as she turned the big machine on, and she grinned broadly as the engine roared to life, making the tractor vibrate. He helped her find the right gear, and after one or two fitful starts, the tractor lurched into motion. Lori had the steering wheel in a death grip as she maneuvered the big rig onto the dirt road that led to the peat field.

"I'm doing it!" she shouted, her eyes shining. "If only my father and brothers could see me now!"

Her grin was contagious, and Flynn felt his own spirits lighten as he watched her. The dogs ran ahead of them, and the sheep that grazed on either side of the road lifted their heads as they passed, unperturbed by the noise. Below them, the saltwater inlet shimmered beneath the morning sun. A breeze carried the salt-tinged scent of the sea, and flocks of seagulls wheeled high overhead. When they finally reached the edge of the peat bog, Flynn showed Lori how to turn the tractor off before helping her down. Beside the deep, black trench where the peat was harvested stood dozens of neatly stacked peat bricks.

"We'll start with these piles first," Flynn said, indicating the closest stacks. "They'll spend the summer months drying out in the peat shed, ready for next winter." Reaching into the trailer, he withdrew an armful of large mesh bags and handed one to Lori. "Just throw the bricks into the bags, and I'll load them onto the trailer."

Lori stood for a moment, an empty sack dangling from one hand as she gazed out over the landscape, a dreamy expression on her face. Brody rolled on his back in the nearby grass, his back legs cycling furiously, while Rob sniffed a stack of peat. "It's so beautiful here," she finally said, turning toward him. "I can understand why you might never want to leave."

"It's pretty special," Flynn agreed. "If only—" He broke off, unwilling to finish the thought.

*If only I could turn a profit.*

*If only you could stay.*

*If only.*

"If only what?" Lori asked, watching him.

But Flynn shook his head. Let her make what she wanted of it. After a moment, she bent to pick up a peat brick and drop it into the sack. They worked side by side for nearly an hour, and Flynn surreptitiously watched as Lori began filling yet another bag. She had pulled her sweater off and wore a light cotton jersey underneath. Every so often, she would pause to swipe the back of her arm across her forehead. The morning was beautiful, the work wasn't difficult, and the peat was easy enough to handle, but he felt guilty allowing her to do any work at all. Dropping his own bag onto the ground, he closed the distance between them and put his hand on her wrist, stopping her.

She looked at him, expectant. "What?"

He studied her for a moment, seeing the wariness in her eyes. She expected him to stop her, to tell her he would finish bagging the peat, and in a moment of clarity, he realized that would be a mistake. "Nothing," he finally said. "I just thought you might want to take a break. I have some bottled water in the trailer if you'd like."

The breeze and exertion had whipped color into her cheeks, and her eyes were bright as she gave him a swift smile. "No, thanks, I'm fine. I'm actually enjoying the exercise. C'mon, you're falling behind. I'm beginning to think you're purposely letting me do all the work."

He still held her wrist, gently manacled in the circle of his fingers, and he couldn't help stroking the soft skin. "Maybe I should just offer you a permanent position here."

Her hazel eyes widened and her mouth opened, but no words came out.

"Relax, I'm teasing you," he said gently, before she could come back with a cutting rejoinder. While he typically enjoyed their banter, he found he wasn't in the mood for her to cut him down to size today. "As helpful as you've been, you've made your feelings perfectly clear."

"Have I?" she asked, tugging her arm free. Her voice sounded strained and more than a little indignant. "And I suppose you know all about my feelings."

He smiled thinly. "You once said we come from different worlds. You nearly had a panic attack when I suggested visiting you in Chicago. I thought you were just afraid of commitment, but the real reason you balked was because you were already committed."

"No."

"No, you weren't committed?"

"I made a mistake that day at the hotel, when you said you wanted to see me again," she said. Her tone was tight, as if it cost her to make the admission. "I should have agreed, but I was afraid my father wouldn't take me seriously if he thought I'd spent my time here fooling around with a local. I was here to do a job, not—"

She stopped abruptly, as if she'd said too much.

"Not—what?" Flynn asked, taken aback by how much she'd revealed. He didn't even mind that she'd diminished the time they'd spent together to something as trite and inconsequential as "fooling around." All he heard was her acknowledgment that she'd made a mistake in not staying in touch. All these weeks, he'd been sure her reasons for pushing him away had been because she thought he wasn't good enough for her. Now he wondered if he'd been wrong. "What were you going to say?"

"Nothing," she mumbled. Her face had reddened, and

she refused to meet his eyes.

"C'mon, don't chicken out. I want to hear what you were going to say."

"Can we not talk about this, please?" she begged, turning away. "Let's just finish collecting the peat so you can get over to the hospital and see your dad."

But Flynn refused to be deterred. Catching her hand, he pulled her back toward him. She came up against his chest with a small gasp, one hand pressed in a fist against his chest, as if she could physically hold him at bay. As if. "Shall I tell you what you're so reluctant to say out loud?"

"Fine." Her tone was filled with dramatic exasperation, but Flynn didn't miss the quick flare of alarm in her expression before she quickly hid it. "I can't wait to hear this."

He drew her nearer, sliding one hand to her back as he let his gaze drift over her face. "I think you were about to say you were here to do a job, not fall for an irresistible, devastatingly handsome, brilliantly smart Irishman."

"Ha." She tipped her chin up. "And just where is this paragon? All I see is an annoying sheep farmer who's too full of himself for his own good."

"Then you're not looking close enough."

Her eyes widened slightly and her lips parted, and that was all the invitation Flynn needed. Still holding her loosely, he bent his head. He'd intended for the kiss to be light, but as he eased his lips over hers, she made a small sound and softened in his arms. He felt a surge of satisfaction when she returned the kiss, slanting her mouth across his and sliding one hand around him to clutch the back of his sweater. He stroked deeper, seeking out the secret corners of her mouth as he gathered her even closer. His entire body tightened in response to the hot silk of her tongue, his blood pumping in hard rushes through his veins.

When he slid his lips to the side of her jaw and traced a tender, biting path along the column of her neck, she shivered and arched against him, her breath coming in warm pants against his ear. He sucked at the small, throbbing pulse near the base of her throat, and she gasped his name and pushed her hands beneath the edge of his sweater. The coolness of her fingers against his heated skin brought him back to his senses, reminding him of where they were. Reluctantly, he disentangled himself from her and put some distance between them. Lori's eyes were slightly unfocused, her color high as she stared at him.

"Was that supposed to convince me?" she asked, crossing her arms under her breasts. She sounded breathless and a little sulky, as if maybe she hadn't wanted him to stop.

"If it didn't, I can try again."

She made a small scoffing sound. "There's more to a relationship than kissing, Flynn."

God, he hoped so, because he wanted to do so much more than just kiss the sharp-tongued woman standing before him. "Are we in a relationship?" he asked instead. "Because if we are, you should probably let your eejit fiancé know."

"He's not my fiancé. I told you I refused him."

"And yet, he's getting the ring resized and plans to propose to you again."

"It's not my fault if he won't take no for an answer. Do we really need to talk about this right now?" she demanded. "Let's just finish bagging the peat, so you can go see your father."

Without waiting for his reply, she grabbed a bag from the ground and determinedly began filling it with peat bricks. Flynn watched her for a moment, wanting to press her about her feelings—for him and the poor bloke back in Chicago—but part of him didn't want to hear what she might say.

Blowing out a frustrated breath, he snatched up his own bag and began filling it with the cut turf. He told himself there was still time. She could still change her mind about returning to Chicago. But in his heart, he wondered if she hadn't already made her decision.

# Chapter Fourteen

WHEN THEY RAN out of bags to fill, Lori opted to walk back to the cottage alone. They'd worked in silence, separately, as if they weren't each acutely aware of the other. Flynn's entire demeanor had turned so cool and remote that it was with a sense of relief she filled her last bag and declared she was returning to the farm. Flynn remained on the bog with the tractor, claiming he needed to cut more turf, but Lori knew the real reason was because he was annoyed with her. He made no objection when both dogs chose to return with her, running ahead along the dirt road that led back to the barn.

She still reeled from the kiss and the verbal exchange that had followed. She wanted to smack her head against something, anything, to knock some sense back into it. She had fallen so easily—so *willingly*—into his arms.

Again.

She'd been about three seconds away from dragging him down to the soft, spongy grass and giving him whatever he'd wanted right there on that windswept hillside. Thank goodness he'd had enough sense to end the kiss and put some space between them, because she'd been incapable of doing so. It seemed whenever she was with him, all she wanted to do was kiss him. Now, as she approached the barn, Flynn's younger brother, Declan, stood in the outdoor enclosure, examining a small flock of sheep.

"Hey," he greeted her, looking up as she approached. "Gone for a walk, have you?"

"Yes." Lori folded her arms across the top rail of the fence and watched him, unwilling to admit she had been on the bog with Flynn, kissing him as if her life depended on it. "What are you doing?"

He straightened and indicated a jug of dark liquid and a large plastic syringe hanging on the fence. "That's a deworming medication. I'm checking for worms and trimming hooves."

"Do you check every ewe?"

"I do, yeah." She watched as he pulled the lower eyelid of one sheep downward, exposing the pink skin inside. "See how her eye is more red than white on the inner eyelid? That's a good indication she's worm-free, so I'm not going to give her any medicine." Lifting one of the sheep's back feet, he examined her hoof before pulling a small clipper out of his back pocket. "She could use a trim, though. This helps prevent a pocket from forming where dirt and dung can collect."

Lori watched Declan for several minutes, appreciating how deftly he handled the animals. The sound of an approaching vehicle caused her to straighten and turn around. A large multipassenger van slowly lumbered toward them along the gravel road.

"Who is that?" she wondered aloud.

"No idea," Declan said as he opened the gate and stepped out of the pen.

The van came to a stop near the barn and a man climbed out of the driver's side. "Good morning," he called, smiling. "I hope we're not trespassing, but we were driving by your farm and wondered if we might take a closer look at your sheep?"

Declan frowned. "I beg your pardon?"

The panel door on the van slid open and a seemingly endless stream of young children tumbled out, their faces alight with excitement. Lori glanced in alarm at Declan, whose expression was a comical mixture of surprise and confusion.

"I'm Mike Hurley," the man said, walking toward them with his hand extended. "We're from America, upstate New York. Been here for five days and the kids have had their fill of cities and museums, so we decided to head into the country."

Swiping his hands on the seat of his jeans, Declan shook the older man's hand. "Declan O'Rourke," he mumbled.

"Good to meet you. This is my wife, Deanna, and my brother and sister-in-law, Frank and Ellen." Two women and another man had exited the van, looking slightly embarrassed but hopeful.

"Nice to meet you," Declan replied, still looking bemused. "How can I help you, exactly?"

The kids—Lori counted seven of them—had made a beeline for the sheep enclosure and now they hung on the fence exclaiming over the animals, while Rob and Brody circled around them, tails wagging cautiously.

"We were hoping the children might be able to see your sheep," Deanna explained, stepping forward. "I hope it's not an imposition. They got so excited when they saw the baby lambs in the field."

One glance at Declan told Lori he was about to send the family packing. Before he could speak, she stepped forward. "We'd love to show you the farm," she said, smiling brightly. "Wouldn't we, Declan?"

She almost felt bad for him. He looked so uncertain. "Uh, we don't usually give tours."

"We could pay you, of course," Mike said.

Declan glanced at the children, who watched the exchange with eager expressions, and finally blew out a hard breath. "Yeah, sure. Fine."

"Would you be interested in a sheepdog demonstration?" Lori asked. "Brody and Rob are the smartest dogs in Ballylahane, and Declan would love to demonstrate how they work." She gave Declan an encouraging look. "After that, if you're interested, maybe the kids would like to bottle-feed a lamb?"

This suggestion was met with a chorus of excited cries from the children and grateful smiles from the parents.

"Thank you so much," Deanna said, coming forward. "You don't know how much we appreciate this. We couldn't come all the way to Ireland without visiting a sheep farm, but most of the farms require advance reservations. We didn't realize, and we waited too late."

"It's no problem," Lori assured her, hoping Flynn didn't decide to return before the family had left. She couldn't imagine he would approve.

"But you're American too?" Deanna asked.

"I am," Lori said without elaborating that she was as much a visitor to the farm as they were. Declan had gathered the children around the enclosure as he began explaining life on a sheep farm. "Why don't you join your family, and I'll prepare some warm bottles of milk for the lambs?"

She ducked into the barn before anyone could engage her in further conversation, quickly mixing warm formula and pouring it into bottles, ensuring one for each of the children. When she came out of the barn, the sheep were no longer in the enclosure. Declan stood on the crest of the hill, issuing commands to Rob and Brody as they expertly guided the flock across the fields. The children seemed enthralled as Declan explained what the dogs were doing, and how they would bring the sheep back into the nearby pen. The family clapped when the demonstration was over and spent several minutes gushing over the dogs, who accepted the attention as their due.

Inside the barn, the children swarmed the lambs, picking them up and giggling as the animals tried to squirm away. Lori showed them how to hold the bottles and then handed one to each of the children, laughing as the lambs pushed against them in their eagerness. Their delight was contagious. Declan even agreed to take photos of the family with their smartphones.

"If you come outside, we can take some pictures with the water in the background," he suggested once the bottles were empty.

As the visitors obediently followed Declan out of the barn, Lori collected the empty bottles and placed them in the sink before turning on the hot water. Mike Hurley hung back from the rest of the group and came to stand beside her.

"That was fantastic," he said. "Really. Thank you."

"I'm glad you enjoyed it," Lori said with a smile. She pushed her sleeves up and began washing the bottles.

Reaching into his pocket, he withdrew a wad of euros and extended it toward her. "Frank and I think this is a fair amount, but I'll let you decide."

Startled, Lori dried her sudsy hands on a towel and took the money before realizing how much was there. "Oh, this is too much," she protested, extending the money back toward him. "I can't accept this."

"Sure you can," he said. "You just gave our kids a day they'll never forget, maybe the best day of the vacation so far.

Please, take it."

"If you're sure . . ."

"I am. Thank you."

She watched as he left the barn and then absently fingered the wad of bills. She'd thought ten euros per person was fair, but he'd given her much more. She pushed the money into the pocket of her jeans and stood in the open door of the barn to watch as Declan snapped pictures of the group. They insisted on including Rob and Brody in the photo shoot, and Lori smiled because they all looked so happy.

The sound of the tractor drew her attention away from the visitors and toward the farm road. While the vehicle had seemed enormous when she'd been sitting in the driver's seat, Flynn somehow managed to make the machine appear small. He pulled the tractor alongside an outbuilding and killed the engine, his eyes fixed on the strangers. Climbing down, he strode in their direction, and Lori hastily moved to intercept him.

"Flynn—"

"What's going on? Who are these people?"

"Visitors. From America."

His head swiveled in her direction. "Visitors?"

"Yes. Their kids wanted to see the sheep, so we gave them a tour."

He braced his hands on his hips and stared at her as if she was speaking a foreign language. "You gave them a tour."

"Yes. Well, me and Declan. But I didn't give him much choice and—" He began to walk away and she hurried beside him. "Oh, Flynn, if you could have seen their faces when they fed the lambs!"

"You fed the lambs?" He sounded incredulous. He stopped and turned to face her. "They were just fed a few hours ago. They didn't need feeding again so soon."

"They seemed hungry enough, and I only filled the bottles halfway," she said, knowing it was a poor defense.

"We. Don't. Give. Tours." He spoke with exaggerated patience, as if she were a child, but Lori ignored his deliberate condescension.

"Not true. You gave Rachel and me a tour the last time I came to Ireland."

"That was different, and you know it. You should have sent them away." He started to turn away and then spun back. "What gives you the right?"

For a moment, Lori was too surprised to respond. He hadn't raised his voice, but the expression in his eyes told her he was disappointed. Instead of backing down, she tipped her chin up and stood her ground. "I know the farm is in trouble, Flynn. I saw this as an opportunity to show you there's a way to bring in extra income."

He narrowed his eyes. "What do you mean, 'the farm is in trouble'? How would you know anything about it, unless—"

"I saw the ledgers you keep in the back room of the

barn."

His eyes widened, his expression one of astonishment. "You snooped through my private papers?"

"If they're so private, why do you keep them in the barn? Honestly, anyone could see them."

He tipped his head down, his gaze boring into hers. "They *were* kept in the cottage until I invited a wee, interfering female to move in, so I brought them into the barn instead."

He meant herself, of course. She glanced at the group, who were still absorbed in taking pictures and seemed oblivious to the small drama playing out by the tractor. "They'll be gone in a few minutes, and you can have your precious privacy back."

"Privacy," he repeated drily. "What a concept."

He began to walk away, but Lori forestalled him with a hand on his arm. He looked pointedly at her hand and then at her face.

"Be nice to them," she pleaded softly. "What happened is not their fault—it's mine, and I'm sorry. I had no business letting strangers tour the farm, and I apologize. If you want me out of the cottage and off the property, I'll understand."

"What?" He looked at her in bemusement. "No, absolutely not. My biggest concern is the liability. If one of those kids was to get hurt, we could lose the farm."

"Of course," she said, contrite. "I didn't even think about that. But I don't think that will happen. Their mothers seem very protective. Oh, I almost forgot." Reaching into her back pocket, she withdrew the folded wad of money and held it out to him. "They insisted on paying for the tour."

"No, I can't take that."

Lori reached for his hand and pressed the money into it. "Of course you can. Look at their faces. They're so happy. The father told me this might be the best day they've had so far."

"Fine, you keep it."

"If you don't want it, I'll give it to Declan. My point is, you could easily supplement your income if you open the farm to visitors. Deanna, over there, told me she tried to make a reservation at several other sheep farms, but they were all completely booked. What does that tell you?"

Flynn gave her a wry look. "Americans have low expectations for what constitutes fun?"

Lori gave him an exasperated look. "If you scheduled just three tours a day during the spring and summer months, I think you'd be surprised how well you'd do."

"I already told you—I don't have time to pander to tourists. I'm happy if other farms are doing well, but I've no interest in becoming a destination for day-trippers. But since they're here now, I intend to put them to work."

"Flynn—"

He pinioned her with a meaningful look and pushed the wad of bills back into her hand. "We'll talk later."

With his jaw set and his stride purposeful, he walked toward the group. Bracing herself for the worst, Lori followed him. But when she reached the group, Flynn was shaking Mike's hand and accepting his effusive compliments regarding the dogs, the sheep, the lambs, and even herself with an ease that would have fooled anyone into believing he welcomed visitors to the farm every day.

"So," Flynn said, looking at the children. "I've just spent the past hour collecting peat, which is what we burn in our fireplaces instead of wood. Can any of you tell me what peat is?"

Several small hands thrust into the air, and they excitedly began talking over each other. Lori exchanged a bemused look with Declan, who shrugged.

"Who wants to see a real peat bog, and—if you're very lucky—help cut some turf logs?" Flynn asked. "I need all the help I can get, and you look like a strong, healthy bunch."

The response was overwhelmingly positive, and Flynn actually looked pleased as he led the group toward the barn to be fitted for rubber boots.

"I don't have enough sizes for the wee ones," he said, sorting through the array of boots he kept in the back room. "But at least the ladies won't ruin their shoes."

"Oh, that's so thoughtful of you," Deanna said, beaming at him as if he were her own personal hero. "The kids are all wearing sneakers, so they're fine."

"It's a bit of a walk and it can be mucky," Flynn warned.

"Trust me, they won't care," Mike assured them. "Be

good to run off some of their excess energy."

As the family followed Flynn out of the barn and across the yard, Declan came to stand beside her.

"That went better than I expected," he said, staring after the retreating group.

"At least he didn't throw them off the farm." She extended the money toward him. "Here, this is for you, from Mr. Hurley. Thanks for what you did with the herding demonstration and the lambs and taking the photos."

He took the money, his eyebrows raised. "Seriously? They gave you this much?"

"Considering you dropped everything to show them around, I think it's fair. Those kids will talk about this visit for weeks, I'm sure."

Declan considered the money in his hand. "Supposing we *were* interested in opening the farm to tourists," he said cautiously. "What would that entail?"

"Getting your brother to agree," she said drily. "After that, if the rest of your family supports the idea, I'd think you'd need a business plan, permits, insurance, and a website. I'd be happy to look into it for you, if you'd like."

"No, but thanks. I can't ask you to do that while you're here on vacation."

"You're not asking," Lori replied. "I'm offering."

Declan looked bemused. "Why would you do that? What's in it for you?"

"Maybe nothing. Maybe everything."

# Chapter Fifteen

STEPPING INTO MALLONE'S Pub, Flynn took a moment to let his eyes adjust to the dark interior. He'd spent the afternoon visiting his father at the Letterkenny hospital and had received a call from Conall during the drive home, inviting Flynn to meet him at the pub for a pint.

He'd arrived early and there was no sign of Conall. But there, sitting in a corner booth with two men Flynn didn't recognize, was his brother Shane. Papers and what looked like a topographic map were spread across the table. Glancing up, Shane spotted him and quickly scooped the documents together and shoved them inside a legal-sized folder. Flynn crossed the room.

"Hey, Flynn," Shane said, standing. The two men with him rose to their feet. "I thought you were at the hospital."

"I was. What's this, then? A business meeting?"

To his surprise, two spots of ruddy color stained Shane's cheeks. "Yeah, nothing to concern you, though." He turned to the two men. "This is Patrick Donnelly and Brian Foster. This is my brother Flynn."

Flynn shook their hands. "Happy to meet you. What's

the business you're here to discuss?"

"I'll tell you about it later," Shane promised. He looked at the two men. "We're finished here, aren't we?"

"We are, yeah," Patrick said. "I think the plan is a good one, Mr. O'Rourke. A win-win for everyone. We'll send someone out to the farm in the next few days, if that works."

Shane avoided Flynn's curious gaze. "It should do. I'm heading back there now, so I'll walk with you to your car. See you later, Flynn."

"Yeah, see you later."

Shane collected the folder and tucked it under his arm before all three men made their way toward the exit, passing Conall as he walked through the door.

"Who were those lads with Shane?" Conall asked, looking over his shoulder at the retreating men.

"Dunno, but I've not got a good feeling about it. Shane is making some kind of deal and I get the sense it concerns the farm, yet this is the first I've heard of it."

They pushed the empty glasses to the edge of the table and slid into the vacated booth.

"Maybe they're buyers for the mussels," Conall offered.

"Could be, but he had what looked like a map of the farm."

"Doesn't he own part of the farm outright?"

"Yes. Dad deeded him the land that his house sits on, as well as four hundred feet of waterfront so he can run his operation separate from the farm. In return, he pays Dad a percentage of his profits each year." He sighed. "Right now, that's about all that's keeping the farm afloat."

"How's your dad doing?"

"Holding his own," Flynn replied. "Mam is staying with her sister in Letterkenny so she can be close to him until the doctors say he can come home."

"Do you know when that might be?"

Flynn shook his head. "No. He's in isolation until his blood count normalizes, but the doctors don't know when that might be."

"Is your uncle still here?"

"Yeah, he's making the rounds, visiting family. I think he'll stay until Dad's out of the woods before he heads back to the States."

"Speaking of which . . ." Conall hesitated. "How long is Lori planning to stay?"

Flynn sharpened his gaze on his friend, pushing down his sudden alarm. Had she said something to Rachel? Was she planning to leave the farm? Or Ireland? "Why do you ask? Did you hear something?"

Conall shrugged. "Rachel seems to think you two have had a falling-out."

"What? No, not exactly." Flynn frowned and shifted uncomfortably, recalling his earlier exchange with Lori. "She invited an American family to tour the farm and feed the lambs, knowing I'm not keen on hosting tourists."

"Really? That doesn't sound like something she'd do."

Flynn smothered a snort, because it was exactly the kind of thing Lori would do. "Okay, maybe she didn't invite them onto the farm, since they drove onto the property without warning and asked her if they could see the sheep, but she didn't turn them away. Instead, she asked Declan to do a demonstration with the dogs, and then let them each bottle-feed the lambs. There were *eleven* of them." He paused, recalling the chaotic morning. "It was a full-on American invasion, and she led the charge."

Conall laughed. "Sounds fun, actually."

"I'll admit I was annoyed when I first saw them, but they were a fun bunch." He didn't add that his mood had already nose-dived following his conversation with Lori about the guy in Chicago. When he'd arrived back at the farm and had seen the group of American visitors, he'd taken his irritation out on her, which hadn't been fair. "I might have been a little harsh with Lori when I saw the tourists. I blamed her, accused her of overstepping."

"I'm sure she meant well."

"She did. I'll figure out a way to make it up to her."

Conall raised his hands. "Don't need to hear the details, mate."

"Sightseeing," Flynn said, scowling. "I'll take her sightseeing. I thought I'd bring her to see the Kilclooney Dolmen stones tomorrow and maybe the cliffs."

"I'm sure she'd like that. What about the waterfall?"

Just the mention of the Assaranca waterfall brought

memories rushing back of the day he'd brought Lori to see the falls during her initial visit to Ireland. It seemed so long ago now, and yet not even two months had passed. With sudden clarity, Flynn realized that was the day he'd fallen for her, completely and irrevocably. He'd actually believed she might feel the same way, a notion she had swiftly debunked when she'd declared they had nothing in common, and that she didn't want to stay in touch after she returned to Chicago.

"She's already seen the waterfall."

They looked up as a waitress paused by their booth to clear away the empty glasses. "Can I get you lads something to drink?" she asked.

"Two pints of Guinness, please," Conall said. After she left, he leaned back and considered Flynn. "Well, as far as the tourists go, was there really any harm done? I'm sure the Americans enjoyed themselves."

"Whether they did or didn't doesn't matter. I don't want strangers tramping all over the property. With my luck, they'll post photos all over social media, and I'll have a line of tourists stretching down the road, demanding to be let in."

Conall's grin was unsympathetic. "You should be so lucky."

"Even if I was interested in opening the farm to visitors—which I'm not—Ballylahane is too far off the beaten path. How much business would we really draw? Most tourists don't come much farther north than Galway or Connemara."

"I don't know," Conall mused. "County Donegal is becoming more attractive for outdoor enthusiasts, and your property is pretty special. People would pay money just to stand on the hillside and admire the views."

Flynn narrowed his eyes at his friend. "Have you been speaking with Lori? Because you're starting to sound like her."

Their beers arrived, and Conall slid one glass toward Flynn. "Maybe you should start listening."

"Even if I were to agree—and I haven't said I will—it could be years before I get the approvals."

Conall's eyes crinkled in amusement, as if he knew Flynn was just throwing up roadblocks. "At least keep an open mind about it."

"I'm nothing if not open-minded," Flynn said grumpily.

"Oh, sure you are," Conall agreed, his eyes gleaming with humor. "You're about as open as a closed door without a key."

"Fine, I'll think about it," he promised. "I know when I'm outnumbered."

LORI AVOIDED GOING to the barn the following morning, telling herself her reluctance had nothing to do with her anxiety about seeing Flynn, although her insides were tangled in knots at the prospect.

She'd disappointed him.

He'd been generous enough to invite her to stay at the farm, and she'd repaid him by inviting tourists onto the property, against his explicit wishes. Worse, he believed she was keeping Seth dangling on a hook for her own perverse enjoyment. And that kiss . . .

He'd promised they would talk later, but she wasn't ready to face him.

She'd spent most of the night on her laptop, and although her eyes felt gritty with fatigue, she hadn't been able to get more than a few hours of sleep. Now she sat at the kitchen table, researching the legal requirements for opening the farm to visitors. The process didn't seem nearly as complicated or lengthy as she'd originally believed. If the O'Rourke family agreed, they could potentially begin accepting visitors as soon as next spring, with annual earnings anywhere between fifty and eighty thousand euros.

Glancing at her watch, she saw it was already ten o'clock, and yet she was still in her pajamas. Flynn hadn't come by the cottage to check on her or see why she hadn't come down to the barn that morning. She felt both disappointed and relieved. Disappointed, because spending time with him had become the highlight of her days since she'd been on the farm. But there was a certain relief in not seeing him, too, knowing he was likely still upset with her. She felt embarrassment and remorse about looking through the farm ledgers. Worse, she had encouraged the Americans to tour the farm when she knew he would disapprove. If he was still annoyed with her, she'd rather not know.

Which was why she'd thrown herself into the task of putting together a draft business plan for the farm, as well as a comprehensive list of the legal hoops the family would need to negotiate if they did eventually decide to open the farm to tourism. Maybe he wouldn't be interested in seeing the report. Maybe he would toss it back to her with disdain, but she wanted to show him he had options. It was the only way she could think to make amends.

Pushing her chair back, she filled the kettle with water and put it on the boiling plate, and then stood staring out the window over the kitchen sink. The sky was a clear, cloudless blue. She could see the long sweep of green meadow and the glittering blue water below, and the tiny blobs of white that were the sheep as they meandered over the landscape. Directly beneath the window, the rhododendrons were in full bloom, a brilliant splash of red and purple against the backdrop of sea and sky, and Lori understood why Flynn couldn't leave. She wasn't sure she could leave, either, when it came right down to it.

She jumped when her phone rang and hurried over to the table to pick it up, groaning when she saw the caller ID. For scant seconds, she battled with her conscience before she answered.

"Seth," she said, smiling through gritted teeth. "How's the new job?"

"I can tell by your tone you're still upset," he said, sounding petulant. "It's been a week, Lori. Why haven't you answered my calls? Or my texts?"

Just hearing the hurt and belligerence in his voice made her cringe. "I talked to you the day after I got here."

"No, you gave me the bum's rush," he said. "I'm talking about all the times I've called since then."

"Oh, did you call after that?" she asked weakly. "The reception here is terrible. What time is it, anyway? It must be the crack of dawn over there."

"I wanted to be sure to catch you. I'm worried about you, Lori."

"There's nothing to worry about," she assured him. "I'm with Rachel, and I'm fine."

"Are you staying with her at the B&B?"

"No, actually, I rented a little cottage outside of town."

There was a brief silence. "Just how long are you planning to stay?"

"I'm not sure. I don't see any reason to rush home."

"Don't you?" His question was pointed.

"Look, Seth—"

"No, don't say anything," he interrupted. "I think I understand what you're going through, and I'm willing to give you this time to sort it out."

Lori barely resisted the temptation to end the call. "Gee,

thanks."

"Your dad and I are both worried about you." His tone was patently patronizing, as if she were a child. "I know you're disappointed that I got the commodities manager position, but running away isn't the answer. In fact, it only demonstrates you weren't ready for the job. Come home, Lori. You've had some time to think things over and now that you're less emotional, I think you'll agree marrying me is a good bet."

Lori didn't hear what he said next because her blood pounded hot and loud in her ears, blocking out everything else. She took several deep breaths, willing herself to calm down.

"Seth, we both know you and I are not going to work," she managed. "I already told you I'm not going to marry you, and I meant it."

"So you're just going to come back to work, and I'm supposed to pretend there was never anything between us?"

*Because there never was anything.* At least, Lori amended silently, nothing that should make either of them consider marriage.

"I'm not coming back to my old job." The words were out of her mouth before she knew she was going to say them, but once they were said, she realized it was the truth. She wasn't going back, not to her old job, not to Chicago, and most definitely not to Seth.

"You're not serious. What else would you do?" Seth demanded, sounding genuinely baffled.

Lori's mouth fell open, and she had to snap it shut or risk saying something she knew she'd regret. Did he truly believe she had no options aside from marrying him or working for her father? "Actually, I have something pretty fabulous lined up over here," she fibbed. "So I'm going to take some time to explore it and see where it leads."

"Is it another guy? Is that it? Because I sensed you might have met someone the last time you were over there." He lowered his voice, as if he didn't want someone overhearing him. "Don't throw away a good thing for someone you barely know, Lori. Some country hick who has no idea who you are or what you come from. If this is your way of making me jealous, then you've succeeded, okay? Is that what you want to hear? I know some girls like to play those games, but you're better than that."

Lori was silent for several seconds as she struggled to contain her rising irritation. "I have to go, Seth. Tell my father I'll call him later, okay?"

"I'm right, aren't I?" he persisted. "You've met someone, but you're making a mistake if you think he'll make you happy. Whoever he is, he's probably just looking for a free ride or an easy road to—"

"Goodbye, Seth." She disconnected the call and stood for a moment to marshal her chaotic emotions. She half expected him to immediately call her back, but her phone remained silent, and with a sigh, she dropped it onto the table next to her laptop.

The kettle began to whistle on the stove, so she made herself some coffee and was just preparing to sit down again when someone knocked on the door. Loudly. Imperiously.

Her heart leaped, and for one crazy second, she thought it might actually be Seth, materializing at her door to batter down her resistance. But a furtive peek through the lace curtains over the sink revealed Flynn standing on her doorstep, looking large and imposing. Drawing a deep breath, she set her coffee cup down and quickly smoothed her hair before she opened the door a crack to peer out at him.

He scowled when he saw her. "Are you ill?"

"No."

"Good." Without warning, he shouldered his way in, forcing her to step back or get plowed under.

"What are you doing?" she spluttered indignantly, closing the door behind him.

"I might ask you the same thing." He raked her with a narrowed, silver glance. "Why aren't you dressed?"

"I'm on vacation. I don't have to do anything if I don't want to." She refused to feel self-conscious at being caught in a pair of stretchy shorts that clung to her butt and thighs, but when his gaze drifted over her bare legs, heat gathered beneath her skin and seeped all the way to her toes. She resisted the urge to tug the hem of her T-shirt down. "What are you doing here, anyway?"

"I've come to take you sightseeing."

"Really? I thought maybe you'd changed your mind after yesterday."

He scowled. "Why would I?"

Lori felt her eyebrows shoot upward. "Because you were pretty upset with me, that's why."

"I don't like that you snooped through my private papers, but I think I understand why you did it. As far as the tourists go, I'm willing to forgive you."

Lori only just resisted the urge to roll her eyes. After her conversation with Seth, she was so done with masculine arrogance. "Thank you," she said instead.

"Get dressed. I'll wait."

Her glance flicked unwillingly to her laptop, hoping her screensaver had kicked in. "Where are we going?"

"You'll see."

She moved toward the bedroom, glancing back at Flynn to make sure he wasn't looking at her laptop. To her dismay, he was staring in unabashed interest at her backside. Realizing he'd been caught, he gave her a leering grin. Lori fled, but she couldn't deny that her spirits buoyed at seeing him, and the prospect of spending a day in his company was, if she was honest, thrilling. She dressed quickly, pulling on slim-fitting jeans and low-rise boots, pairing them with a long-sleeved white shirt tucked in at the front. She rolled the sleeves back and then quickly ran her fingers through her hair, leaving it loose around her face. She applied a swift coat of mascara and her signature red lipstick and took a deep breath, surveying herself in the bathroom mirror. When she returned to the main living area, Flynn was standing by the sink, drinking her cup of coffee as he contemplated the scenery.

"Glad to see you made yourself right at home," she said drily.

"Well, it is my home, so . . ." He considered her over the rim of the coffee cup. "You look nice."

She could have said the same about him. She'd become accustomed to seeing him in sweats or work clothes. Today he wore a pair of dark jeans with a soft-gray T-shirt under a black leather biker jacket that emphasized the impressive width of his shoulders and accentuated his gray eyes. The recent haircut she'd given him looked good too. He'd made an effort to tame the unruly waves, which perversely made Lori want to push her fingers through the thick strands and mess them up.

"You clean up pretty good yourself," she commented. She collected her handbag from where she'd left it on a kitchen chair and casually closed her laptop, hoping Flynn hadn't seen what she'd been working on. "Ready when you are."

Setting down the coffee cup, he indicated the door. "Then let's go."

"Where to, exactly?"

"I told you, you'll just have to wait and see."

"Really?" She paused at the door and looked at him.

"Not even a hint?"

"Not even a hint." He held the door open for her. "They say anticipation is ninety percent of the fun."

As Lori followed him down the path to the car, she couldn't help but think he was wrong; the anticipation of spending time with Flynn could never match the excitement of the actual experience, and therein lay the problem. She was hopelessly addicted.

# Chapter Sixteen

"WE CAN TAKE my car," Lori offered as she followed Flynn down the cottage path.

"Thanks, but I'll drive," he said, anticipating her reaction when she saw his chosen mode of transportation.

They reached the bottom of the path and Flynn knew the precise instant she spotted the motorcycle parked near the barn. She stopped. "Is that yours?"

"It is." He'd learned to ride a motorcycle in secondary school, and he'd owned this beauty for just over two years. He'd been waiting for the weather to improve before he took it out, and today promised to be glorious. Nothing could beat sightseeing from the back of a motorcycle, and Flynn couldn't wait to share the experience with Lori. But he could see she didn't immediately share his enthusiasm.

"Don't look so scared. You're going to love it," he assured her. "Have you ever been on a bike before?"

She shook her head. "No, and you don't want me starting now. I'm afraid I'll make you get into an accident."

Flynn laughed. "Give me—and yourself—more credit. Just do what I do. When I lean into a corner, you lean with me. That's the only trick. Follow my movements and don't work against me, and we'll be fine." He strode toward the powerful-looking machine and retrieved a jacket that lay across the seat. "Here, put this on."

Lori accepted the jacket, smoothing her hand over the supple leather. "Whose is it?"

"It belongs to my mum." Seeing her dubious expression, he resisted the urge to pull her into his arms and reassure her. "Trust me—she doesn't mind you borrowing it, and it will keep you warm. Here, give me your purse. I'll stow it in the side bag."

Obediently, Lori handed her purse to Flynn before pulling on the leather jacket. She was smaller than Maureen O'Rourke, but curvier, and Flynn watched surreptitiously as she attempted to zip it closed over her bust.

"Yeah, that looks fine," he said when she succeeded. "Is it comfortable?"

Lori stretched her arms experimentally. "A little snug across the chest, but otherwise, it's a good fit. Thanks."

Two helmets sat on top of the seat, and Flynn handed one to Lori. He watched as she put it on and fastened the clasp beneath her chin and lowered the visor before he secured his own headgear and slid on a pair of sunglasses. Straddling the bike, he rocked it free of the kickstand and switched it on, loving the smooth purr of the engine.

"Climb on," he called, and stood to give Lori more room. She clutched his arm as she clambered onto the seat behind him. When she was settled, he sat down again, acutely aware of her slim legs bracketing his thighs. "Comfortable?"

"Yes, but where do I hold on?" she asked over his shoulder.

Reaching back, Flynn found her hand and pulled it forward until it rested on the flat of his stomach. "You hold on to me."

His stomach muscles contracted involuntarily when both her arms came around him, and he could feel her pressed warmly against his back. He eased the bike from its parking spot and onto the gravel road that led past the sheep fields and beyond the cottage. When they reached the main road, he turned toward the coast and opened the throttle, gratified when Lori clutched him tighter. The air was fragrant with the coconut scent of the flowering gorse bushes that bloomed on either side of the road. Beneath that, there was the fresh, briny smell of the sea.

"Doing okay?" he called to Lori.

She hugged his back and he felt her chin come to rest on his shoulder. "It's wonderful! Amazing!"

They roared along the cliff road, passing small houses, a pub, and the occasional B&B, before turning inland. They traveled for less than ten miles when Flynn slowed down and pulled into a parking lot near a church surrounded by farmland. Turning the engine off, he waited as Lori climbed down.

"Where are we?" she asked, removing her helmet.

"We're in Kilclooney." Raising the bike onto its kick-stand, he removed his own helmet and climbed off. "Were you warm enough?"

"Yes, thanks, but I thought most bikers wore the full leather suits over here."

"They might do if they're touring," he replied. "I tend to stay local, so a good jacket is sufficient." Opening the saddlebag, he withdrew a bicycle lock and threaded it through both helmets before securing them to the frame of the motorcycle. Withdrawing her handbag, he handed it to her. "The helmets will be fine, but I'd feel better not leaving your purse here."

"So where are we going, exactly?" Lori asked, securing her handbag across her body.

Flynn held out his hand. "Come with me."

She tucked her hand into his, and Flynn led her across the street and alongside a small house, where a narrow path went through the yard to the fields beyond.

"Should we even be here?" Lori asked. "I feel like we're trespassing."

"The house belongs to Mrs. McNelis, and she doesn't mind the foot traffic, so long as you close the gate behind you."

"Is this another secret ring fort? Why are all the local attractions found on private property? This feels so intrusive, I'm not sure—"

Flynn stopped, torn between exasperation and amusement. "Would you feel better if I knocked on her door and asked for permission?" He indicated the distant fields, where a group of people were making their way back to the main road. "Look, there are others doing exactly what we're doing. This is the only way to get to the dolmen."

"The what?"

"You'll see."

Without releasing her hand, he unlatched the gate at the back of the yard and drew Lori through. They made their way across several fields, and although the ground was spongy, Flynn was gratified to see it wasn't muddy. Lori suddenly pulled him to a stop.

"Oh," she breathed. "I see it."

Looking ahead, Flynn saw the dolmen in the distance. Sitting at the top of a gentle rise, the stacked stones resembled some sort of prehistoric beast rising out of the ground.

"It almost looks like a bird getting ready to take flight," she observed.

Flynn considered the dolmen, which consisted of three massive, upright stones supporting an enormous capstone that featured a surprisingly graceful upward curve. "I don't know," he mused. "I've always thought it looks like a dolphin."

"Actually, you're right," she agreed. "How old is it?"

"Archeologists think it's from the Neolithic period, so more than five thousand years old."

As they drew closer, Lori realized there was a second, smaller monument nearby. "Is that another dolmen?"

"It is, yeah."

Lori released his hand and stared at the largest dolmen in amazement. "How do you suppose they raised the top stone into place?"

"That's the mystery, isn't it?"

She glanced at him, a half smile curving her mouth. "It's hard to believe there are still mysteries in the world."

"There is no mystery so great as a woman's heart."

She looked questioningly at him. "Yeats again?"

"No, I just made that up."

Lori laughed and punched him lightly on the arm. "We're not that mysterious, actually."

He gave a noncommittal grunt.

"If you had sisters, you'd feel differently," she assured him.

"You have four brothers," he pointed out. "Does that make you an expert on men?"

She pulled a face. "No. Just their bad habits, unfortunately."

Recalling his own youthful behavior with his two rambunctious brothers, Flynn laughed. "I'll try not to meet your expectations. As far as the dolmens, they're also called portal tombs, and archeologists believe they mark burial sites."

They slowly circled the dolmen, admiring it from different angles. The ground surrounding the stones was lumpy and strewn with large rocks, and after Lori stumbled twice, Flynn took her hand and tucked it securely into the crook of his arm.

"Thank you," she said, flushing a bit. "It's hard to look up and still watch where you're going."

"No worries," he said easily. "I've got you."

They nodded to an older couple who had also made the hike out to see the rocks.

"Would it be disrespectful to take a picture under the capstone?" Lori asked, keeping her voice low.

"No, I don't think so." Releasing her hand, he waited as she fished her phone out of her purse and handed it to him. Then, stepping carefully between the upright stones, she stood beneath the stone pillars. She was short enough that her head didn't quite touch the bottom of the capstone. Leaning forward, she grinned at him.

"I feel so small!"

"That's because you are so small," he said, and snapped several quick pictures of her.

"Would you like me to take a photo of the two of you together?"

Flynn turned to see the older couple standing nearby, watching them with indulgent smiles. "Sure, that would be great, if you don't mind."

"Not at all," the woman assured him. Taking the camera, she waited as Flynn attempted to position himself near Lori.

"I'm too tall to fit underneath," he said, frustrated. He

moved to the upturned part of the capstone, where there was more room. "I'll just stand here."

"Go on and stand beside him, luv," the older woman said, gesturing for Lori to join him. "That's it. No, get closer. Now, put your arm around her. Perfect."

Flynn smiled, happy to have Lori tucked against his side with her arm around his waist as the woman took photos. "Something for your scrapbook," he murmured, smiling at her.

"Who says I have a scrapbook?"

"Something for your book of conquests, then."

She glanced up at him from beneath her lashes. "Is that what you are? A conquest?"

"You've vanquished me completely. I have no choice but to surrender."

Before she could respond, the woman stepped forward with Lori's phone. "There you are. I think I got some good ones, but check to be certain."

Flynn peeked over Lori's shoulder as she swiped through the pictures. "They're perfect," Lori assured the woman. "Thank you."

"Are you newlyweds, then?" she asked.

"What?" Flynn gave a startled laugh, even as Lori hastened to deny it.

"Ah, my mistake," the woman said with a chagrined smile. "You just have that look about you, so I assumed. Sorry."

After she and her husband wandered over to the second dolmen, Lori fussed with her phone and Flynn noted how she avoided looking at him.

"Did that embarrass you?" he asked, amused in spite of himself.

"You have to admit, it was a little awkward." She glanced at him. "It's like asking a chubby woman if she's pregnant. You don't do it unless you're absolutely sure."

Flynn didn't laugh, because he was sure. Absolutely. Whatever the woman had seen, she hadn't been wrong, at least not where he was concerned. Wordlessly, he took the phone from her hands and scrolled through the half dozen or so pictures the woman had taken. One photo had caught him looking at Lori in a way that could easily be mistaken for infatuation. Or love. He was tempted to delete it, but then thought . . . what the hell? He handed the phone back to her and watched as she studied the photos.

"They did come out nice." She enlarged one photo with a swipe of her fingers and peered more closely at the image. "Why do you have to be so handsome?"

For a moment, Flynn had no response. He wasn't vain about his looks, but hearing Lori say she thought he was attractive lightened his mood.

"I think that might have been a compliment," he finally said with a wry grin. "I'm going to take it as one."

She slid him an amused glance. "Don't let it go to your head."

"Tell you what . . . let's make a wish."

"What?" She gave a bemused laugh. "Why?"

"The locals believe if you toss a stone onto the capstone of the dolmen and it stays on top, your wish will come true."

"Okay, I'm game."

They spent the next five minutes hunting for the perfect stones, and when they'd each found one, Flynn drew her back from the dolmen to a spot where he thought they would have the best chance of success.

"Just throw it onto the top?" Lori asked, hefting her stone experimentally.

"Just give it an underhand toss," Flynn confirmed. "Here, I'll go first."

Testing the weight of the stone, Flynn eyed the distance to the top of the dolmen before he gave it a soft lob. The rock made a perfect arc through the air and clattered onto the top of the dolmen and was still.

"Oh! Sheer luck," Lori exclaimed.

"Uncanny skill, you mean."

She gave him an absorbed look. "Did you make a wish?"

"I did."

"Tell me."

Flynn laughed. "I can't tell you, or it won't come true. C'mon, take your turn."

Lori groaned and pushed a lock of hair away from her face as she eyed the dolmen. "I was never good at sports."

"This just requires some gentle finesse. You'll do great."

"But what if I miss? I really, really want my wish to come true."

Flynn understood; he'd made a wish that had nothing to do with his dad's health or the prosperity of the farm. His wish had been motivated by his own selfish desires, and he desperately hoped it would come true.

"Don't think about it too much," he advised. "Just give it a toss."

She looked adorable as she squinted up at the dolmen, her face scrunched up in an expression of focused intent. She made three practice swings of her arm, and then, before she could release the stone into the air, Flynn grasped her around the waist and hoisted her upward so that she was almost on eye-level with the capstone. Lori gave a small squeal of surprise, but gave the stone a gentle toss. It landed near the middle, but then rolled toward the curved edge of the capstone, and Flynn was sure it would fall off, but to his amazement, it stuck. Lori gave an excited squeal and thrust both arms into the air as Flynn lowered her back to the ground.

"Does that count?" she asked. "Are you allowed to get a helping hand, or does that negate the wish?"

"I don't recall anything that says you can't get a boost," Flynn said, chuckling. "Nice job."

"Thank you." Then she caught his hand with a swift grin. "Quick, let's get out of here before it changes its mind and decides to roll off. That way, my wish will still come true."

Laughing, Flynn allowed her to drag him away from the stones. "What did you wish for?"

She cast him a reproving look. "If you can't tell me your wish, there's no way I'm going to tell you mine."

"Fair enough."

But as they circled the second dolmen, Flynn wondered what it was she had wished for. To return to Chicago? To obtain the coveted position of commodities manager somewhere back in the States? To leave him again? Each thought was more depressing than the last.

He thought of his own wish. He wanted just one thing.

Flynn wished Lori would stay.

# Chapter Seventeen

WHEN THEY FINALLY left the dolmens, Lori expected Flynn would want to head back to Ballylahane and was surprised when they turned out of the church parking lot and headed in the opposite direction. She wasn't about to complain, though. She enjoyed riding behind Flynn with her arms wrapped around him. Despite having never been on the back of a motorcycle, riding with Flynn felt completely natural. He handled the bike with an easy confidence that made her feel safe. She could feel every subtle shift of his body as he maneuvered the bike along narrow coastal roads, past dramatic views of green fields and shimmering sea. Wanting to feel the wind on her face, she'd pushed her visor up and instead wore her sunglasses. Without the plastic barrier, she kept getting tantalizing whiffs of Flynn, and he smelled amazing, a masculine elixir of clean soap and spicy aftershave with underlying notes of leather and cedar. She wanted to inhale him.

"Where are we going?" she asked, propping her chin on his shoulder so she could shout into his ear.

"There's a little fish shack about thirty minutes from

here," he called back. "I don't know about you, but I'm getting hungry."

"Sounds good!" She tightened her arms around him, determined to savor every minute of the short ride. They passed through small villages and flew past fields of sheep and donkeys until the air began to change and Lori caught the enticing scent of the ocean. Then they rounded a bend in the road, and she saw they were at the head of a long harbor. A series of industrial-sized piers marched along one side of the harbor, and dozens of brightly painted fishing boats bobbed on the water. The town itself was a colorful array of buildings and churches, all facing the port. Flynn drew the bike to a stop near one of the piers and raised himself up to allow Lori to climb off.

"This is so cute!" she exclaimed as she pulled her helmet off and ran her fingers through her hair. "Where are we, exactly?"

Flynn rocked the bike onto its kickstand and climbed off before unfastening his helmet. "This is Killybegs, the largest fishing port in Ireland."

The harbor was wide and long, and Lori could see where it emptied into the ocean beyond. While there were numerous small sailboats on the water, she could also see working fishing boats and enormous trawlers. The harbor was a hive of activity as fishermen took advantage of the sunshine to spread their nets out to dry on the quays or unloaded their catch onto the wide, concrete piers, where they were put onto forklifts and transported into a long, low building that looked like a processing center. The main road ran alongside the harbor and an assortment of restaurants and hotels.

"Where is this fish place?"

"Just down the road." After securing their helmets and jackets, he led the way past the quays to a wide pedestrian boardwalk where a small crowd of people had gathered in front of what looked like a walk-up fish shack. They joined the queue and Lori saw the small, portable food truck was actually called The Seafood Shack. The aroma of fried seafood and French fries made her mouth water and her stomach rumble, reminding her she'd skipped breakfast that morning.

"Oh, that smells amazing. I didn't realize how hungry I was until just now."

When they reached the window, Flynn ordered fish and chips for both of them, along with two cans of Guinness beer. The smiling girl gave him the beer, two plastic cups, and a slip of paper with a number on it, and they sat down on the low wall that separated the boardwalk from the water. Flynn cracked both cans and poured the beer into the cups, handing one to Lori.

"I have some bottled water back at the bike, if you'd prefer," he offered.

"Maybe later," she said, taking an appreciative sip. "Mm, delicious. Do you come here very often?"

"Not really. I only come during the off-season. They do a

brisk business during the summer months, and I'm not the most patient of guys. I don't fancy waiting forty minutes for a piece of fish, so I tend not come out here during tourist season."

"This isn't tourist season?"

Flynn laughed. "Not yet. It's still early days. Once June rolls around, it'll be a different story. Then you'll see long lines of people until September."

"So even though we're pretty far north, this part of Ireland sees plenty of tourism?"

"I'd say so. If Conall is to be believed, more people are heading this way every year, drawn by the outdoor activities."

Lori let her gaze drift over the harbor, taking in the unique fishing town. Overhead, gulls wheeled and cried, hoping for a handout or an opportunity to pilfer seafood from the fishermen or the tourists.

"I can see why," she said quietly. "It's beautiful here."

"During the summer, the town has a street festival to celebrate the fish catches and to perform the traditional Blessing of the Boats." He paused, smiling. "Conall actually worked on one of the fishing boats here in Killybegs until he realized he suffered from motion sickness."

Lori gaped at him. "Is that true? I'm having a hard time imagining it. Does Rachel know?"

She could easily see Flynn decked out in yellow waterproof overalls and a thick sweater, with his dark hair ruffled by the wind and salt spray, but she had a harder time imagining Conall in the same scenario.

"It's a true story, and I've no idea if Rachel knows. I think he only managed it for a few summers before he gave it up. To hear him talk about it, he spent most of his time hanging over the railing, casting up his breakfast."

Lori started to laugh. She couldn't help herself. "Poor Conall. No wonder he decided to keep his feet on firm ground instead."

Flynn was staring at her in an arrested sort of way, and suddenly self-conscious, she bent her head and took a sip of her beer.

"You should do that more often," he said, his voice low.

"What, drink?"

"No, laugh. You've a rare smile and a laugh that makes me want to—" He broke off, as if he'd said too much. "Never mind."

But Lori wouldn't be put off. She was intrigued enough to want him to complete his thought. "No, finish what you were about to say."

He looked at her then, his silver eyes clear and intent. "You have a wonderful laugh. Amazing, really. It makes me want to do or say something absolutely ridiculous just to hear it again. I like seeing you smile. I want to be the one who makes you laugh like that."

Mesmerized by what she saw in his eyes and moved by what he'd shared, Lori found it impossible to look away. But before she could respond, the girl at the walk-up window called his number, and he stood.

"That's us. I'll be right back."

Lori took the moment by herself to draw in a steadying breath, aware that her heart was skipping a little erratically, and no wonder. Flynn O'Rourke had just told her she had a rare smile and that he wanted to be the one to make her laugh. It wasn't a declaration of love, but his words spoke to Lori in a way that banal tributes to her beauty never could. When he returned, he carried two cardboard boxes patterned to look like old newspaper.

"Here you go," he said, handing one to Lori. "I got you the large portion, but just eat what you can. No pressure."

Opening the box, Lori saw two large, golden pieces of fried fish on a bed of French fries with small containers of tartar sauce and ketchup. The smell alone made her believe she could devour the entire thing in one bite.

"I'm totally onto you, you know," she said as she placed her box on the wall between them.

For a moment, Flynn looked alarmed. "What do you mean?"

"I know why you got me the large portion. Because you'll have dibs on whatever I can't finish."

"Ah," he said, his expression relaxing into a rueful grin. "Yes, you're right. Sorry. I'm completely transparent. Leave me some chips, would you?"

Unable to suppress a smile, Lori punched him playfully

on his arm. "You'll be lucky if I leave you so much as a single, measly French fry." She inhaled deeply. "This smells amazing."

In fact, it tasted amazing too. Lori broke off a chunk of delicate fish and ate it, nearly moaning with pleasure. "Oh, this is delicious."

"Best seafood around," Flynn confirmed, breaking off chunks of fish and dipping them into his tartar sauce before eating them. "It doesn't get any better than this. Great food, great view, and—" He gave her a meaningful look. "Great company."

Lori flushed with pleasure. "Thanks. I feel the same way."

Flynn lifted his cup of Guinness and touched it against hers. "Here's to today."

"To today."

"May there be many more."

Lori didn't answer, too flustered to do more than bend her head and sip her beer. When they had finished eating—and Flynn had been correct in guessing that Lori wouldn't be able to finish her meal—he disposed of their empty boxes, cups, and cans, and they made their way back to where he'd left his motorcycle.

"I guess we'll be heading back now?" she asked, even though it was the last thing she wanted to do. The entire day had a magical quality to it, and there was a part of her that hoped it might never end.

"If that's what you want," Flynn said slowly. "But if you have a little more adventure in you, there's something I'd like to show you. It's about thirty minutes from here. We won't be able to spend much time there because I do have to get back eventually, but I think we can spare another hour."

"What is it?"

"You'll see when we get there," he said, and handed Lori her helmet and jacket.

Balancing herself on Flynn's arm, she climbed onto the back of the motorcycle as if she'd been doing so her entire life and not just the past few hours. But settling herself against his back with her thighs bracketing his and her palms pressed firmly against his rock-hard stomach, it felt both familiar and exciting. Soon they left Killybegs Harbor behind and were zooming through the countryside.

They passed through towns with names like Castlecarn and Meenderrygamph until Flynn turned onto a road that wound steadily upward, bordered on either side by yellow gorse bushes, flowering rhododendrons, and fields of fleecy sheep. Eventually, they reached a flat area with parking lots and a small visitors center. Beyond the parking lots, Lori saw a paved road that ascended steeply into the surrounding hills. Flynn pulled the motorcycle to the curb near the building and climbed off.

"Wait here," he said, pulling his helmet off. "I'll be right back."

She watched as he disappeared inside the building. Tourists were slowly making their way up the road, many of them using walking sticks and carrying backpacks. When Flynn reappeared, he wore a satisfied smile.

"I thought we might have to leave the bike here," he said. "But they told me we can take it to the top."

"Is that not normally allowed?" Lori asked, looking at the number of cars in the parking lots.

"Not without a badge on your vehicle," he confirmed. "But the guy who runs the center belongs to our running club. We're not staying long, and I paid the parking fee anyway."

"I can hike up," Lori assured him, feeling uncomfortable about being given preferential treatment.

"Sure you can," Flynn said, his eyes lit with amusement. He climbed back onto the motorcycle and soon they were making their way up the road, which was so steep that Lori clutched Flynn tighter, half-afraid she would fall off the back of the bike, but grateful he had not asked her to hike up. They continued to climb, the tires of the motorcycle spitting dirt and gravel as the pavement ended and the road grew steeper. Then, suddenly, they rounded a bend and the road ended. Lori felt her jaw drop.

Killing the engine, Flynn pulled his helmet off and raised himself up on the seat so Lori could climb off. She did, hardly aware of doing so. Flynn hung his helmet over the handlebar and then leaned back against the bike with his arms crossed, watching Lori with amusement.

"Are you going to take your helmet off or just stand there, staring?" he asked, a smile quirking one corner of his mouth.

"Oh!" She fumbled with the fastening until Flynn pushed himself away from the bike and brushed her fingers aside, deftly unlatching the helmet and removing it for her. "Sorry," she said. "I seem incapable of doing anything right now but staring at this incredible view!"

Flynn smiled, seeming pleased with her reaction. "It is pretty amazing," he said, following her gaze.

They were at the top of a high cliff, with the entire Atlantic spread out before them. The cliffs stretched out to the right for as far as Lori could see, rising out of the crashing surf like an ancient fortress. A viewing platform had been built on the edge of the cliff and they walked over to it and stood in silence for several long moments. Far below them, she could hear the thunderous crash of the surf against the rocks. The air was salty and cool against her skin.

"I've never seen anything so majestic," Lori breathed. "Thank you for bringing me here."

"You're welcome."

"What are these cliffs called? I know we're too far north for the Cliffs of Moher."

"You're right. These are the Slieve League cliffs, and they're almost three times higher than the Cliffs of Moher." He pointed to their left, where, in the far distance, a flat-topped rock formation rose from the horizon like the prow of a massive ship. "That's Ben Bulben, near Sligo. Do you remember we passed it when we drove to Galway the last time you were here?"

"I remember you spouting some poetry about it," she said, bumping her shoulder gently against his arm. "Someone must have told you women like that sappy stuff."

"Is it working?" He slanted her a hopeful glance.

It was, but Lori didn't dare tell him so. The more time she spent in Flynn's company, the harder it was to consider returning to Chicago. Even harder to recall Seth's face or remember why she had wanted the commodities manager position so badly. Everything she'd thought she wanted seemed unimportant now. Standing at the cliff's edge with the complex, infuriating, irresistible man beside her, Lori couldn't think about much except that she was in serious trouble. What was it Rachel had said? *Sometimes you need to take a leap of faith.* As she glanced down, the drop was dizzying and Lori felt herself sway just a little. Almost immediately, Flynn's hand was at the small of her back, steadying her.

"Sometimes it can get to you," he said quietly.

"What can?" Her voice sounded breathless even to her own ears.

"The height. Maybe take a step back, away from the edge."

*Too late.* She'd already plummeted over the precipice, falling headlong into whatever this thing was with Flynn.

He hadn't removed his hand from where it rested warmly against her back, and without conscious thought, Lori
turned toward him. He was even closer than she'd realized,
and she instinctively reached out to steady herself, only
realizing her mistake when her palm encountered his chest—
his warm, hard, supremely muscled chest. She found herself
staring at the notch at the base of his throat, where his pulse
visibly throbbed in a rhythm that matched the hard beats of
his heart beneath her hand. That sensual hollow that seemed
to beg for her lips. Unable to resist, she touched the indent
with her mouth, hearing his swiftly indrawn breath.

"Flynn," she breathed, and then she was pressed against
all that masculine heat and strength as his arms closed
around her and his mouth descended over hers.

She'd thought the kiss would be hard and demanding,
but Flynn devastated her with his gentleness, fusing his lips
softly with hers and teasing her with his tongue. The effect
was a lush merging that had Lori aching for more. She slid
one hand to the nape of his neck and cupped the heated
skin, exerting gentle pressure as she tried to deepen the kiss.
But Flynn kept his exploration slow and searching, until Lori
couldn't prevent the small, needy noises that rose in her
throat. Only then did he give her what she wanted, sinking
his tongue deeper into her mouth as his hands slid down to
cup her hips and pull her closer.

The kiss was *hot*. Raw.

Lori's blood surged in sultry pulses through her body

until even her toes felt saturated in heat. She pushed her fingers into his hair, loving the coolness of the thick, silken layers. She lost track of where they were or how long they stood locked together, trying to absorb one another. It wasn't until Flynn dragged his mouth from hers and tucked her face against his chest that she became aware of a group of noisy tourists making their way along the path toward them.

"Didn't think you'd want an audience." His voice vibrated beneath her ear, deep and a little rough, his accent more pronounced.

Lori smiled against his chest as laughter bubbled up. Her legs felt unsteady, and she curled her fingers into the leather of his jacket, grateful for his support. "If they'd been five minutes later, who knows what they might have seen?"

Flynn gave a mournful groan. "Timing is everything."

Lifting her head, Lori smiled at him. "We definitely need to work on that."

As the tourists joined them on the viewing platform, Flynn took Lori's hand and drew her farther down the path that snaked along the cliff edge.

"So, are there any poems about this place?" she asked in an attempt to regain her composure. "If I know you, you probably have several memorized."

He laughed softly and pinched the bridge of his nose. "That predictable, am I? As it turns out, I do recall one," he mused. "'With a bridge of white mist / Columbkill he crosses, / On his stately journeys / From Slieveleague to

Rosses.'" He shrugged. "There's more, but that's the only verse that references the cliffs."

"What does it mean? Who is it crossing the bridge of white mist?"

"The fairy king. The poem is called 'The Fairies,' by William Allingham. Columbkill Lough is a lake in County Donegal and the fairy king must cross over the lake as he travels from Slieve League to the Rosses."

Lori stared at him, impressed. "When did you learn all this?"

Flynn looked mildly embarrassed. "I took a poetry class in college, mostly Irish and Gaelic poets. Allingham is Scottish, but I was interested in the poem because it referenced this region."

"I'd love to hear the rest of it."

Flynn laughed. "Yeah, well, maybe another time. It's a charming poem, but a bit lengthy. I'm not sure I'd do it justice."

Lori didn't press him further. They stayed at the cliffs for another fifteen minutes, admiring the view and watching the seabirds soar overhead, until finally, Flynn said they should return.

Lori sighed, taking one long, last look at the ocean before turning to look at Flynn. "I wish we could stay."

"Maybe we can come back."

"I'd like that."

She hadn't yet told Flynn that she was considering staying in Ireland. There were so many details to work out first, and she couldn't shake a sense of foreboding that something might happen to ruin her fledgling plans. Maybe the Irish government would refuse to grant her a visa, or she'd discover there was no market for handmade Irish goods. Maybe Flynn wouldn't want her to stay, which would be the icing on the cake because the more time she spent with him, the more she realized her reasons for wanting to stay had less to do with her business plan and everything to do with wanting to be with him.

She'd even wished for him at the Kilclooney Dolmen.

"Are you okay?" he asked, pulling her out of her reverie.

"Yes," she assured him. "But there's something I want to tell you, and I'm not sure how you're going to feel about it."

They were walking back toward the motorcycle and he slanted her an amused glance. "Sounds serious. Have you gone and invited more tourists to the farm? Or let the flock loose to run free across the countryside?"

She knew he was teasing her, but she couldn't prevent an uneasy laugh. "Of course not."

"Well, then let's hear it." He handed her a helmet just as his phone began to ring. Pulling it from the front pocket of his jeans, he glanced at the display and held up one finger. "Hold that thought. I really need to take this. Sorry."

"No, of course," she murmured, already having second thoughts about telling him about her plans. He turned partially away from her as he answered the call, but Lori could hear the strident tones from the other end. Flynn frowned and tried to interject several times unsuccessfully.

"Declan," he finally said, his tone slicing through his brother's tirade. "I'm on my way. I'll be there within the hour."

As he disconnected the call, Lori could see his expression had tightened. "Is everything okay? Is it your father?"

Flynn thrust his helmet on and climbed onto the bike before kicking it into life and putting a hand out to assist Lori. "No. It's my brother Shane. He's selling the farm out from under us."

# Chapter Eighteen

A S FLYNN NEGOTIATED the road that led to the farm, he
saw several vehicles parked near the barn and a group of
men standing on the knoll that overlooked the water. He
parked the bike near the cottage and waited as Lori climbed
off.

"Who are they?" she asked, eyeing the group as she removed her helmet.

"Developers," he said darkly.

He couldn't believe his brother had the audacity to bring
them onto the farm without letting him know, as if Flynn
had no stake in what happened with the family property.
Hanging his own helmet on the handlebar of the motorcycle,
he stripped out of his leather jacket and waited as Lori did
the same, never taking his eyes from the group. Shane turned
briefly in his direction before returning his attention to a
map that had been spread out on a nearby folding table.
Flynn recognized two of the men from the earlier meeting
with Shane at the pub. Today they'd been joined by three
additional men. One of them carried what looked like
surveying instruments and another held a drawing tube, used

to carry maps or blueprints. He was pointing down the hill to the waterfront and making sweeping gestures with his arm. Flynn couldn't hear his words, but he already knew he wouldn't like them.

Seeing Flynn, Declan separated himself from the group and trotted across the grass toward them, the two dogs at his heels.

"You've got to stop this," he burst out when he reached them. "He's going to lease the land to these jokers for some kind of adventure center for tourists. They're talking about building a massive lodge and cabins down on the shoreline and having overnight summer camps with ziplines and kayak excursions on the water. It's absolute bollocks, Flynn. I'm sure this isn't what Dad envisioned when he gave him the land."

"It's okay, Declan." He clapped a hand on his brother's shoulder. "I'll take care of this."

"What are you going to do? Shane owns the land free and clear. He can do with it as he likes, and we'd have no say about it."

"That's not how this is going to work," Flynn assured him. "I'll go talk to them."

"Well, I guess I'll head up to the cottage," Lori said, reminding Flynn that she was still there, watching the exchange with an expression of growing unease.

"No," he replied before she could step away. "You should come with me."

He saw the surprise in her hazel eyes and then the quiet concern. "This is a family matter, Flynn. I'm not sure it's my place—"

"I want you there."

After a brief moment, she nodded. "Okay."

The men turned as they approached, and Flynn saw a flash of guilt cross Shane's face before he quickly recovered and schooled his features into an expression of welcome. Flynn wasn't fooled.

"What's going on?" he asked, keeping his tone neutral, even friendly.

"You remember Patrick Donnelly and Brian Foster." Shane indicated the two men standing nearest him, and Flynn was gratified to see they each looked chagrined. "And these other gentlemen are with Atlantic Engineering and Survey Consultants."

"Great." Flynn kept his hands firmly in the front pockets of his jeans, making it clear he had no desire to shake hands. "What brings you lads out to the farm?"

He knew the answer, of course, but he wouldn't make this easy for Shane.

"Ah, we're just taking a look at the property, taking some pictures, and doing some land surveys," volunteered one of the engineers.

"For what purpose?"

"Flynn, can we talk about this later?" Shane asked, shooting an apologetic smile at the other men.

"No, Shane, we can't. If you're going to lease our land to these blokes and turn the farm into some kind of tourist attraction, I deserve to know about it."

"My land," Shane said, his voice flat. "Not yours. Mine."

"And what about access? Your property only extends along the water. Will your new business venture require an access road through the farm?"

"We're planning to create a separate entry road about a quarter of a mile away. I'll ask Dad for an easement and ensure the road doesn't impact the farm. That's part of why the surveyors are here today."

"So Dad knows about your plans?"

Glancing at the other men, Shane said, "Excuse me for a moment, gentlemen."

Taking Flynn by the arm, he drew him away from the other men. Declan and Lori followed them.

"Dad is the reason I'm doing this," Shane bit out.

"I don't understand."

Shane shot a meaningful glance at Lori, who was hanging back and looking uncomfortable. "Maybe we should keep this private. Family only."

Flynn knew Lori would like nothing better than to re-treat to the safety of the cottage, but there was a reason he wanted her there. "Sorry, but anything you have to say can be said in front of Lori."

Pinching the bridge of his nose, Shane blew out a breath. "Okay, fine. Look, the farm is just barely holding on, but

Dad's medical bills are going to put us in the red. Deep in the red. If we don't do something now, we might not recover."

"You're not telling me anything I don't already know," Flynn said tersely.

"This agreement will save the farm." Shane's expression was earnest. "Do you know how much Patrick and Brian are willing to pay to lease the land for an adventure center?" He paused. "Fifty thousand euros per year. Think about it, Flynn. Think about what that income would mean for the farm and for Dad. We wouldn't be giving up our rights to the land either. It would be a twenty-year lease, with an annual adjustment based on the cost of living. That's over *one million euros*."

Flynn relaxed marginally. He'd been prepared to hear worse, that Shane had sold his share of the farm to investors, or that he'd leased the land for some ridiculously exorbitant amount that Flynn wouldn't be able to argue against. The thought of leasing any portion of the family's land to an outside venture went against everything he believed in, but he at least understood and appreciated his brother's motivation.

"What if I told you there's a way we can bring in extra income without leasing the land? Do you really want to see an adventure center built down by the water?" he asked, gesturing toward the pristine view. "To have cars and people coming and going at all hours?"

They stood in silence for a moment, looking at the un-spoiled landscape. Flynn tried and failed to envision a clubhouse, a visitors center, bunkhouses, and parking lots bordering the sparkling blue inlet. That kind of enterprise would undermine everything his family had tried so hard to preserve.

"If you have a better idea, let's hear it," Shane said.

Flynn held out his hand to Lori, beckoning her closer. "Actually, it's her idea, and it's a good one. Tell him about your plan, Lori."

He saw the astonishment on Lori's face before she quick-ly recovered and gave him a look of bemused pleasure. "Which plan are you referring to, exactly?"

"The one I saw on your laptop this morning while you were getting dressed. The one that allows us to share our love of sheep farming with the public, while earning money."

Lori gaped at him. "You saw that?"

"I did, including the draft business plan you drew up." He turned to his brother. "Lori believes we can open the farm to tourists during the spring and summer months and bring in the same amount of money your land lease would generate. Possibly more."

Shane looked skeptical. "How? That kind of income is unreliable. Just look at what COVID did to tourism. What if that were to happen again? If the country went into another lockdown, these investors would still legally be bound to pay us our annual rent."

"If we went into lockdown again, their business would go bankrupt, and you'd be fighting for your money in court," Flynn argued.

Shane raked a hand through his hair. "Even if it was possible, how is it any better than my plan? You'd still have strangers tramping all over the place."

"But in this case, you would decide when and how many," Lori interjected. "The business case I created is based on three one-hour tours per day over a six-month period, and you could limit the number of people to whatever you're comfortable with, but I estimated ten to fifteen people per scheduled tour. At fifteen euros per person—and that's a conservative amount—you could potentially earn between seventy and one hundred thousand euros per year, and you wouldn't need to build access roads or parking lots or additional structures."

"Why would anyone be interested in coming to a sheep farm?" Shane asked.

"Trust me, they'll come," Lori replied with a confident smile.

"She's right," Declan interjected. "We had a family of eleven visit the farm a few days ago, and they not only handed over a wad of cash for the privilege, they seemed happy to do it."

"Really?" Shane still appeared unconvinced. "So did they just walk around and look at the sheep?"

"Declan did a sheepdog demonstration, and they each

got to bottle-feed a lamb and Flynn took them out to the bog to cut peat." Lori clasped her hands together, looking hopeful. "They said they had tried to book reservations at several other farms, but they were all sold out."

Shane gave a huff of laughter. "Seriously? And you think this could really be profitable? What about liability? And marketing?"

"I've taken all of that into consideration," Lori assured him. "There would be some initial start-up costs, of course, but you would earn that back the first month you open."

"Listen, tell your friends you need some time to consider their offer," Flynn said quietly. "Then let's sit down, and Lori can show you the research she's done. After that, we can make a decision as a family, yeah?"

Shane rubbed the back of his neck, looking undecided. Finally, he blew out a hard breath and nodded. "Okay, sure. I'll just finish up here and let them know I haven't made any final decisions yet."

"Great," Flynn said, and extended his hand to his brother. "You won't regret it."

Shane shook his hand. "This isn't me giving my approval," he said. "This is me saying I'm willing to listen."

"That's all I'm asking," Flynn assured him. If someone had told him just a week ago that he'd seriously consider opening the farm to tourists, he would have told them they'd lost their minds. But what he'd seen in Lori's draft business plan had seemed promising. Best of all, he could decide when and how often to run the tours in order to minimize any disruption to the farm operation. And if opening the farm to tourists meant Lori would stay to ensure a smooth transition, he'd do it. He'd do almost anything to keep her in Ballylahane.

"Well, I should go and take care of the lambs," Flynn said after Shane had rejoined the group of men.

"Already done," Declan said.

Flynn looked surprised. "Thanks, I appreciate that."

Declan shrugged. "Yeah, of course." He gestured toward the others. "I'll stay with Shane and make sure he doesn't get talked into doing anything crazy."

"Why didn't you tell me you looked at the business plan I drew up?" Lori asked as they walked back toward the barn.

"Because I didn't want to be accused of snooping." He pretended to wince as she playfully smacked his arm. "At least now we're even."

"But I thought you didn't want tourists tramping all over the farm," she persisted. "Why the change of heart? Don't get me wrong—I'm thrilled that you're going to consider it. Shocked, but thrilled."

"Because everything you said makes sense. Inviting tourists to visit the farm on my own terms is a better option than the one Shane offers. Can you imagine what this place would be like if there were buildings, roads, and parking lots down by the water? No thanks. If Donnelly and Foster want an adventure center, let them find somewhere else to build it."

Looking at the views of the surrounding hills and water, Flynn couldn't imagine spoiling it with construction. Opening the farm to a few groups of tourists seemed a better option and a small price to pay. There was even a part of him that had enjoyed showing the American family around the property, and he liked to think they'd left with a newfound appreciation for sheep farming.

"Do you have time to come up to the cottage?" Lori asked. "I can't imagine you were able to look at much of the business plan this morning, and I have some other ideas I'd like your opinion about before we pitch this to Shane."

She'd said *we*. As if they were a team. As if, maybe, she had some stake in this. Something that felt like hopeful joy threatened to bubble up, and he quickly tamped it down. He'd gotten ahead of himself once before, only to have her set him abruptly back on his heels. He wouldn't make the same mistake again. He'd promised himself he would go slowly this time and not overwhelm her. He needed to be certain of her feelings, and while he believed they'd reached a new level of awareness and intimacy in their relationship, she hadn't said she would stay. More than anything, he wanted to ask what her motives were and why she cared what happened to the farm, but was reluctant to put her on the defensive or, worse, drive her away. Instead, he gestured toward the cottage.

"Lead on. I'm all yours."

She cast him an inscrutable look before she made her

way up the path and opened the door to the cottage. "Can I get you something to drink?"

"Sure." He pulled out a chair and sat down at the kitchen table and waited as she poured them each a glass of lemonade before sitting beside him and pulling her laptop closer. They were near enough that their shoulders brushed, and he could smell the light, enticing fragrance he'd come to associate with her. Everything about her fascinated him, even her slender, white fingers as they flew over the keyboard. She'd painted her nails a pale shade of pink that reminded Flynn of candy. He wanted to nibble on those delicate fingertips.

"So this is the plan," she said, pulling the document onto the screen. She elbowed him. "Are you even paying attention?"

He dragged his gaze from her hands to her face. "Uh-huh, I am."

She eyed him for several long seconds and must have sensed the direction of his thoughts because color bloomed in her cheeks and she quickly averted her gaze. "Okay, well, make sure you are. This is important."

They spent the next hour reviewing the business plan and making changes to those bits that Lori had drafted based on estimates, but where Flynn had the facts.

"Do you think your family will agree to do this?" Lori asked when they had finished.

"I can't see why they wouldn't. Shane understands something needs to change if the farm is to survive and I know him well enough to believe he doesn't relish the idea of an adventure center down by the water. He was only doing what he thought he had to in order to keep the farm."

"The important thing is to ensure Shane, Declan, and your parents see the benefits of bringing tourists to the farm," Lori said earnestly. "We want your entire family to be on board with this."

"Don't worry. I'll ensure they are. What about marketing? That's going to be a big part of making this a success."

"That's true. Look, I drafted a website for you." She pulled up a page dominated by a photo of the farm's sweeping vista. Emblazoned across the top were the words, *O'Rourke Family Sheep Farm*. "Don't mind the content—it's just a placeholder until we finalize the page. I've included a mock link to where people can make reservations and online payments, so that's something you won't need to worry about. I can also create accounts for the farm on all the social media platforms, but someone will need to update the postings each day to keep it relevant. We'll need to work with organizations like Booking.com, Tripadvisor, GetYourGuide, and all the other travel sites in order to maximize your exposure, but that should be easy enough."

Flynn was floored. Even in a rough draft format, the website exceeded anything he could have imagined, and the photos she'd included of the farm, the barn, the sheep, the dogs—and even himself—were vibrant and engaging.

"What's this?" he asked, indicating a link that said *Gift Shop*. To his surprise, Lori seemed embarrassed and quickly scrolled past the link.

"Oh, that's nothing."

But when he saw her expression, Flynn's antennae went up. "No, go back. I want to know more about that."

"Fine." Lori gave an exaggerated exhale. "It's just an idea I had, but you don't need to do it if you don't want to. I just thought how cute it might be if you transformed one of the smaller outbuildings into a gift shop."

"A gift shop?" Flynn repeated in dismay. "What would we sell? Wool remnants, dirt and dung included at no extra charge?"

She did turn to look at him then, and beneath the indignation, Flynn sensed a vulnerability in her and suspected this was more important to her than she was letting on. "No, of course not." She hesitated and then abruptly stood. "Come with me, but I swear if you make fun of this in any way, I will absolutely never forgive you, Flynn O'Rourke."

Mystified, he followed her into the spare bedroom that adjoined the kitchen. Spread out on the bed and dresser were a vast array of items, everything from hand-thrown pottery, woolen sweaters and scarves, to jewelry, bath and beauty products, as well as candles and assorted artwork.

"What is this?" he asked cautiously, mindful of her warning. "Souvenirs? Gifts for your family?"

"Well, yes," she admitted. "Some of them, anyway. The

thing is, these are examples of handmade items that tourists look for when they come to Ireland. I purchased all of this from local craftspeople at the festival. I'd like to start an online shopping site for handmade Irish gifts. But then I thought, what if you also carried these products here, on the farm? Even nominal sales would benefit the crafters, as well as the farm."

Flynn was quiet for a moment, his mind racing. Lori had suggested a gift shop on the farm the first time she had visited. He knew she'd once managed the retail shop at her father's company, so he understood why she believed this might be a good idea. What he couldn't see was himself or Declan running a retail gift shop, no matter how small. While he hated to disappoint or discourage her, he had no interest in managing a store.

"Sorry, but I'm not in the retail business. Who would manage it? How would we keep items stocked? How would the crafters get paid?" He spread his hands. "I'm not saying it's a bad idea. I'm just saying I don't think it's practical. I'm a farmer, Lori. I don't know anything about running a shop, nor do I particularly want to."

"Well, that's the thing," Lori said, picking up a small sheep figurine tufted with real wool and turning it over in her hands. "You wouldn't need to."

Flynn stilled, not daring to hope. "Then who would?"

She looked at him, and a tentative smile curved her mouth. "Me."

# Chapter Nineteen

AFTER DROPPING HER bombshell, Lori watched as Flynn's expression registered puzzlement and then dawning understanding.

"What are you saying? That you're planning to stay here in Ireland?"

Lori couldn't tell if the prospect thrilled him or terrified him. She wanted to fling herself against his broad chest and tell him yes, she intended to stay because there was no place she wanted to be except with him. Instead, a vestige of lingering uncertainty kept her rooted where she stood.

"I'm not sure," she hedged. "There's a lot of red tape involved in staying, since I don't have a visa. But I could easily hire someone to keep the shop stocked and ensure the crafters get paid," she said. "That is, if you do decide to open the farm to tours."

Flynn's expression was inscrutable. "If I did agree to all that, I'd have to insist that you run it. There isn't anyone else I'd trust."

For a moment, Lori couldn't form a response, and when she was able to find her voice, it came out sounding breathless. "Well, of course I would run it."

Flynn took a step closer, his eyes intent. "I meant I would want you here, not sitting at a laptop on the other side of the Atlantic. I want your living, breathing presence, Lori, not some virtual oversight performed through monthly Zoom calls."

Her heart had begun a hectic step dance inside her chest, and she couldn't seem to drag her gaze away from his. "In that case, I—I would need a visa and a place to live."

Flynn made a small sound of dismissal. "Easy enough."

"I would need to go home and settle some things, move out of my apartment, and say good-bye to my family."

"Fine. I can come with you." His mouth tilted into a wry smile. "I've always wanted to see Chicago."

Lori stared at him in bemusement. "Why?"

"Why do I want to see Chicago?"

"No." She shook her head, waving away his words. "Why do you want to come with me? Why do you want me here?"

When he spoke, his voice was gentle. "Don't you know, Lori? And here I thought you had me all figured out."

She stopped breathing, hardly daring to hope. But as she moved to step into his arms, someone banged heavily on the door to the cottage, startling her so that she stepped hastily back.

"Expecting someone?" Flynn asked before he crossed to the door and swung it open.

Still in the spare bedroom, Lori pressed her hands against

her flushed cheeks and tried to contain her tumbled emotions. *He wanted her to stay.* What other revelation had he been about to tell her before they'd been interrupted?

"Lori." Flynn's voice cut into her thoughts. "There's someone here to see you."

Something in his tone caused alarm bells to go off in Lori's head, and she took a moment to gather her composure before joining Flynn by the door. A man stood on the walkway, looking impatient. A taxi idled on the gravel drive behind him.

"Seth," she exclaimed in dismay. "What are you doing here?"

"What do you think? To fetch you home," Seth said, his eyes flicking between Lori and Flynn.

"What? No, I'm not going home, at least not yet, and not with you."

"Listen," Flynn said, looking at her. "You have some things you need to figure out, so I'm going to make myself scarce and let you do that."

"No, Flynn, wait," she pleaded softly. "Stay. I didn't ask him to come here."

"Maybe not, but he obviously cares about you, or he wouldn't be here." He touched her lightly on the arm. "I'll be in the barn."

Before Lori could protest further, he stepped out of the cottage and down the walkway, giving Seth a curt nod as he passed. He shoved his hands into the front pockets of his jeans and hunched his shoulders, and it took all of Lori's restraint not to chase after him.

"So that's him, huh?"

"Excuse me?" Lori dragged her attention back to Seth.

"That's the guy you're dumping me for."

He looked and sounded so weary that Lori felt a pang of guilt. "Come into the house, Seth. You and I need to talk." She gestured toward the taxi. "Do you want to let it go?"

"No, something tells me I won't be staying long."

"When did you get in?" she asked.

"I landed in Dublin this morning and, after checking into the Grand Arms Hotel, had the taxi driver bring me here."

"Are you saying you were here—in Ireland—when you called me this morning?"

"Yes."

"Did you take a taxi all the way from Dublin?" she asked, aghast. She had done the same thing the first time she'd visited Ireland, but she'd had no idea how far Ballylahane was from the Dublin airport, or how much a taxi would cost. Back then, she hadn't cared. But so much had changed in the ensuing weeks.

*She* had changed.

"Never mind," she continued. "Ask your driver if he needs a break. I'll make you both a cup of coffee."

"I think I'm going to need something stronger," he muttered, and after speaking to the taxi driver, followed her into the cottage. He stood for a moment, looking around. "Nice place. Is he staying here with you?"

Opening the fridge, Lori pulled out a can of Guinness and busied herself pouring it into a pint glass. "Don't be like that, Seth. Flynn was good enough to rent the cottage to me when every hotel and B&B in the area was booked."

"So his name is Flynn."

"Yes, Flynn O'Rourke."

Seth snorted. "Of course it is."

Handing Seth his glass, she watched as he took a long swallow. Despite looking jet-lagged and aggravated, he still managed to radiate an air of entitlement and wealth. While most people would choose to wear casual clothing for a transatlantic flight, Seth wore a tailored wool jacket and khakis that appeared remarkably uncreased, given his recent travel. His only concessions to personal comfort were the loosening of his tie and unfastening the top two buttons of his shirt. His light-brown hair was cut in a classic Ivy League style, swept to one side and kept in place with a strong hold product. She couldn't help but compare him to Flynn. The two men were as opposite as day and night.

"What are you doing here, and how did you find me?" she finally asked.

"I'm here because you refuse to answer my calls," he said, giving her a direct look. "I stopped at the McDermott mill and Rachel told me where you're staying."

"Oh." Lori took a moment to process this information.

"How long are you planning to stay?"

"Long enough to talk some sense into you. I also told your father I'd meet with Seamus McDermott while I'm here and take a look at some of the new tweed designs. We're meeting for dinner later."

The knowledge that he was partly here on business as her father's newly hired commodities manager should have stung, but Lori felt nothing, not even a small amount of resentment. He could have the job with her blessing.

"I'm happy to hear you didn't come all this way strictly for me. I know how much you wanted the job, and I'm actually glad you got it. But since I've been here, I've discovered what it is I really want too."

"Let me guess—Flynn O'Rourke." He said the name flatly, without emotion.

"I want to be my own boss," she said, ignoring his comment. "I've decided to start an online business for handcrafted Irish products."

He gave her a blank look. "Great. You could do that from anywhere. You don't need to stay here for that."

"That's just it, I do. In fact, I want to stay here. I'm happy here, Seth. And yes, a big part of that has to do with Flynn O'Rourke."

"I get it. I really do. He has a sort of Heathcliff vibe to him that I'm sure is very appealing. But does he really know you? Can he make you happy?"

She tipped her chin up. "He does and he can."

Seth set his glass down on the table. "You're not thinking this through, Lori. Your life—your family—is in Chicago. I'm in Chicago. Come back with me." Reaching into the breast pocket of his jacket, he withdrew a small velvet jeweler's box. Flipping it open, he tilted it toward her so she could see the oval diamond surrounded by a halo of smaller diamonds. "I had this resized. Try it on."

She pushed her hands behind her back. "I'm sorry, Seth. I've already made up my mind."

He gave a bark of disbelieving laughter and snapped the box closed. "Do you really think you can be happy on a sheep farm in the middle of nowhere? C'mon, who are you trying to kid? This is a joke, right?"

Lori frowned. "No, it's not. I'm completely serious. I thought I came back here because I didn't get the commodities manager position and needed time to reassess my life. But now I know it's because this is where I'm meant to be. I fell in love with everything about Ireland the first time I came over here. I even fell in love with Flynn. I was just too blind to see it. After I returned to Chicago, all I could think about was how much I wanted to be back here. You getting the commodities manager position is the best thing that could have happened because it forced me to figure out what I really want. And everything I want is right here."

In an uncharacteristic gesture that spoke volumes, Seth thrust his fingers through his hair, uncaring that he caused the perfectly groomed layers to stand on end. "I don't get it.

I really don't. I can give you everything, Lori. If you give me a chance, I'm sure I could make you happy."

On a surge of sympathy, Lori stepped forward and took his hands. "It's okay, Seth. All you need to understand is that I *am* happy. I'll call my dad tonight and explain everything to him. He'll understand."

"He'll be disappointed. He thought you and I—" He broke off, looking embarrassed. "I was really hoping to become part of the Woods family."

"Trust me," Lori said drily, "you're my father's right-hand man. That's even better than family. I really am happy you got the job—you'll do great." She gave him a tentative smile. "We're good, right?"

He frowned, seeming uncertain. "Are you sure? I don't like leaving you here."

Lori laughed softly. "Where? Here, in the middle of paradise? There's no place I'd rather be."

After a moment, he blew out a hard breath. "Okay. Fine. You're probably right. You and I weren't going to work. You're too stubborn, and I like getting my own way. Tell Flynn I wish him luck with that."

"Trust me, he knows."

"Okay, well, that's it then." He gave her a rueful smile. "Give me a hug before I go."

She stepped into his arms, grateful that he wasn't going to make a bigger deal about her refusal to marry him or return home with him. Grateful that he was leaving.

"I'll let your father know you look well," he said as he stepped back. "I'll tell him you look—happy."

She watched from the doorway as he made his way down the path and climbed into the taxi. Then, with a final lift of his hand in farewell, the vehicle slowly made its way back toward the main road before it disappeared from sight. Drawing in a deep breath, Lori turned toward the barn.

She found Flynn standing inside with his back to the doors. He was bent over a worktable, painting something that Lori couldn't see. For a moment, she just watched him, admiring the broad shoulders and muscled contours of his back.

*Hers.*

If he would have her.

"Hey," she said quietly, stepping into the shadowed coolness of the barn.

He turned quickly, and for just an instant, Lori saw the raw relief on his face before he relaxed his features into a smile.

"There you are." He leaned back against the worktable and braced his hands on the edge as he watched her approach. "I heard the taxi leave. Are you okay?"

Lori nodded, tucking a strand of hair behind her ear. "Yes. I think he's finally accepted the fact that he and I were never going to work. You were right about that."

Flynn cupped a hand around one ear. "Sorry, I didn't catch that last bit. What was it you said?"

Lori closed the distance between them and socked him lightly on the chest, but then let her hand remain there, resting over his heart. "I said you were right. Although, in my own defense, I did tell him I wouldn't marry him—several times, in fact. But he said he's here to meet with Seamus, so his trip wasn't all about me."

Flynn took her by the shoulders and pulled her close, sliding his big hands up and down her arms. "Trust me, *mo chailín*, it was absolutely all about you."

What she saw in Flynn's eyes made Lori's breath catch. "What makes you so sure?"

"Because I would have done the same. The only difference is I would have been on the very next flight to Ireland after I learned you'd left." Lifting one hand, he slid it along her jaw, rubbing his thumb gently against her cheek. "How have you not guessed?"

"Guessed what?"

Flynn smiled, a slow, sensual curving of his mouth as he searched her eyes. "Today, at the dolmen, I wished for you to stay here with me. I'm completely, ridiculously in love with you, Lori. I have been since the day I first saw you, right outside this barn."

"But you were so rude to me," she managed, her heart thudding through her veins in slow, hard pulses.

"Well," he said, amusement lacing his voice, "it was that, or kiss you senseless, and I didn't think you'd appreciate that."

"You'd have been wrong," she breathed, sliding her hands over his chest and leaning up to press her mouth against his. "It's what I've always wanted. I wished for you too."

Flynn slid his arms around her, pulling her into the vee of his thighs before pushing one hand into her hair as he plundered her mouth with deep kisses, stroking his tongue against hers until her legs went boneless.

"Like that?" he murmured, lifting his head.

Lori nodded. "Exactly like that." Leaning back in the circle of his arms, she let her gaze drift over his face. "I love you, Flynn O'Rourke."

"Say that again."

"I love you, even though you're impossible."

"And you're the most aggravating woman I've ever met. You make me crazy."

She gasped when he hauled her back against his chest and renewed kissing her, nuzzling the tender skin beneath her ear with his face and making her shiver.

"Come up to the cottage with me now," he said, his voice low and rough. "Let me love you."

"Yes." She was helpless to resist him, had waited too long for him to deny him anything. But as he drew her away from the table, her eyes fell on the project he'd been working on. "Wait, what's that?"

Flynn paused and turned back. On the table lay a rustic sign with the words *Woolly Wonka* painted on the wood in bright-red letters.

"If we're going to open the farm to tourists," he said, "I thought we should have a mascot."

"Oh, Flynn," she cried, clutching him. "He can stay?"

Flynn chuckled. "He can stay. He'll have his own enclosure right outside and he'll be the first one to greet tourists as they enter the farm."

"Thank you," she whispered fervently, hugging him hard around the waist.

"Of course, I'll be expecting something from you in return."

Lori tipped her face up, a smile curving her mouth. "Anything."

"Marry me."

Lori knew she should be wary about agreeing to marry someone she'd known for such a short time, but after her experience with Seth, she was more than certain about her feelings.

"There's nothing I want more," she assured him, moving deeper into his embrace. "I'm exactly where I belong, right here with you."

# Epilogue

*One Year Later*

"WE COULD HAVE had a double wedding," Flynn remarked, watching as Rachel and Conall swayed together beneath an enormous wedding tent adorned with garlands of flowers and hundreds of fairy lights, while a string quartet played in the background. Rachel was luminous in a classic A-line wedding dress of white organza overlaid with delicate Irish lace. Conall looked dashing in a black tuxedo, his hair as bright as a new copper penny. Neither of them could stop smiling at the other. They'd chosen to hold their reception on the same hilltop where they had first met, where Conall had once rescued Rachel from a bog hole.

"A double wedding would have been fun," Lori said, her arms looped around Flynn's neck as they danced. "But then I couldn't have been Rachel's maid of honor, and you couldn't have stood up for Conall."

"That's true," he said, smiling at her. "I like that our own wedding will be at the top of Carraig O'rga—the Hill of Gold, surrounded by our family and friends."

"Just so you know, I'd marry you in the barn with only Woolly Wonka as our witness, if that's what you wanted," she said softly, her fingers stroking the warm skin at the nape of his neck.

"Never," he said. "You deserve a day that's all yours, and I want everyone to see what a lucky man I am."

They'd opted for a sunset service on the hill where the Beltane festival had taken place, where the setting sun would turn the sky to molten gold before giving way to deepening hues of purple and indigo as the moon climbed into the night sky.

Looking back, the past year had been a whirlwind of activity, getting both her online business and the farm ready for customers, as well as obtaining a visa and moving her entire life from Chicago to Ballylahane. Her parents had been dismayed by her decision until they'd met Flynn. Now it seemed hard to imagine there had ever been a time when he hadn't been part of the family, playing golf or sailing with her father and brothers, or charming her mother with his stories and his appreciation for her cooking. There had been days when Lori had been sure this moment would never arrive, that her fledgling business would bomb, that they wouldn't get the approvals and permits needed for the farm, that his father wouldn't pull through. Flynn had been her bulwark through it all, never wavering in his belief that everything would work out. And it had, beyond all expectations.

"Any regrets?" Flynn asked softly, bending his forehead to hers.

"Just that we didn't elope a year ago, when you first proposed," she said, only half teasing. She'd continued to live in the cottage during the past year, but Flynn had insisted on staying in the family farmhouse until after the wedding. Recently, however, he'd begun moving his personal things into what would soon be their shared home. With each item he introduced, Lori found herself more impatient to begin their married life together. Now she lifted her hand from his shoulder to admire the flash of her engagement ring, a simple solitaire in a gold setting. She couldn't wait for their own wedding day, to see Flynn's expression as she walked toward him to exchange vows.

"Just one more month," Flynn said, reading her thoughts. "After that, you're mine."

"I've been yours since the day we met," she said softly. "But I'm glad we waited so that our family and friends can be here. And your dad . . . especially your dad."

John O'Rourke had made a full recovery and had been enthusiastic about opening the farm to tourists. They had been conducting daily tours for less than four weeks, but their reservation numbers had already increased and Lori felt certain that once the summer season began in earnest, they would sell out.

"He loves you, that's for certain," Flynn said. They both looked over to where Flynn's parents were dancing together. John O'Rourke looked healthy and happy as he twirled his wife in his arms. "But not nearly as much as I do."

Lori couldn't speak for the emotion that threatened to overwhelm her, so she did the only thing she could—she kissed him with all the love she felt for him. When he finally lifted his head, his breathing was unsteady and patches of ruddy color rode high on his cheeks. "Maybe you're right—we should have eloped." He groaned, pulling her closer into his arms.

"Look," she said softly, directing his attention to where the moon hung suspended in the night sky, its reflection shimmering on the water below. "How beautiful."

"Very beautiful," he agreed.

Something in his voice made Lori look at him, only to find him watching her and not the moon. "You're missing it," she complained.

"No, *mo chailín*," he said, his voice low. "I'm not missing anything. Everything I need—everything I want—is right here in my arms."

And bending his head, he kissed her beneath the Irish moon.

# The End

Want more? Check out Rachel and Conall's story in
*Kiss Me Under the Irish Sky*!

Join Tule Publishing's newsletter for more great reads and
weekly deals!

If you enjoyed *Love Me Beneath the Irish Moon,*
you'll love the other book in the…

# Love Always, Ireland series

Book 1: *Kiss Me Under the Irish Sky*

Book 2: *Love Me Beneath the Irish Moon*

*Available now at your favorite online retailer!*

# More Books by Karen Foley

## The Riverrun Ranch series

Book 1: *Swipe Right for a Cowboy*

Book 2: *Counting on the Cowboy*

Book 3: *How to Catch a Cowboy*

## The Glacier Creek series

Book 1: *A Hummingbird Christmas*

Book 2: *Montana Defender*

Book 3: *Montana Firefighter*

Book 4: *Montana Protector*

*Available now at your favorite online retailer!*

# About the Author

Karen Foley admits to being an incurable romantic. When she's not working for the Department of Defense, she loves writing sexy stories about alpha heroes and strong heroines. Karen lives in New England with her husband, two daughters, and a houseful of pets.

Thank you for reading

# Love Me Beneath the Irish Moon

If you enjoyed this book, you can find more from all our great authors at TulePublishing.com, or from your favorite online retailer.

TULE
PUBLISHING

Made in the USA
Middletown, DE
09 May 2023

30314410R00175